Praise for Ray Keating
and his Pastor Stephen Grant Thrillers...

Murderer's Row was named KFUO's BookTalk "Book of the Year" in 2015.

"The author packs a lot into this frantically paced novel... a raft of action sequences and baseball games are thrown into the mix. The multiple villains and twists raise the stakes... Stephen remains an engaging and multifaceted character: he may still use, when necessary, the violence associated with his former professions, but he at least acknowledges his shortcomings—and prays about it. Action fans will find plenty to love here, from gunfights and murder sprees to moral dilemmas."

- Kirkus Reviews on *Murderer's Row*

The River was a 2014 finalist for KFUO's BookTalk "Book of the Year."

"A gritty, action-stuffed, well-considered thriller with a gun-toting clergyman."

- Kirkus Reviews on *The River*

Marvin Olasky, editor-in-chief of WORLD magazine, lists Ray Keating among his top 10 Christian novelists.

The host of KFUO radio's BookTalk calls Ray Keating "a great novelist."

"Mr. Keating's storytelling is so lifelike that I almost thought I had worked with him when I was at Langley. Like the fictitious pastor, I actually spent 20 years working for the U.S. intelligence community, and once I started reading 'The River,' I had to keep reading because it was so well-crafted and easy to follow and because it depicted a personal struggle that I knew all too well. I simply could not put it down."

- Kenneth V. Blanchard
The Washington Times review of
The River

"Thriller and mystery writers have concocted all manner of main characters, from fly fishing lawyers to orchid aficionados and former ballplayers, but none has come up with anyone like Stephen Grant, the former Navy Seal and CIA assassin, and current Lutheran pastor. Grant mixes battling America's enemies and sparring with enemies of traditional Christian values, while ministering to his Long Island flock. The amazing thing is that the character works. The Stephen Grant novels are great reads beginning with *Warrior Monk*, which aptly describes Ray Keating's engaging hero."

- David Keene, former president of the American Conservative Union, former president of the National Rifle Association, and current opinion editor at *The Washington Times*

U.S. Congressman Peter King said *Warrior Monk* is "a fast-moving, riveting read right out of today's – and tomorrow's – headlines."

"*Root of All Evil?* is an extraordinarily good read."

- Paul L. Maier,
best-selling novelist

"Ray Keating has a knack for writing on topics that could be pulled from tomorrow's headlines. An atheist mayor-elect of NYC? I could envision that. Pastor Grant taking out a terrorist? I could see that."

- *Lutheran Book Review* on
An Advent for Religious Liberty

"This novel is a fascinating read with a murder mystery, unique and exceptional characters, and wit... With multiple layers and a complex plot, the novel moves forward with a smooth and even pace."

- *SeriousReading.com* on *Murderer's Row*

"I miss Tom Clancy. Keating fills that void for me."

- *Lutheran Book Review* on
Murderer's Row

"Perfect for anyone interested in the real life assault on religious liberty that's taking place right before our eyes."

- Tyrel Bramwell,
author of *The Gift and the Defender*, on *An Advent for Religious Liberty*

Wine Into Water

A Pastor Stephen Grant Novel

Ray Keating

Blessings!

Ray Keating

For more information:
Keating Reports, LLC
P.O. Box 596
Manorville, NY 11949
raykeating@keatingreports.com

ISBN-10: 1515274950
ISBN-13: 978-1515274957

Author's Note

On the stylistic matter of whether or not to capitalize "he" or "his" when referring to God the Father or Jesus, I have used the *Lutheran Service Book* for various parts of the Divine Service, which capitalizes. In terms of Bible passages, my choice of *The Lutheran Study Bible (ESV)* does not capitalize. In other parts of the book, I generally have followed the lead of *Lutheran Service Book*.

For

Beth, Jonathan and David

who provide love and support

Previous Books by Ray Keating

Murderer's Row: A Pastor Stephen Grant Novel (2015)

The River: A Pastor Stephen Grant Novel (2014)

An Advent for Religious Liberty:
A Pastor Stephen Grant Novel (2012)

Root of All Evil? A Pastor Stephen Grant Novel (2012)

Warrior Monk: A Pastor Stephen Grant Novel (2010)

Discussion Guide for Warrior Monk:
A Pastor Stephen Grant Novel (2011)

Nonfiction selections...

Unleashing Small Business Through IP:
The Role of Intellectual Property in Driving
Entrepreneurship, Innovation and Investment
(Revised and Updated Edition, 2016)

Unleashing Small Business Through IP:
Protecting Intellectual Property, Driving Entrepreneurship
(2013)

"Chuck" vs. the Business World: Business Tips on TV
(2011)

U.S. by the Numbers:
What's Left, Right, and Wrong with America State by State
(2000)

New York by the Numbers:
State and City in Perpetual Crisis (1997)

D.C. by the Numbers: A State of Failure (1995)

"When the wine ran out, the mother of Jesus said to him, 'They have no wine.' And Jesus said to her, 'Woman, what does this have to do with me? My hour has not yet come.' His mother said to the servants, 'Do whatever he tells you.'"

- John 2:3-5 (ESV)

"I am the true vine, and my Father is the vinedresser. Every branch in me that does not bear fruit he prunes that it may bear more fruit. Already you are clean because of the word that I have spoken to you. Abide in me, and I in you. As the branch cannot bear fruit by itself, unless it abides in the vine, neither can you, unless you abide in me. I am the vine; you are the branches."

- John 15:1-5 (ESV)

"And he took the cup, and when he had given thanks he gave it to them saying, 'Drink of it, all of you, for this is my blood of the covenant, which is poured out for many for the forgiveness of sins.'"

- Matthew 26:27-28 (ESV)

Prologue

Twenty years ago

Stephen Grant decided to savor the moment.

He sipped the aromatic, earthy white Hermitage wine. Bottled 15 years earlier, it came from grapes grown on slopes above the French town of Tain on the banks of the Rhône River.

While swallowing, Grant took in his surroundings from the rooftop of the Loews Hotel in Monte Carlo.

He looked down at the Formula One cars fighting an unnatural restraint in order to make hairpin turns. As was always the case when observing excellence, Grant admired the drivers' skills, as well as the expertise of those who built and maintained these machines. His ears recognized the vast difference between these engines versus other so-called high-performance cars, not only in terms of power, but also the precision and responsiveness needed to compete in the Monaco Grand Prix.

He then turned to look out at the yachts anchored in the harbor and beyond in the Mediterranean's azure waters. The Principality of Monaco might be tiny, about the size of New York's Central Park, Grant reflected, but what it lacked in space, it more than made up for in terms of wealth.

The weather was near perfect, with clear cerulean skies and bright sun. After all, this was May in Monaco. Grant chuckled to himself, wondering if the residents and their guests would allow for anything less. Looking out at the crowds populating the grandstands that were wedged in along the hillside road course, he didn't doubt estimates that the city's well-heeled population of 30,000 jumped by six or seven times during race weekend.

Grant's gaze then found the woman next to him, who had her right hand slipped through the bend in his left arm. Paige Caldwell's long black hair, steely blue eyes, freckles, full pink lips, and athletic body melded into a unique beauty. Grant had become thoroughly familiar with each of her traits. Their partnership had moved rather quickly from the strict professionalism of working together for the Central Intelligence Agency to the addition of physical intimacy.

The CIA had spared no expense in making sure that Grant and Caldwell fit in naturally to the Monaco landscape. Grant had even been immersed in a couple of months of training in both wine tasting and poker.

This also meant a shared room at their hotel, the Hôtel de Paris Monte-Carlo, and an expense account to finance the best food and drink offered in the city, along with ample time at the tables of the Casino de Monte Carlo. Grant was pleased that his winnings from the last few days actually would turn a profit for the Agency on this particular case.

The assignment also required fine attire. The strong, six-foot, black-haired, green-eyed Grant looked at ease in a Burberry taupe sports jacket made of a wool, silk, linen and cashmere blend, accompanied by a crisp white shirt with thin pinstripes, and dark pants. Caldwell was striking in an Oscar De La Renta black, sleeveless blouse, and short white skirt with black polka dots. She carried a black Gucci handbag.

Grant and Caldwell, indeed, fit together.

The two also were equipped with the tools of their trade. A Glock 20 comfortably rested in a holster in the small of Grant's back. And strapped at the highest point possible of Paige Caldwell's left thigh was a Taurus PT-25. Grant knew that she liked a larger handgun. He also understood that no matter the weapon, Paige was deadly, and always had his six.

For good measure, the CIA made sure that, through a variety of affiliations, Grant and Caldwell had access to a wide choice of events in order to keep close eyes on the couple they were tracking.

Jacques Lafleur and Dasha Pudovkin made for an odd and potentially dangerous partnership from the CIA's perspective.

Lafleur was ex-French intelligence, having served in the General Directorate for External Security, or DGSE. His early retirement certainly was not unusual in France, nor was his deepening interest in a wide variety of wines. In fact, as Caldwell and Grant followed Lafleur around Monaco for several days, the ex-DGSE operative gave most of his attention to wine experts and expensive vintages, rather than drivers and their cars.

What made the DGSE and CIA, along with the British MI6, take notice was Lafleur's new companion. Dasha Pudovkin was about 20 years younger than Lafleur. This was Monte Carlo, and a beautiful, tall, blond woman in her twenties with a distinguished, balding man in his late forties was anything but out of the ordinary. Troubling was Pudovkin's former work for the KGB.

From the roof of the Loews Hotel, Grant and Caldwell watched Lafleur and Pudovkin hosting two other couples on the deck of one of the smaller yachts in the harbor. Again, the focus seemed to be on the wine and food, rather than the cars racing nearby.

Moving leisurely about the dock was the third person in the CIA's team. Edward "Tank" Hoard was dressed in security attire related to the race, which made his massive, sculpted, Schwarzenegger-like body appear less out of place. While Grant and Caldwell wore microphones, Hoard was able to sport an earpiece. Tank could hear Paige and Stephen, but not the other way around.

As Grant glanced down at the Formula One cars, Caldwell whispered, "Our friends." She nodded at the yacht where Lafleur and Pudovkin seemed to be kissing each of their guests good-bye. In no particular rush, the two descended from the top deck, then over the side and down a short ladder into a small boat tied to the larger vessel.

Grant whispered, "I trust you're seeing this, Tank."

Hoard removed his cap and wiped his forehead, signaling affirmative back to his fellow team members.

The boat moved at an appropriate speed away from the dock and into the harbor, while Formula One engines roared in the background.

Caldwell slipped her arm around Stephen's waist, and moved her face close to his ear. She whispered, "Where the hell are they going?"

"Not sure."

Lafleur guided the boat past the assorted seafaring vessels of some of the world's wealthiest individuals.

While Caldwell and Grant continued to watch from atop the hotel, Hoard moved toward a small, but speedy classic mahogany runabout that was part of the team's toolkit for the day. He hovered near the boat, while trying to casually watch their targets.

 Lafleur moved the boat through the large harbor opening into the Mediterranean waters.

Caldwell whispered, "Tank, it might not be a bad idea to get our own boat moving."

On the dock below, Hoard untied the runabout, jumped in, and started the engine.

Anchored beyond the harbor entrance, a handful of super yachts lazed in the sunshine. Grant spotted Lafleur's destination. It was a tri-deck yacht with a helicopter parked on the craft's helipad.

Following his gaze, Caldwell asked, "And who owns that lovely yacht?"

Indeed, who? The answer came to Grant as he absentmindedly took another drink of his wine. He looked at the glass, and what Lafleur and Pudovkin were doing became clear.

"This isn't about spies sharing or stealing secrets. It's not about national security."

Paige said, "Are you going to let me in on your revelation?"

Grant hesitated, as he went over the theory one more time in his head. "It's a heist. That's Sir James Blasingame's yacht. Tonight, after the race, Blasingame will be hosting an auction of some of the most expensive wines in the world. And he's doing so on that yacht."

Lafleur pulled next to Blasingame's vessel, and he and Pudovkin were helped on board by one of the crew.

Blasingame and friends are somewhere else watching the race. Skeleton crew, at most. And Lafleur's got someone on the inside.

Grant announced, "Crap. Let's move."

As they pushed past Grand Prix revelers, Caldwell asked, "Where are we going?"

Grant offered an answer to both Caldwell and Hoard. "Tank, get that boat around to the waters at the other end of the hotel. You're going to pick us up."

Grant assumed Hoard got the message.

As their pace quickened going by the pool, Caldwell declared, "Are you kidding? We're going over the side?"

"If we want to catch those two. Anything else will be too slow. My guess is that they're grabbing the wine, with help from the inside, and planning to leave on that helicopter."

Hoard already had the runabout moving at top speed, exiting the harbor, and then banking hard. He was heading toward the part of the hotel that jutted out into the Mediterranean.

Once they moved beyond other partygoers who were not all that interested in the race, Grant and Caldwell accelerated to jogging toward the other end of the hotel's roof.

Caldwell called out, "Are these waters deep enough to drop five floors?"

"Probably. I'm sure it'll be fine," Grant answered.

"Probably? You're not exactly doing much for my confidence."

"Just jump out far, and make sure your knees are bent and flexible."

"Thanks. Whatever would I do without you?"

As they reached the end of the building, neither hesitated. They vaulted the short wall, and began their descent toward the shimmering sea. Before hitting the water, Grant spotted Hoard approaching in the runabout.

Tank expertly took the runabout from nearly full throttle to a stop within a few feet of where Grant and Caldwell sprang back above the water line. Hoard used his massive strength to snatch each person from the waters with what appeared to be little effort, and then reaccelerated the boat. "Everybody okay?"

Caldwell answered, "I think so."

As he drove, Hoard said, "Blasingame's wine?"

Grant replied, "Looks that way."

As Caldwell was shedding her soaked clothes, she asked, "Change of clothes, Tank?"

"In the green locker." He glanced over his shoulder at Caldwell, who was now down to nothing but her rather skimpy underwear, removing the holster strapped to her thigh.

Grant advised, "Let's focus on the task at hand, Tank" – though he glanced at Paige as well.

"Relax, Stephen."

As she slipped on black pants, Caldwell said, "Now, now, boys, let's not fight."

After pulling on a shirt, she dragged out a silver locker. Once opened, it revealed assorted handguns, ammunition and holsters. "Now for something with more kick than that pissant Taurus PT-25."

Grant replied, "Hey, the PT-25 serves its purpose."

"You might be right," Caldwell said. Then she held up a black handgun. "But like you, I'll take a Glock 20, thank you very much." She slipped a cartridge into the weapon with evident pleasure.

"Get ready people," announced Hoard as they approached the yacht.

As Caldwell worked to finish her tasks, including picking up the discarded PT-25, Hoard again skillfully slowed the runabout, nudging aside Lafleur and Pudovkin's smaller boat, gaining position next to a ladder coming down the side of the much larger vessel.

* * *

In the hallway outside the yacht's formidable vault, Lafleur and Pudovkin paused after placing the last precious bottle in the protected cases, and looked at each other. Lafleur said, "Regrettably, it sounds like we have company." He looked at the tall crewman in white, and said, "You will have more to do to earn your considerable cut, Mr. Gaborik."

Lafleur then looked at Pudovkin, "We know what must be done. I'll see you topside, Dasha."

She nodded and smiled in response.

*   *   *

Grant whispered, "No one watching? Loading the wine, I guess." He led the way up the ladder, and then pulled out his Glock. Caldwell and Hoard quickly followed.

Hoard silently signaled that he would head up the stairs to the second deck. Caldwell indicated her intent to take the main deck, leaving Grant to follow Hoard with the intention of moving up to the third level.

Caldwell watched for anyone emerging as her team members advanced. Once they were up the staircase, she crept forward to a sliding glass door. Her movement was cautious since the doors were mirrored. Anyone inside could see out, but it was impossible for her to see inside.

On the second deck, Hoard paused as Grant headed to the next set of stairs, and scanned above. When Grant was halfway up the steps, a door next to the staircase swung open, and out bolted a tall man dressed in white crew attire. Before Hoard or Grant could truly react, the man was hurling himself up the staircase at Grant. The two landed hard on the stairs, with Grant taking the brunt of the force. Gaborik leaned on Grant while raising a fist in the air, with the clear intention of driving it into the back of Grant's head. But as the fist started its descent, Hoard's body seemed to fly into the crewman. Tank's arms wrapped around Gaborik, and locked together. The two crashed over the other side of the staircase and down onto the yacht's railing. They then tumbled into the waters of the Mediterranean.

Grant regained his breath, and grabbed the Glock that had fallen out of his hand. He looked over the side.

Below in the water, Hoard had already wrapped his arms around the crewman's neck.

Tank's got it under control.

* * *

While Gaborik was entertaining Grant and Hoard, below on the main deck Caldwell reached out and quietly slid the door open. She took a step forward, with the Glock held in front of her. But a foot wearing a hard, pointed shoe emerged without warning from around the corner, landing with considerable speed on Paige's chin.

Caldwell fell back, struggling to stay on her feet. She dropped the Glock while reaching out with her arms, trying to regain her balance. But the disorientation would not allow it. She did manage to turn and steady herself on her hands and knees, with her head hanging down.

Pudovkin sauntered over. She kicked the Glock away, and then drove another foot into Caldwell's side.

As Caldwell lay on the deck facing skyward, Pudovkin squatted next to her. She said in a heavy Russian accent, "American, I assume. You stink like an American." She paused. "My partner would prefer that I render you unconscious, and we leave with our treasure. He is squeamish about such things. But I am not that way. You are ... ah, how do you say it? ... a loose end."

She pulled out a knife concealed in a pocket on her right pant leg. But with the thud and then splash of Hoard and Gaborik going over the side of the yacht, Pudovkin glanced up.

Caldwell took the brief moment to act. She coiled and then swung her right leg, returning the favor of foot to the face.

Pudovkin tumbled backward, stopping against the railing of the yacht. She jumped to her feet, knife still in hand.

By this time, though, Caldwell had snatched the small Taurus PT-25 out of the holster strapped to her right calf. She pulled the trigger.

The small caliber shot found Dasha Pudovkin's beautiful face, and had enough energy to take the former KGB operative over the side and into the water.

Caldwell shook her head, got to her feet, and wiped blood away from the corner of her mouth. She moved to the railing, and started scanning the waters below. She declared, "And you carried the stench of an arrogant Russian bitch."

From the other side of the vessel, she could hear Tank calling out for assistance. She darted in that direction. But the sound of two gunshots rang out from above. Caldwell spun away from moving to Hoard, and headed toward the stairs.

*   *   *

Grant had turned away from Hoard in the water, and climbed to the third deck, which sported a small pool.

A pool onboard a boat struck him as oddly superfluous. Beyond the pool was a wide ladder to the helipad.

Lafleur was on the platform, bending over to move the last of five containers onto the helicopter. The aircraft's engine was on and humming.

Grant pointed his Glock, and called out, "Don't bother, Lafleur. You're done."

The Frenchman hesitated while holding the case, and looked down at Grant. He replied, "I assume you are CIA?"

"Very good."

"Just go away. There is no threat to the U.S. here. This does not concern you."

Grant knew Lafleur had the advantage of the high ground. The closer he moved, the more the angles would work against him. Grant would be able to see less of what Lafleur was doing, especially once the former DGSE agent put the container down. "Law breaking concerns me."

Lafleur sighed. "Ah, you're one of those justice-minded Americans. You're like John Wayne, no doubt."

A shot rang out from the main deck below. Grant knew Paige had done her job, or more accurately, he hoped that she had.

As Lafleur bent to put down the container, Grant moved quickly forward, going around the pool while keeping his gun trained above.

Lafleur announced, "I'm sorry, my friend." He pulled out a gun.

The two men fired simultaneously.

Grant's shot narrowly went wide.

Lafleur's bullet, however, cut into Grant's upper arm.

Grant almost stayed on his feet, but while staggering, he hit the side of the pool, and went over the low edge into the chlorinated water.

Stupid-ass pool.

He regained his balance in four feet of water, and jumped over the sidewall. The engine and rotors of the helicopter were now roaring. Grant sprinted to the ladder, and bounded up with the Glock still in his hand.

The helicopter was now some twenty feet in the air, and rising. Lafleur looked down on Grant through the front window, smiled, gave a saluto, and banked the helicopter away from the yacht.

Grant lowered his gun without firing.

Caldwell arrived next to him. "And he has the wine?" She held the Glock in one hand and the PT-25 in the other.

Grant nodded.

"Well, at least I got Pudovkin. She went over the side. You were right. The PT-25 did its job."

While watching the helicopter move away, Grant said, "He had the nerve to say this didn't concern us, and that we should just go away."

"And you said?"

"I told him that law-breaking concerns me."

"You actually said that?"

Grant turned to Caldwell, "Of course, I did. He compared me to John Wayne."

Caldwell laughed. "How fitting." She looked at his arm wound. "You might need a BAND-AID there."

In frustration, he ignored her comment and returned his gaze to the sky.

Hoard's distant call could be heard. "Hey, anybody? A little help?"

Grant took in a deep breath. Amidst the roaring engines of the Grand Prix of Monaco, the helicopter continued to shrink in the blue sky. *Son of a bitch.* "Okay, I guess we better fish Tank and his prisoner out of the drink."

Chapter 1

Present Day

Duane Ellis could have clutched his U.S. Senate seat from California until only death wrenched it away.

Why not? After all, Ellis was articulate, well educated, and handsome in an odd Elvis Presley kind of way. He also happened to be a liberal in a liberal state, and the beneficiary of considerable wealth created by his grandfather decades ago in the Golden State.

The only blemish on his record was standing uncomfortably close to a recent scandal that included the murder of a U.S. senator from New York. In that sordid case, however, Ellis looked on as an unknowing political dupe. The voters of California would not have cared, perhaps granting him only 55 percent of the vote rather than his usual 65 percent, give or take a few percentage points.

But the scandal affected Duane Ellis in unexpected ways. To the surprise of his wife, Janice, he spent more time at their California home, rather than in their Capitol Hill townhouse. He also took more time talking with her than with his staff, fellow senators, lobbyists and media – which also took Janice off-guard.

Over several weeks, with the help of Janice, Duane Ellis worked through how the scandal unnerved him. He went on to recognize a long naiveté about many of his own actions and relationships in government over the years. Duane entered a mini-depression, as he lost an unwavering, unquestioned faith in what he thought he had been accomplishing.

Ellis stunned the California political establishment and alarmed the national party leaders when he resigned from office. Fellow Democrats were displeased, worrying about having to scramble to find a suitable replacement. But that didn't last too long, as the governor appointed a prominent Democratic member of the House of Representatives who surely would hold the Senate seat in the next general election.

Ellis' enthusiasm for politics had evaporated. But it was replaced by a renewed focus on his family, and newfound joy in one of the family businesses – Ellis Vineyard in Napa Valley. The vineyard was one of the enterprises that his grandfather had built toward the end of his life. Duane had taken it for granted, generally using it only for the occasional photo op.

So, on this late September evening, the former chairman of the Senate Foreign Relations Committee stood in the valley floor's deep, fertile soil, alongside his wife and employees, cutting bunches of Cabernet Sauvignon grapes, and laying them in shallow containers to prevent the grapes from being crushed. It was obvious that Ellis undertook this task lovingly, and with little, if any, regret about leaving behind power politics just over three years earlier.

Ellis also came to the valley to participate in and oversee the rest of the grapes' journey. He helped at the sorting tables, weeding out unripe, moldy or otherwise damaged grapes. The conveyor belt then took the fruit to the crusher-destemmer where the grapes, as the name indicated, lost stems and were crushed. Next, the grapes, including skins, were pumped into a stainless steel open-top fermenter, where yeasts started the work of alcoholic fermentation. Over the coming days and weeks, sugar levels would fall and the alcohol would rise. The next stop would be the aging process in oak barrels for as long as 18 months, and then on to being carefully and lightly filtered, bottled, laid in bins for further aging, then labeled and sent off to the market.

Ellis oversaw all of it.

During this year's harvest, the first vintage he guided from start to finish also happened to be ready to go on sale. Ellis looked at one of the bottles of Cabernet Sauvignon resting in the middle of his desk. He smiled broadly.

Of course, a list existed of individuals who would receive a complimentary bottle or a case for various reasons, such as reviews, retail consideration, or as thanks for help and support provided to Duane, his family, or the Ellis Vineyard. Interestingly, only a small handful on that list came from Ellis' old life in politics – a few staff members and colleagues with whom he had real friendships, rather than mere relationships of political convenience.

Few, if anyone, would have expected economist Jennifer Grant to be on the list. While he was in the Senate, Ellis and Grant disagreed on just about every issue having to do with the economy and the federal budget. But Jennifer reached out after Ellis had resigned from office with a sincere pledge of help, if needed. Subsequently, Ellis wound up speaking with Jennifer about government, and with her husband, Pastor Stephen Grant, about questions of faith that Duane had started to ponder. The Grants and Ellis struck up a friendship. Jennifer helped Ellis think more clearly about government, its proper role, its limitations, and its dangers, while Stephen guided him to a nearby church.

Ellis lifted the bottle of wine off his desk and slipped it into the last open slot in a case. He read over the brief note he'd just finished writing.

Dear Jennifer and Stephen,

I trust you are both well, and that this case of Cabernet Sauvignon hopefully will make life a bit more enjoyable.

It's the first vintage that I was blessed to take part in from start to finish. I think I'm more excited about this than perhaps anything I was involved in during my time in the Senate. No, strike that. I know I'm more excited - at least at this point in my life. As we've discussed, funny how one learns and gains perspective through both trials and blessings.

I hope you take time to enjoy at least a couple of the bottles, perhaps over dinner here and there. And, Stephen, if you choose to use any of the bottles for Communion at St. Mary's, Janice and I, and the rest of our team at Ellis Vineyard, would feel blessed and humbled. Once again, I appreciate your guidance and thoughts for my WineCon presentation.

I look forward to seeing both of you at WineCon in New York City.

Sincerely,
Duane

Within a week, five of the dozen bottles of Ellis Cabernet Sauvignon made their way to St. Mary's, with four left behind at the Grants' home and another three presented to friends.

*   *   *

By the time Pastor Grant reached the late service on Sunday morning, the temptation of slipping into mechanical speaking, singing and action tugged at him. But the central acts of the Divine Service pulled him back. When rote threatened, reading the Gospel to the congregation got him refocused. The sermon, even on its third delivery for the weekend, never failed, out of necessity, to get him fully engaged.

Then came the time for the Words of Institution to be said over bread and the wine in Holy Communion.

The wine had been created by nature, human ingenuity and deliberate care at Ellis Vineyard in California, and then readied by additional sets of hands for the Divine Service at St. Mary's Lutheran Church in Manorville on Long Island. And it was about to play its part in a miracle.

It probably would have surprised many of his parishioners that Grant ranked as something of a skeptic about many, if not most, contemporary claims of miracles. Whenever he drove past a local church with a sign proclaiming "Tuesday Night Miracles Service," he shook his head. When Jennifer was with him, he usually would sarcastically announce, "Who knew that miracles were so common that you could count on some each Tuesday night?"

Subsequently, the conversation would generate reflection on his belief in the miracle of the Holy Spirit calling each of us to Christ and saving faith through the Gospel, and the miracles occurring through Baptism and during the Lord's Supper at St. Mary's each week.

Well, I guess miracles do come weekly. But Scripture is pretty clear about when and where. Indeed, Christ has told us where we can find and, yes, depend on miracles.

Grant once again stood at the altar looking down at the bread and wine, understanding, yet not fully comprehending, the miracle at hand.

He said, "Our Lord Jesus Christ, on the night when He was betrayed, took bread, and when He had given thanks, He broke it and gave it to the disciples and said: 'Take, eat; this is My body, which is given for you. This do in remembrance of Me.'" Grant raised the bread, bowed his head, and a bell rang.

He then proclaimed, "In the same way also He took the cup after supper, and when He had given thanks, He gave it to them, saying: 'Drink of it, all of you; this cup is the new testament in My blood, which is shed for you for the forgiveness of sins. This do, as often as you drink it, in remembrance of Me.'" Grant raised the chalice, bowed his head, and a bell rang, once again.

It was the most profound of moments, a sacramental mystery and miracle of bread, wine, and the body and blood of Jesus Christ, celebrated by Christians around the globe for nearly two millennia. Stephen Grant understood perfectly well that this was not about him, or any power he possessed. It was only through Christ's word and power. Yet, at the same time, it never failed to humble Grant to be some part of the moment.

Chapter 2

Few people can say they spent each workday at their dream job. But Kenneth Osborne could say that about two careers. He had moved from one dream job to a second.

His first career as an FBI special agent lasted for more than 20 years.

Osborne attended and excelled at Dartmouth. No one in his old-money family understood the decision to join the FBI after graduation. They apparently ignored his incessant emphasis on right and wrong from a very young age. Failing to appreciate his dream and the importance of the work, they proclaimed, in less-than-hushed voices not too far away from Ken's ear, "We expected so much more than the FBI."

But Barbara, the woman he married, understood Ken. At the same time, however, Barbara's relief was apparent when her husband decided to retire from the Bureau, and use his family money to pursue the next dream. Barbara told friends that she could finally rest easy at night. Ken was safe.

Once into retirement, he launched his second career. Within three years of opening in Manhattan's Gramercy Park, the Osborne Tavern claimed one of the most diversified wine lists in the city, with inspired, informed selections from France, Germany, Italy and Australia, not to mention California, New York and Virginia. Barbara was at his side throughout, and this time, the rest of his family also approved.

It was 2:00 in the morning, and as usual, Ken was about to lock up. Barbara and the staff had gone home earlier. He had just finished cleaning up, checking on a few orders, and doing another quick tally of the day's receipts and cash. Talking to no one else, Ken declared, "Not bad."

His cellphone rang. He looked at the screen, and answered, "Yes, Barb, I'm finally going to leave."

Her voice shook. "Ken, someone broke into the house."

"Barb, get the hell out of there." He stood up from the office chair.

"No one's here."

"Are you sure?"

"Yes. Ken, the only room disrupted is your office."

"What?"

"They grabbed the desktop computer, and your drawer of files is gone."

Ken paused. "They had to be after the investigation."

"That's what I thought, too."

"Call the police. I'm on my way."

Barb answered, "Okay." They ended the call.

* * *

Before Barbara Osborne could dial 911, a voice came from behind her. "Put the phone down, Mrs. Osborne."

She sucked in air, and did as she was told.

When the end of the gun barrel touched the back of her head, her body started to tremble. Barbara whispered, "Please, no, I have..."

That was the end of her plea, as the trigger was pulled. Barbara Osborne's body fell forward, with her face crashing down onto the hardwood floor.

Before leaving, the two intruders moved quickly through a couple of other rooms, taking money, jewelry and other valuables.

* * *

After the call ended, Ken sat back down, and pulled open the top drawer, sweeping in the cash, receipts and other paperwork that had been spread on top of the desk. He looked up when a voice declared, "Get up, Mr. Osborne. Let me see your hands."

Ken stopped, and then stood up. Two men in suits and trench coats were pointing guns at him. Osborne asked, "What do you want?"

The shorter of the intruders replied, "Information."

"Take whatever you want." Osborne backed slowly away from the desk.

"We will, of course. But then there's the problem of the information in your head."

Ken stopped, and looked at the two men. "You're really going to kill a former FBI agent over bottles of wine?"

The taller man laughed. "You're smart, but yes, that's the idea. I know it's hard, believe me. You should have left those FBI investigative skills behind in retirement. But you just had to poke around."

"There'll be hell to pay."

"Not something you'll have to worry about."

The only weapons available to Osborne were bottles of wine from Byrd Nest Vineyards, perched on the edge of a table that he now leaned against. Without turning away from the intruders, Ken reached back, grabbed a bottle in each hand, and bolted forward.

He moved to throw one bottle, while getting ready to swing the other. But neither action ever had the chance to be initiated.

The intruders fired several times.

The two bottles hit the floor first. Glass shattered. Red wine sprayed outward.

Ken Osborne then fell. His blood began to ooze into the wine, but the two didn't really mix. The darker, denser blood pushed against the light-bodied red wine.

As Ken lay on the floor of the Osborne Tavern, the dream was over. Life began to slip away. The shorter assailant stood over him, and fired two more shots into his head.

They grabbed the cash, and made more of a mess in the office. But by the time they exited the building into the rainy night ten minutes later, their two assigned goals were achieved. Information contained in a laptop was acquired, and the information in Ken Osborne's head was lost with his life.

A black sedan waited in the wide alley at the back of the building. The two men got in the car. The driver headed east, and then south on FDR Drive. The car crossed the Williamsburg Bridge, and the assailants disappeared in Brooklyn.

Chapter 3

"Are you all right?" asked FBI Supervisory Special Agent Rich Noack.

The call about Ken and Barbara Osborne came in the middle of the night. Noack told his wife what had happened while getting dressed, and then left to drive to Trent Nguyen's home.

In the few short years working together, Noack and Nguyen had become good friends, sometimes grabbing a drink after work. Hockey also was a shared passion, and a few nights earlier, the two men had gone to the Verizon Center as Noack's Washington Capitals faced off against Nguyen's San Jose Sharks. Their families occasionally got together for dinner or a holiday as well.

Nguyen's first partner coming out of Quantico was Ken Osborne.

"To be honest," answered Trent, "I'm not sure. I'm numb, pissed off, and want to nail whoever did this."

The men sat quietly nursing beers for a few minutes at Nguyen's kitchen table. Trent had pulled a couple of bottles from the refrigerator after the initial shock of what Noack relayed began to retreat.

These were imposing men. Nguyen was slim but powerful; stood at six feet two inches; and possessed an alert mind. He also ranked as one of the most decorated individuals in the history of the FBI, exhibiting professionalism and leadership skills that earned the trust of colleagues. Born in Saigon to an American nurse and Vietnamese businessman, Nguyen's love of the United States earned him the nickname Captain America among his fellow agents. That love of country nearly rivaled Nguyen's adoration for his wife and two children.

Still, Noack's combination of a strong personality; a slightly overweight, thick, six-foot-six-inch frame; and bald head managed to make Nguyen almost seem small. Noack often came across as the quintessential no-nonsense supervisory agent, but his words and actions also revealed a compassion for victims that clearly drove his work.

Each man was an FBI "lifer," with Noack having about ten years on Nguyen.

Their profession briefly took over the conversation, with Nguyen asking Noack for the details of what happened. After getting that information, the conversation went quiet.

Trent broke the silence. "I dread waking Zoe and telling her. Barbara helped her adjust to being married to an FBI agent in the early years."

Noack didn't respond immediately. He eventually asked, "Didn't you mention helping Osborne out a few weeks ago with something?"

Nguyen nodded, and took another sip of beer. "The restaurant Ken owns ... owned ... gained quite a reputation for having one of the best wine lists in the city. But he recently ran into a problem with some counterfeits. He spent significant dollars on wines that turned out to be fakes. That didn't sit well with a business owner who happened to also be former FBI. I connected Ken to a guy I know pretty well in the New York office who deals with counterfeit goods."

Nguyen went quiet again. He shook his head, and added, "You know what? She didn't say it, but I could see how relieved Barbara was when Ken retired. No doubt, she thought he'd be safer. And now they're both dead."

Noack paused, and then asked, "What do you think this was about?"

Nguyen downed what remained in the beer bottle. "I need to know more. But from what you said, it sounds like grabbing cash and valuables might have been a lame attempt to make it seem like Ken and Barbara were targets of some kind of coordinated robberies. My gut says too professional for such a small payoff. Sounds like they probably left behind some valuable bottles of wine, for example. This was about something Ken worked on while at the Bureau, or maybe he was on to something with the counterfeit wines."

"Agreed," replied Noack.

Chapter 4

The weather camouflaged the fact that it was the first Monday in October on the South Shore of Long Island. It was a sunny 76 degrees with the slightest of breezes at 10:30 in the morning. The high for the day was expected to top 80. Only the position of the sun in the sky revealed the actual time of year.

Zack Charmichael bent over the ball on the ninth green at West Sayville Golf Course, which was separated from the Great South Bay by a slim strip of marsh. He pulled his putter back slowly, and then accelerated the head forward. The ball rolled smoothly, started to slow and bend to the left. It then dropped in the hole.

The rest of his foursome of clergy members offered their approval.

"Nice putt, Zack," said Stephen Grant.

Ron McDermott declared, "Well done."

"Sweet birdie," added Tom Stone.

After the others putted out on the par 4, they each shared their scores while walking off the green. Stephen's par was next best after Zack's birdie, followed by Tom's bogey and a triple bogey by Ron.

As they pulled handcarts across a narrow road walking to the tenth tee, Tom looked at the scorecard. He announced, "So, that birdie gave Zack a 48 on the front.

Stephen had a 40. I shot a 43, and that triple put you at 48, Ron, tied with Zack."

"Thanks, Tom, I know," replied Ron with a slight edge in his voice.

"Geez, it would be embarrassing if Zack beat you, considering that he only really took up the game last year, and you've been playing for ... well ... how long?"

Zack leaned closer to Stephen and said, "They really do enjoy giving each other a hard time."

Stephen laughed. "You only noticed now?"

Ron looked at Tom, and said, "I wish nothing but the best for Zack on the golf course, but you, however, not so much."

Tom retorted, "But I'm willing to help you. Maybe some putting lessons? You know I've broken 80 now a few times since I improved my putting."

"Ouch," announced Stephen, who knew that struck a nerve with Ron. Tom had gone from atrocious putter to respectability after switching to a cross-handed grip. Before that alteration, Ron usually beat Tom, and by a healthy number of strokes. Naturally, Ron would tweak Tom about those victories. But golf karma being what it is, Tom now regularly beat Ron, and Tom took great delight at reminding his friend and competitor of this new golf reality.

While others occasionally were surprised at the interactions between these two clergy members, Stephen understood that the constant banter and ribbing was all about their friendship. In fact, despite their surface differences, Tom and Ron would do, and in the past had done, anything for each other. That, in fact, was the case with all four men.

Stephen said, "You have the honor, Zack."

Zack Charmichael was the youngest of the foursome at 30. His thick, somewhat purposefully messy, brown hair, and dark, rectangular glasses were perched atop a thin, five feet seven inches. The combination made him appear even younger than he was. While a friend to all three, his links ran deepest with Stephen and Tom. Zack served as the assistant pastor at St. Mary's Lutheran Church in Manorville, where Stephen was senior pastor – though Grant made sure that the titles "assistant" and "senior" were basically ignored. And Zack would become Tom's son-in-law after marrying Cara Stone in five days.

After teeing up his ball, Zack's swing reflected his personality. It was fast and exuberant. The ball started high and left on the short, fairly straight par 4, and then the slice took hold. The ball eventually landed in the hard, light rough to the right of the fairway, bounced across the road, and eventually came to rest in the fairway of the ninth hole.

As he stepped onto the tee, Stephen said to Zack, "Good luck with that."

Zack smiled and shrugged in response. Golf had only become an interest after he arrived at St. Mary's. Zack was from Seattle. His lengthier interests included being a fan of the Mariners, Seahawks, and especially the Vancouver Canucks; and a big-time technology, video game and comic book nerd.

To say that Stephen Grant was a unique Lutheran pastor risked gross understatement. His youth growing up just outside of Cincinnati, however, was very Middle America. His father, Douglas, delivered Coca-Cola products, and his mother, Samantha, was a librarian. The tight family was active at church, and Stephen attended parochial school, played baseball and golf, practiced archery, read a great deal, and followed the Reds and Bengals. While studying history at Valparaiso University in Indiana, Stephen's interest in weapons expanded beyond archery, and he began to seriously train his body as well. Graduation led to the Navy and the SEALs. Not long after the devastating loss of his parents in a car accident, the

Central Intelligence Agency approached him. Grant joined the Agency, subsequently using his skill set in ways that belied the title of "analyst."

Ron, Tom and Zack knew some of Stephen's basic background, and even saw him undertake actions in recent years that did not exactly fit with the "clergy" job description. At the same time, though, his friends knew no real details of what Grant did as a SEAL or a CIA operative.

As he readied to strike the golf ball, Grant's general fitness made him look like he was in his mid-late thirties, rather than actually being a bit north of forty-five. The ball seemed to jump off his three wood – made of metal, of course. It drew ever so slightly, landed on a slight down slope, and rolled up just short of the green.

Tom watched the ball disappear from sight, and said, with admiration apparent, "That was a monster hit."

Stephen said, "Thanks," and picked up his tee.

Tom Stone, the rector at St. Bartholomew's Anglican Church in Eastport, had eight years on Grant, and also served as best man at Stephen's wedding just a few short years earlier. Tom grew up in southern California, and was a longtime surfer. Seemingly, whenever the temperature topped 60 degrees, and Stone was off-duty from his priestly responsibilities, he could be found in a Hawaiian shirt and shorts. Shorts and a polo shirt with Hawaiian floral design were the order of this day. While his hair had moved to pure white, Stone generally was healthier in recent years after losing considerable weight at the behest of his wife, Maggie, and their six children, who now ranged from mid-teens to late twenties. Cara, the oldest, was engaged to Zack.

Tom also possessed a quick laugh and laid-back personality. That meant some were surprised by his deep understanding of and passion about theological matters. In addition, Tom exhibited strong leadership in the Church.

That was clear when he guided St. Bart's out of the Episcopal Church, due to that church body's decline into revisionism, and into the Anglican Church in North America.

In general, Tom shared an enthusiastic outlook on life, like his soon-to-be son-in-law, though tempered by experience. His golf swing, for example, was quick, but far more controlled than Zack's. Using a hybrid and dropping the ball on the grass without a tee, Tom took a three-quarters back swing and then inflicted a crushing move on the ball, followed by a somewhat shortened follow through. The ball sailed straight down the middle of the fairway.

As Ron moved to tee up his ball, he said to Tom, "Nice."

"Thanks."

As a Roman Catholic priest, Ron had completed what had been an ecumenical trio of traditional Christians prior to Zack coming along. Grant, Stone and McDermott initially came together as part of a local clergy group that got together to discuss various articles and topics raised in *Touchstone* magazine, which focused on Christian orthodoxy. The group eventually drifted apart, but Stephen, Tom and Ron formed a deep friendship. And for several years now, they tried, as schedules allowed, to have breakfast together three days a week, or as was the case on this day, once in a while play some golf. They shared devotions, usually from a volume of *For All the Saints*, and offered each other support. They discussed a wide array of topics, ranging from sports and movies to politics and theology.

Ron was ten years younger than Stephen, and served at St. Luke's Roman Catholic Church and School. In contrast to the easygoing reputation of his friend Tom Stone, first impressions of Father McDermott – he definitely was not a "Father Ron" – were that he was tough and standoffish. His muscular, stocky five-feet-six-inches and close-cut blond hair had the effect of reinforcing such notions. But once parishioners and others got to know McDermott, they found a priest who cared deeply about his friends and flock, including the students and families at St. Luke's School. As proven time and again, Ron stood willing to act, and sacrificed much for others.

In contrast to Tom's shorts and Hawaiian shirts, one only seemed to find Ron out of the collar when on the golf course, swimming, or, at times, relaxing in the church rectory.

Ron's ball sat on a high tee, and he swung a long driver with an oversized head. The ball was launched into a big draw that when it eventually landed back on earth took two large bounces, and left Stephen's ball behind as it rolled onto the green.

Tom shook his head after he spotted the ball rolling up on the green. "Crap, you drove the green. With that shot, you have silenced all taunting and criticism from me for the rest of the round."

Ron chuckled, and said, "Yeah, right, that'll be the day." He turned his attention to Zack as the four began walking down the fairway. "So, are you and Cara ready for the weekend?"

"As ready as we can be, I think. As you can imagine, Cara is in charge, and I'm in full agreement mode."

Tom interrupted, "You've learned very quickly how to treat my daughter."

Zack smiled, and continued, "Some family and friends actually start arriving from out of town on Wednesday, including my family. The Friday rehearsal dinner is set, and Tom and Maggie have been incredible in terms of making everything happen." He looked over at Tom. "And I know I'm repeating myself, but thanks. It's much appreciated."

Tom answered, "Are you kidding? We're happy that we can do this. It's my little girl's wedding."

Ron said, "Oh, jeez, you're not going to tear up, are you?"

Zack queried, "You guys are still set for Thursday night?" He received nods in response. Stephen had worked with Zack's best man, who was back in Seattle, to arrange a bachelor party that involved dinner in Manhattan and tickets for the Canuck's very early season visit to Madison Square Garden to take on the Rangers.

Ron said, "Hey, I hadn't thought of this before." He looked at Zack. "Does this mean you're going to start calling Tom 'dad'?"

Stephen added, "Good question." He looked at Zack. "Well?"

Tom interjected, "I told him that 'sir' or 'Father Stone' would suffice."

Zack ignored that comment. "Cara and I agreed that 'mom' and 'dad' were reserved for our respective parents, and that we'd stick with first names for the in-laws."

"Understandable," replied Ron. "But it would have been fun and somewhat unnerving to hear you suddenly calling Tom 'dad.'"

Zack said, "I agree. And now I have to go find my ball in the ninth fairway."

They eventually reassembled on the tenth green, with Ron crouched behind his ball, lining up a downhill, roughly 30-foot eagle putt.

Tom asked, "Have you ever had an eagle before?"

Ron shook his head.

"Some pressure then."

"Shut up, Tom."

Stone smiled, and added, "Well, that was uncalled for."

As his three friends fell silent, Ron took his stance. It was clear from the size of his back swing that the ball was struck too hard. If it missed the hole, the ball would roll off the front of the green. But the putt hit dead center. The ball struck the back of the hole, popped slightly up into the air, and fell in.

Ron pumped his fist, and proclaimed, "Yes!"

He received enthusiastic congratulations all around.

Stephen shook his head, adding, "Had it all along, right?"

Ron's smile grew wider. "Darn straight."

Chapter 5

Most people struggled to figure out Larry Banner's age. He had looked old for a long time.

That worked to his advantage as a money manager. People trusted their retirement income to his gray hair – not to mention his fine suits, perfect grooming, and large Wall Street office populated by yacht-racing trophies. And since that hair had gone completely gray by his mid-thirties, Banner built a long, lucrative career. Of course, his stellar investing track record helped as well. Time and again, Banner knew when and where to move his clients' money. His timing, for example, was perfect during the financial crisis of 2008, as he shifted from stocks to bonds a week before the Dow plummeted in late September. By early spring the next year, his clients were back in stocks, riding the wave of loose monetary policy higher for several years. For those who knew him for any extended period of time, Banner had earned the reputation of market guru, with an air of agelessness – looking not all that different at 63 than he did in his late thirties.

When asked about the trophies, Banner would respond, "I dabble in such things." It sounded arrogant, but it was true. Wine and poker ranked as his true passions. He had won poker tournaments around the world.

This evening, though, was about wine.

For opening such a rare, expensive bottle, the group at Banner's spacious Upper West Side apartment in Manhattan was unusually small. In addition to his daughter and son-in-law being in attendance, Colin Wiggs, a well-known New York master sommelier, and Pearson Gerards, a columnist for a premiere wine-tasting website, waited to savor a bottle of Merlot from 1929. The website also sent along a photographer, who would be taking pictures but not tasting.

The five were seated at a large round table in Banner's high-ceilinged library. The photographer had taken shots of the bottle. He then clicked away as Banner relayed the history of how this bottle, along with two others he had purchased at auction, had been taken from the Bordeaux region of France by the Nazis. The three bottles were found at the end of the war among Hitler's massive stash of stolen wine – some half-a-million bottles – hidden in his Eagle's Nest high in the Bavarian Alps. Banner smiled, and added, "In one of those moments of fitting justice in history, this wine was found and liberated by de Gaulle's soldiers."

The photographer took pictures of the smiles and anticipation on each person's face while Wiggs opened the bottle with some ceremony. Of course, as the owner who paid $405,000 to purchase the bottles at auction, the first glass was Banner's to swirl, eye, smell, and finally, taste. He said nothing; his face expressionless.

Wiggs asked, "May I, Larry?"

Banner nodded.

Wiggs had a slight build, but a disproportionately large, round head and a bulbous nose, which was insured for $1 million. With the photographer clicking away, after examining the wine against a white background and then swirling the liquid with enthusiasm, Wiggs pushed his considerable nose into the glass, closed his eyes, and breathed in deeply. He paused rather dramatically. After taking a sip and sloshing the liquid around his mouth, he declared, "Oh, my." He looked at Banner, who remained inscrutable. Wiggs took another deep sniff and test-filled sip. He turned to the other guests. "One never knows with a vintage this old. After all, so much depends on the bottle's history; the various environments it passed through. At first, there was the age." He smiled broadly. "But then, the fullness bursts forth. There is a wondrous complexity here, a marvelous sweet, full-bodied mix of cherry, vanilla, plum and a hint of licorice." Wiggs turned back to Banner. "It is miraculous, Larry, and I thank you for the privilege of tasting this precious bit of history."

Banner nodded.

The website's columnist basically echoed Wiggs' assessment.

Banner's daughter and son-in-law appreciated wine, but claimed no expertise. His son-in-law was upbeat about the vintage, while Banner's daughter smiled cordially while watching her father closely.

Dinner followed the tasting. The columnist largely drove the conversation, asking Banner about his background, history as a wine collector, and how he came to own the Merlot.

At the end of a seemingly successful and pleasant evening, Banner exchanged thanks with Wiggs, Gerards and the photographer; and a bit later, shook his son-in-law's hand firmly, and assured his daughter that all was well.

Alone, he returned to the library, sat down, and stared at the Merlot bottle. He picked up and looked closely at the cork, and then turned his attention back to the bottle, meticulously examining the label and glass.

Banner put the bottle back down, and went to the temperature and light-controlled room that served as a wine cellar. He performed a similar examination of the remaining two unopened Merlots.

After returning to the library, Banner reached for his smartphone.

* * *

As his iPhone played Brad Paisley's "Celebrity," Stephen Grant looked up from his book. He saw the name on the screen, smiled and answered the call. "Larry Banner?"

"Hello, Stephen."

"It's been a while. How are you?"

Banner replied, "A long time, Stephen. I'm well. And you?"

"Good."

"I need your help with something that I would prefer to keep quiet, at least for the near term. Can we meet?"

What's this about? Very clandestine. "You recall what I do now, right? Is this a matter of faith, Larry?" Grant would have been both pleased and surprised if Banner answered in the affirmative.

"No."

"What is it, then?"

"I'd rather we meet, and very soon, if possible."

Okay, nothing more. "Do you still have the Manhattan apartment?"

"Of course."

"Well, I'll actually be in the city tomorrow night. I can get in a bit early and come by, if that works?"

"Perfect. I appreciate it."

"How could I say 'no' to one of my mentors?"

They chose a time and ended the call.

Stephen placed the phone back on his nightstand.

Jennifer, who was lying next to him in bed, looked over from the book she was reading. "Mentor?"

"At the CIA. Larry Banner."

"Who? I thought you said Tony Cozzilino was your mentor at the Agency?"

"Coz was, without a doubt. Larry was a consultant."

"And?"

"Larry had fascinating expertise that the Agency needed, but only on the rarest of occasions."

With a slight smile as she folded her arms, she replied, "Is this one of those things you can't tell me about, or are you just trying to annoy me?"

Jennifer Grant was thin, had short, dark auburn hair, fair skin, sharp facial features but for a slightly upturned nose, and offered a bright smile. For good measure, she possessed a welcoming personality, a keen sense of humor, and an intelligence that helped to make her a respected and sought-after economist.

Jennifer also was eight years younger than Stephen, and had been married previously. That marriage to Ted Brees, once a Long Island congressman and now a U.S. senator, ended due to Ted's affair with his chief of staff, Kerri Bratton.

In the end, if it can be said that two people were meant for each other, it would be Stephen and Jennifer Grant.

Stephen said, "You know when you ask me how I know so much about wine, and where I learned my poker skills?"

"I don't know if I ever exactly said 'poker skills.'"

Stephen laughed. "Do you want to know or not?"

She tossed the book aside, rolled over, and placed her head on his chest. "Yes, of course."

"Well, early on, the Agency identified me as having some potential in those areas. You know, for possible undercover work. They sent me to Larry, and I gained a passable level of expertise – or at least a level of skill that I could fake it really well – from him during two intense months of training."

"'Intense'? Wine and poker? That sounds just brutal. How did you ever survive?"

"I know. It wasn't easy. Poker against some of the best players in Las Vegas. Wine in California, France, Manhattan and Germany. And both wine and poker in Monte Carlo. The wine, of course, had to come with just the right food pairings; after all, this was comprehensive training."

She rolled her eyes. "And how did Mr. Larry Banner gain expertise in such areas?"

"The old-fashioned way. He earned a boatload of money, and pursued his passions along the way. From what I understand, he also gained some friends in government, which somehow led to the Agency occasionally sending a trainee his way."

"Sounds like some movie fantasy."

"Maybe. But I can say without a doubt that Larry's training saved my life at least twice. And unfortunately, I still can't tell you the details in those cases."

"Hmmm." Jennifer shifted her body, brushing her nose gently against his. "A sexy man of mystery."

"And a breathtakingly beautiful woman."

They both smiled, and wrapped their arms around each other.

Chapter 6

I guess it's been 15 years. Stephen noted that little in terms of basic décor had changed in Larry Banner's apartment, including the incredible vista of skyscrapers and Central Park.

As they entered the living room, Grant was drawn to look out the floor-to-ceiling windows. "Still a beautiful view."

Banner replied, "Thanks. Please, take a seat."

"How are the markets treating you, Larry?"

"I have no complaints about the financial markets. And how is the God business going?"

Grant smiled. "I have no complaints, either."

"Good to hear. You know, your decision to become a pastor surprised me."

"Yes, I know. You said that when I first told you many years ago."

"I did, and it still surprises me to this very day. Why no collar tonight, by the way?"

"I'm on my way to dinner with some friends, and then the Rangers game."

Banner seemed to ignore that response, and went on, "I know I never told you this, Stephen, but you were by far the best student the Agency ever sent me. Most of the time, I get someone who is learning about either wine or poker.

You and only three others over the years were students of both. And whether here for one or both, you were the best."

"Thank you, Larry."

Banner waved a hand in the air, adding, "But of course, that made your decision to join the clergy even more disappointing."

"I have no doubts about my decision, Larry, and I would hope that you could accept and respect that by now."

"You're quite right. It's none of my business actually."

"Besides, it all didn't go to waste. After all, your lessons helped save my life and my partner's. I also tend to win when playing poker with friends, and have a knack for choosing the right wine for Communion."

That generated a smile from Banner.

Stephen turned the conversation. "So, why do you possibly need my help?"

Banner said, "Come with me."

They entered the kitchen, where four bottles and some glasses were waiting on the marble-topped island in the middle of the room.

Banner picked up an empty bottle, and held it out for Grant.

Grant said, "I hope this isn't going to be a test from my old teacher."

"I wouldn't worry about it. Your old teacher failed the test miserably."

What does that mean? Grant took the bottle, and immediately noted the label. "Impressive. 1929. If memory serves, that was a premiere vintage."

"You still have an excellent memory. Consider these." Banner pointed to two other bottles, not yet opened, on the table.

Grant leaned down without touching. "From the same year. These must have set you back a pretty penny."

"$405,000."

Grant actually whistled softly.

Banner continued, "And I'm pretty sure they are fakes."

"What?"

Grant picked up the empty bottle once again, and looked at it very closely. "Really?" He shook his head. "How did you figure it out? Taste?"

"I had a tasting last night. The guests included a master sommelier and a columnist from a wine-tasting website."

Grant winced slightly in sympathy. "They caught that it was counterfeit."

Banner chuckled sadly. "Actually, they didn't have a clue. They sang its praises. I believe a word used was 'miraculous.'"

"Okay, what am I missing here, Larry?"

"The wine was good."

Grant offered Banner a bewildered look.

Banner said, "It was too good."

"What?"

"The sommelier was absolutely right when he called it 'miraculous.' Given the age of the wine and the journey the bottles supposedly went on, if the wine had faltered, or even become undrinkable, that would not have surprised me. But this tasted fresh, and there was nothing in the aroma to indicate it being bottled so long ago. Nothing had been lost to time."

"Isn't that what you'd hope for paying $405,000?"

"Well..."

The two men were quiet for a few minutes. Grant finally said, "This is one of those subjective, wine-tasting things. Isn't it?"

"In part, perhaps. But then I did some quick wine forensics. Something I should have done, apparently, before I bought the bottles. That's what you get for relying on others, and allowing enthusiasm to overrule prudence."

"And?"

"The glass used for the bottle actually checks out for the twenties. And the cork appears fine as well. Then I came to the label. Nothing looked unusual. For example, it wasn't a sticker, which is where some counterfeiters fail."

"So, what then?"

"I learned recently that paper produced after about 1960, due to the chemicals used, actually reacts when viewed under the right illumination."

Grant replied, "Interesting. Another lesson from my former teacher."

"There's more. Come with me." Banner picked up the open bottle, another unopened vintage, and what appeared to be a flashlight. He led Grant into a large pantry closet, put the bottles down on a small table, and closed the door. It was almost completely dark. "Now, watch."

He shined the light on the unopened bottle, and asked, "See anything unusual?"

Grant looked closely. "No. What am I missing?"

"Nothing. That's a legitimate burgundy from 1947." He turned the light onto the empty bottle. "What about now?"

"Wow. It seems to glow."

"Right. A fake." There was an unmistakable tone of disappointment in Banner's voice.

They came back into the kitchen. Grant asked, "The other two 1929's as well?"

"One is a fake, not the other. At least, not according to my observations here."

Grant smiled. "Well, that's some good news, right?"

"Or, it could be that the other is still a fake, but with a legitimate label. After all, they were in the same lot."

"Hmmm. So, what's the next test?"

"I'd like to have it sent out for Cesium 137."

"And that is?"

"It's a product of the Atomic Age. It's not generated naturally. Instead, it is a radioactive isotope resulting from fission, that is, nuclear testing. And it's pretty much everywhere. So, wine bottled before 1945 should have no

Cesium 137 present. If that wine has Cesium 137 present, then no doubt it's a fake, too."

Grant paused, and then said, "Well, I hope the other bottle is legit, Larry. But again, why did you reach out to me?"

I also want to ask how you got taken given everything you just walked me through? But not the time.

Banner answered, "Paige Caldwell."

"My old partner? What about her?"

"She left the Agency."

"Yes."

"I hear that she has her own firm now that deals with many, let's say, challenges."

"You've heard correctly. Paige has an excellent team. They're professional, skilled in many facets" – and picking up on where Banner was going, Grant added – "and discrete when necessary."

"Do you think they could handle this type of investigation?"

"I have no doubt. Why the cloak and dagger?"

"You must be kidding, Stephen. First, I have a reputation in the wine and business worlds, and this getting out, at least at this point, would do me no good."

"At this point?"

"Yes, I want to find out who did this, haul the shits into court, and make sure they get jail time. But I want the news out once I can make the case, not now when the only story is that I've been taken."

"You said 'first.'"

"You know reason number two. What do you think the CIA's reaction would be if they received word before I have the guilty in hand? They hire me to teach their people about wine and poker, including being able to bluff. When it comes to these wine purchases, I let the excitement take over. I ignored what I teach." He shook his head sadly. "I'm going to have my entire collection evaluated."

"Understood. I'd be more than happy to put you in contact with Paige. She has two partners who are top notch – Sean McEnany and Charlie Driessen."

"Driessen? You're kidding." Banner chuckled.

"You know Charlie?"

"Stephen, you were the best student I ever had. The Agency for some reason sent Driessen to me years earlier."

Grant laughed. "To become a wine expert."

Banner shook his head. "In their delusions, they sent Driessen to learn the finer points of wine and poker. For all of his other skills, whatever they might be, he was one of the worst students the Agency ever sent, in terms of both wine and poker."

Grant smiled. "Thanks for that bit of information. It might come in handy."

Banner nodded in response.

Grant looked again at the two unopened bottles with the 1929 labels. "Incredible."

Banner grabbed the bottle he knew to be fake, held it up, and asked, "Do you want to try a fake Merlot costing $135,000?"

Grant said, "I'm not sure how to answer that."

Banner opened the bottle, and poured two glasses. Banner went through none of the ritual or ceremony. He simply took a big swig, and declared, "Miraculous."

Grant, however, held up the glass in the light, and examined it closely. He swirled the liquid around in the glass, and then brought it to his nose and breathed in deeply. Finally, he took a drink, and moved the wine around in his mouth, letting the liquid spread across taste buds. And he finally swallowed.

Banner said, "Well?"

"If I were here the other night, I'm guessing that I would have been fooled as well. But knowing what I know now, I understand your assessment. This isn't a great wine, but if it really had survived since 1929, the berry sweetness, and particularly the vanilla, would rank as a minor miracle."

Banner said, "And I'm guessing you now rank as a miracle expert given your line of work."

"Funny." Grant took another, larger drink of the counterfeit Merlot, looked at the glass once more, and then simply shook his head. "Unbelievable." He then looked at his watch, and said, "All right, I'll make the introductions for you and Paige, but if there's nothing else, I have to head out to a bachelor party."

"Bachelor party? You said nothing about a bachelor party earlier. I didn't think pastors did such things."

"In fact, it's for a fellow pastor. Dinner and a hockey game. Nobody's going to be sticking dollar bills anywhere they shouldn't."

Banner declared, "You've become boring, Stephen."

"Yes, I guess I have."

Chapter 7

Walking down the center aisle in the nave of St. Mary's Lutheran Church, Cara Stone's smile and twinkling blue eyes were unmistakable even through the light, fine veil.

Her long strawberry-blond hair fell over the shoulders of the bright white wedding dress decorated with tiny pearls. Cara's mother, Maggie, wore the same dress years earlier at her wedding. For any family members or friends who attended both ceremonies, they might have thought they were time traveling, as Cara was the spitting image of her mother.

Cara moved with a combination of grace and eagerness. The same could not be said for her father, who was escorting her unsteadily down the aisle. Tom's eyes were wet, with a few tears escaping onto his cheeks. At the same time, like his daughter, he also wore a big smile, which was matched by Maggie Stone's in the front pew on the bride's side of the church.

Atop the steps leading to the altar in the Tudor-style church, Pastor Stephen Grant waited as the celebrant for the rite of Holy Matrimony. Stephen glanced at the filled pews, where he saw the backs of heads as people watched the bride come forward. The face he was looking for, however, turned briefly to look his way. Jennifer smiled, and Stephen nodded slightly in response before she turned back toward Cara.

As Pam Larson, St. Mary's organist and youth director, continued to play the processional music, accompanied by a brass quartet in the choir loft, Stephen glanced down at Pastor Zack Charmichael, who seemed to sway ever so slightly.

Stephen whispered, "You okay?"

Zack took a deep breath, and answered, "Yeah, of course."

With both sets of eyes now on Cara, Stephen said, "Cara looks beautiful, Zack."

"She sure does."

When father and daughter arrived, Tom raised Cara's veil, kissed her on the cheek, and said softly, "I love you, Cara."

"I love you, too, Daddy."

Stephen asked, "Who gives this woman to be married to this man?"

Tom cleared this throat, and replied, "Her mother and I do."

Cara then stepped next to Zack, and Tom moved to the pew next to Maggie. While Maggie's eyes were moist, another tear leaked from Tom's left eye. Maggie squeezed his hand, and whispered, "Are you going to cry throughout this ceremony?"

"Don't be surprised. I still can't believe that's our little girl getting married."

"I know."

Stephen then read the opening from the *Lutheran Service Book*. He recently had gained an added appreciation for the words as they had become so counter-cultural:

> The union of husband and wife in heart, body, and mind is intended by God for the mutual companionship, help, and support that each person ought to receive from the other,

both in prosperity and adversity. Marriage was also ordained so that man and woman may find delight in one another and thus avoid sexual immorality. Therefore all persons who marry shall take a spouse in holiness and honor, not in the passion of lust, for God has not called us to impurity but in holiness. God also established marriage for the procreation of children to be brought up in the fear and instruction of the Lord and to offer Him their praise.

So has God established the holy covenant that Cara and Zack wish to enter. They desire our prayers as they begin their marriage in the Lord's name and with His blessing.

The wedding party took their seats, as Stephen went to the lectern for the reading. He announced that it would come from John 2:1-11:

On the third day there was a wedding at Cana in Galilee, and the mother of Jesus was there. Jesus also was invited to the wedding with his disciples. When the wine ran out, the mother of Jesus said to him, "They have no wine." And Jesus said to her, "Woman, what does this have to do with me? My hour has not yet come." His mother said to the servants, "Do whatever he tells you."

Now there were six stone water jars there for the Jewish rites of purification, each holding twenty or thirty gallons. Jesus said to the servants, "Fill the jars with water." And they filled them up to the brim. And he said to them, "Now draw some out and take it to the master of the feast." So they took it. When the master of the feast tasted the water now become wine, and did not know where it came from (though the servants who had drawn the water knew), the master of the feast called the bridegroom and said to him, "Everyone serves the good wine first, and when people have drunk freely, then the poor wine. But you have kept the good wine until now." This, the first of his signs, Jesus did at Cana in Galilee, and manifested his glory. And his disciples believed in him.

The hymn "Gracious Savior, Grant Your Blessing" followed, and then Stephen moved into the pulpit for a brief homily.

Grace to you and peace from God our Father and the Lord Jesus Christ.

We're all blessed to be sharing this special day in the lives of Cara and Zack. I've had the good fortune to officiate at numerous weddings over the years, but never before for a couple with whom I am so close. I thank them for asking me to be part of this today.

So, what are we all to make of what Jesus did at the Wedding at Cana? There's a great deal to unpack here, many points that could make this a lengthy sermon.

He paused, and looked knowingly at Cara, Zack and the entire congregation, which generated some laughing. He smiled.

But, I will only touch, briefly, on a few.

Isn't it interesting that the first miracle performed by Jesus was changing water into wine at a wedding? The fact that Jesus is attending and performing His first miracle at a wedding tells us that He is affirming God's institution of marriage, and it reminds us that Jesus blesses Christian marriages to this very day. That's truly wonderful.

And what about Mary's role at Cana, as we're here in St. Mary's Lutheran Church? She, once again, serves as an example of great faith. Her trust is in Jesus. Mary trusts that He has the power to act, and she merely tells others, "Do whatever He tells you."

This is a wonderful lesson at a wedding, since throughout a marriage, along with so many blessings, there also will be trials, questions, and yes, troubles. What to do in the midst of such times? As Mary says, "Do whatever He" – that is, Jesus – "tells you." Of course, that's a lesson for all of life.

And Jesus does in fact perform the miracle of turning water into wine. He does so freely and abundantly, just as His grace flows forth. There is faith here. There is law, as we are to do what God commands. And there is gospel – abundant gifts from Christ.

Finally, Jesus tells the servants to bring over six stone water jars used for the Jewish rites of purification, and to fill them to the brim with water. Jesus changes the water into wine, and not just any wine, but the best wine filled to the brim.

This all points very clearly to what happens when Jesus' hour does come, on the cross, sacrificing and suffering for our sins. His blood washes and purifies us. And when we partake in Holy Communion, it is Jesus' body and blood, received in faith under the elements of bread and wine, that provide forgiveness, and strengthens our faith.

Wine brings joy to a wedding, and wine is part of the joy of Holy Communion.

Of course, it must be noted that this does not mean that Jesus' gifts of love, forgiveness, and salvation are only meant for those who are married, nor do married men and women have an edge over those who are single. Far from it. The gifts of Jesus are for everyone, equally.

The point for this joyous occasion is that Jesus is blessing marriage. With God, of course, this is no mere coincidence. Jesus performs His first miracle of His earthly ministry at a wedding. This should tell us that marriage is something far more than a mere legal contract, more than the whims of the culture, and more than what happens to feel right at a certain moment in time. It is *Holy* matrimony, blessed by God. And this is good news for Cara and Zack, and for anyone blessed in Christian marriage.

Later in the service, after rings were exchanged, Stephen declared with the couple kneeling: "Now that Cara and Zack have consented together in the Holy covenant of Marriage, have given themselves to each other by their solemn pledges, and have declared the same before God and these witnesses, I pronounce them to be husband and wife, in the name of the Father and of the Son and of the Holy Spirit."

The congregation responded, "Amen."

Stephen continued, "What God has joined together, let no one put asunder."

And then came a blessing: "The almighty and gracious God abundantly grant you His favor and sanctify and bless you with the blessing given to Adam and Eve in Paradise, that you may please Him in both body and soul and live together in Holy love until your life's end."

Again, the reply was "Amen."

Cara and Zack rose, and Stephen declared, "You may kiss the bride."

The kiss was met not only with applause, but a few cheers.

Chapter 8

As Zack and Cara kissed, across the Atlantic, a nascent breeze skimmed across the ocean water, came ashore, and gently moved the blond hair of a woman lying next to a long pool. The tan-skinned woman, wearing a tiny white bikini and mirrored sunglasses, stirred ever so slightly.

She turned to look at the person seated at a nearby table. The bald man in his late sixties was dressed in dark swim trunks and an open, short-sleeved, gray silk shirt.

The woman asked, "Jacques, where shall we dine this evening?"

"You make the selection, my dear. You always know best."

She smiled, rose from the lounge, and walked over to the man who was more than thirty years her senior. She leaned down, and said, "You are so good to me." She kissed him, and then walked over to the pool, descended the steps into the warm water, and began to swim.

Jacques Lafleur watched in unmistakable satisfaction. Over the decades, his journey had been anything but predictable, moving from one set of shadows into another. Lafleur had been French intelligence for some two decades, and subsequently went on to operating in the darkness of high-end counterfeit goods, primarily wine, watches and jewelry, though dabbling in other opportunities.

After his wine heist at the Monaco Grand Prix, Lafleur seemed to disappear, going deep underground. Nearly a decade later, he re-emerged with substantial wealth, purchasing this well-protected compound featuring a 9,000-square-foot villa on the Atlantic Ocean in Casablanca. The villa had served as his luxurious headquarters for the past ten years.

Jacques continued to watch as Gabrielle swam laps, until two men and a woman emerged from the Moorish-style home.

Jacques stood, and waved the three over with a smile. He greeted each with kisses on cheeks, saying, "It's wonderful to see you."

Gabrielle emerged from the water, patted parts of her body dry with a thick towel, and joined them at the poolside table. Two servants presented a variety of drinks.

They spent time catching up on rather mundane personal matters. Liam and Harper Casper, who had been married for nearly 15 years, were both from Australia. They met Lafleur at Whitehaven Beach in Whitsundays, and with their blue eyes, Liam's blond hair, and Harper's light brown locks yet untouched by any gray, the couple looked like they still belonged on that white sand.

Anton Lange was a short, extremely obese, red-haired, quiet German, who breathed heavily, yet continued to smoke, eat and drink in copious amounts. The three had worked closely with Jacques since his late underground days, with Gabrielle entering the picture about seven years ago.

The four fell silent when Jacques said, "Well, let's start with you, Harper."

Harper effectively served as the operation's purchasing manager. She had the eye for identifying legitimate and fake watches and jewelry, the right palate for wine, and the mind to assess what would and would not pass muster and have value in the marketplace, and at what price. She proceeded to report on a new, promising watch supplier in Vietnam, and the wine samples that continued to impress her while she was recently in China. "The bottles, labels, and corks are all extremely well done, and our partner has individuals quite skilled in blending and mixing, with the taste satisfying all but the most discerning, and even fooling them at times."

Liam headed up logistics. He added, "Yes, he has proven to be smart, knowing the ins and outs of moving the product in China. This also might serve to reduce costs and risks rather dramatically when it comes to moving wine into the U.S. After all, given the amount of goods being exported to the U.S. from China, it's simply easier to hide the fakes, and our friend has the wherewithal to move large or small amounts."

Anton dealt with all technology matters, from the most ancient of wine storage and aging methods to the most up-to-date computer software aiding in the wine counterfeiting effort. After puffing deeply on a cigarette and breathing out through his nose, Anton noted, "I still have very few complaints as to his" – he breathed heavily in the midst of the sentence – "tech prowess. As we know, he has proven to be quite good. With my help, I will make him even better."

Liam said, "There's more. We were just informed last week that the U.S. operation was further consolidated. The question mark was removed some time ago, so this could allow for a serious ramping up of activity. That would be even better news than the China development – at least in the near term."

Lafleur replied, "That's very interesting."

Liam agreed, "It is."

Lafleur looked more closely at Liam, and asked, "Is there a problem?"

"No. It just took him a while to let us know. I would have rather been informed earlier."

"Again, is there a problem?"

"No. He just wanted to implement the changes, and make sure everything was operating as intended before telling us. In the end, I'm quite pleased. Given these developments, we might be able to close up one of our facilities, perhaps the one here or the one just outside Phoenix."

"Excellent." Lafleur sprinkled a few more questions at the three, and then he turned to Gabrielle. "And what about our friends?"

Gabrielle answered, "I'm sure they will not have any problems with this plan as long as everything continues to comply with both sides of your agreement, Jacques."

Lafleur asked, "The last bit of information we passed along provided dividends?"

Gabrielle replied, "I was told it was valuable."

"Excellent, as it should be." Lafleur smiled broadly. "It looks like all aspects of the business are functioning as expected. Now, Gabrielle and I briefly discussed where we might have dinner later. I left that decision in her more than capable hands." His eyes moved among Anton, Liam and Harper. "But we have some time, so why don't you three change, and join us in the pool?"

Given the amount of time spent at the Casablanca compound over the years, Liam, Harper, and Anton had their own suites in Lafleur's grandiose home. Liam and Harper went inside to change, while Anton remained at the table as a servant refilled his wine glass and brought a tray of caviar with his favorite accompaniments.

Chapter 9

Heavy flaps and heating units stood at the ready for the reception under a massive tent at Li Vineyard on the North Fork of Long Island. But the equipment was not needed. The streak of summer-like weather continued into this October Saturday.

While Cara, Zack and the wedding party were still off shooting pictures, the cocktail party was in full swing on an expansive grass lawn between the tent and the edge of the grape vines. A full bar selection included various wines, but central naturally were wines produced by Li Vineyard. A fruity Chenin Blanc and a dry, zesty Sauvignon Blanc were being featured.

Stephen and Jennifer Grant moved among the guests, including a good number of St. Mary's parishioners. They stopped to join the discussion between Father Ron McDermott and Glenn Oliver.

Glenn's wife, Dana, died from cancer a few years earlier. The short, thin, easy-going black man had just passed the 60-year mark, with his age only given away by gray sprinkled amidst his dark hair. He retired from his Wall Street career early in order to care for Dana. Stephen helped him get through the tough times during and after Dana's battle. The two men became close friends. Now, Glenn was active at St. Mary's, having just been elected congregation president, while also working to grow a new consulting business for start-up entrepreneurs.

Ron and Glenn were debating if New York was destined for another Subway Series, as both Ron's Mets and Glenn's Yankees were in the postseason. Since her Cardinals also made the postseason, Jennifer joined in gleefully. Stephen stood silent, still smarting that his Reds had finished far from even a whiff of the playoffs.

Ron said, "It's all about pitching, and we've got the best rotation."

Glenn replied, "I don't disagree with your point on pitching. But you have to be able to score runs as well. The Yankees and the Cardinals" – he glanced in Jennifer's direction – "can put runs on the board, unlike the Mets."

Ron looked at Stephen. "What do you think?"

"I know how important both are since the Reds couldn't hit or pitch this year, and finished in last place."

Glenn asked Jennifer, "Does he always sulk like this?"

"Actually, Glenn, the only time my take-the-hill husband sulks is when it comes to the Reds and Bengals."

Stephen smiled, kissed Jennifer on the cheek, and said, "True enough."

As the baseball conversation continued, Stephen spotted Cathy Li, owner of the vineyard. She stood off on the side of the festivities, watching apparently to make sure everything was running smoothly.

Stephen said to the group, "Excuse me, I want to see if I can get a moment with the vineyard owner."

As he approached, Stephen held out his hand and said, "Hello, I'm Stephen Grant, the pastor at St. Mary's."

Cathy Li, in her early forties, was lithe, with a narrow face, short dark hair, thin lips, and noticeably long fingers. Her eyes were dark, but her smile sunny. She shook Stephen's hand firmly, replying, "It's very nice to meet you. Nice homily earlier."

"Thanks. You came to the church?"

"Yes. I got to know Cara when my husband was in the hospital. She stood out as a nurse who cared and was good at what she did. We became friendly."

"Your husband, if I might ask, is he all right?"

"Oh, yes, thank you. We had a bit of a scare, but he's doing fine now."

"I'm glad to hear it. Can I ask about your vineyard?"

"I love talking about it."

"How did you get into the wine business?"

"My grandfather came to the U.S. from China, and he worked most of his life in California vineyards. Late in his life, he came to live with us in Queens, with my parents and me, when I was attending college. He's the one I blame for my passion for wine. Anyway, I met my husband at college. He became a lawyer and I was an accountant. Boring, right?"

"Well, I'm a pastor and my wife is an economist?"

"Hmmm. No, accountant-lawyer has you beat."

They both laughed.

Li continued, "We were both pretty successful, and then there were deaths in our families and suddenly these inheritances. And after some hard thinking, we decided to chuck the law and accounting, and we bought this vineyard six years ago, which actually was one of the earliest opened on the North Fork in the 1980s. And of course, knowledge of accounting and the law help a lot."

"I'm sure. Was it the right choice?"

She smiled even more brightly. "I liked accounting. People laugh at that, but I really did. This, however," she looked around, "I love this. And we've been lucky of late to have good vintages. Growing grapes on this sliver of land between ocean, bay and sound has advantages, especially the soil, but the challenges can be formidable. It is not for the weak of heart. But the weather has been kind the last few years."

"Mind if I ask about counterfeit wines? How much of a problem is it?"

The smile disappeared. Cathy said, "Being relatively new to the business, Li Vineyard has not directly suffered from counterfeits. But it's obviously not good for the industry. And as I mentioned, my husband, Mike, is a lawyer. He used to do intellectual property work – patents, trademarks, copyright and trade secrets. So, recently, some vineyard owners and wine collectors have tapped him to help deal with counterfeits, you know, on the legal front. The problem seems to have stepped up over the past year or so. Mike actually is meeting with someone right now about a counterfeit matter. Of late, he has spent almost as much time on fake wines for others as he has on Li wines. But we're building up another business and goodwill among many in wine circles. So..." Her voice trailed off.

"Interesting."

"Why do you ask?"

"A friend brought it to my attention recently."

Cathy observed, "You know, with Mike dealing so much with the issue, and the reading and your homily on the Wedding at Cana today, it got me thinking."

"How so?"

"These counterfeiters are doing the opposite of what Jesus did. He turned water into the very best wine. They're sort of turning the best wine into something little better than water."

"Wine into water."

"Yes."

Jennifer arrived at Stephen's side, and he made introductions.

Jennifer said to Cathy Li, "This is a beautiful setting, and I love your wine."

Cathy replied, "Thank you. We appreciate that."

"Is Stephen regaling you with his wine expertise?"

Stephen knew his wife was enjoying a bit of private needling.

"We were chatting about the winery and some aspects of the business." Cathy turned to Stephen, and asked, "Do you have some experience in wine tasting?"

"Minimal, and it was a long time ago."

Jennifer smiled, and then announced, "I'm supposed to bring both of you over to the tent. The happy couple is about to be introduced for the first time in public as Mr. and Mrs. Zackary Charmichael."

Chapter 10

"Okay, let's review what we have so far," said Rich Noack, as he lowered his heavy frame into a creaky office chair.

Over the weekend, the two men had moved their base of operations from the J. Edgar Hoover Building in Washington, D.C., to the Jacob K. Javits Federal Building in Manhattan to investigate the murders of Kenneth and Barbara Osborne.

It was early Monday morning when Nguyen sat down across the desk from Noack. "These guys left no traces, nothing to give away anything about themselves at the restaurant or in the home. Money, jewelry, and so on were taken."

"But..."

"But a great deal of value also was left behind, especially at the tavern in terms of some very pricey bottles of wine."

"So, the perps didn't know what they had?"

"Unlikely. They took files and a fairly old desktop from the home, a well-used laptop from the restaurant, and killed Ken and Barbara."

"Right. So, as we speculated initially, they were after information that Ken likely had, while also making sure that neither he nor Barbara would communicate any of that information."

"That seems most obvious to me," said Nguyen.

"It's also highly unlikely that this would be about something that Osborne worked on at the Bureau. He would not have had that information on his personal computers, especially after being in retirement."

"Most likely, but not a definite."

Noack did not respond to that. "And what about his counterfeit wine problem?"

"I spoke with the agent I introduced to Ken, Eugenio Peraza."

"And?"

"Peraza and Ken spoke twice. Peraza basically gave Ken what he had on some of the key domestic and international players the Bureau knows or suspects are in the fake wine business, with the promise that Ken get back to him with anything new."

"Did Osborne come back with anything?"

"The second time they spoke, it was brief. Ken told Peraza that he was poking around some interesting things, and that he would be getting back shortly to arrange a meeting."

Noack shook his head. "And you didn't think of pushing that bit of information closer to the lead when you sat down?"

Nguyen smiled, and shrugged his shoulders. "Hey, we have a process."

Noack asked, "Osborne gave Peraza nothing more?"

"No."

"You have whatever Peraza sent Osborne?"

"Eugenio is sending the files. Should be waiting in my email now."

"Okay, Trent, let's start reassembling Osborne's investigation," Noack concluded.

Chapter 11

By the time Paige Caldwell and Charlie Driessen arrived at the out-of-the-way, exclusive restaurant on the Upper East Side of Manhattan for a lunch meeting, Larry Banner already was waiting at a table.

As Caldwell and Driessen approached, Banner rose to greet them. He extended his hand to Paige. "Ms. Caldwell, I've heard so much about you. It is a pleasure to finally meet."

Caldwell said, "Thank you, Mr. Banner. It's nice to meet you as well." Caldwell added, "And this is one of my business partners at CDM International Strategies and Security, Mr. Driessen."

Paige Caldwell and Larry Banner fit in the surroundings. Caldwell appeared quite comfortable in transforming a fashionable, though rather straightforward black pantsuit with a white button-down shirt into an attention-grabber, while it seemed to be second nature for Banner to wear his gray, three-piece suit. In contrast, Charlie Driessen looked out of place, with a slightly wrinkled yellow shirt, a loose tie, and an ill-fitting brown suit, along with a less-than-tame gray mustache, matched by sparse and scruffy hair.

Banner said, "How are you, Charlie? It's been a very long time."

Driessen shook Banner's hand, and merely said, "Larry, it's been a while."

Caldwell was visibly surprised. She turned to Driessen, and said, "Wait a second, you two know each other?"

Banner interjected, "It was a long time ago. Charlie was a student, briefly." He pulled a chair out for Caldwell, and said, "Please, let's sit down."

As Caldwell went to sit, she offered a short, withering look to Driessen, who quickly averted his eyes.

Amidst casual introductory talk, the trio ordered lunch. Caldwell acquiesced to Banner selecting a wine, while Driessen announced to the waiter, "I'm not a wine guy. A Harp on tap will do, thank you."

Banner said, "I appreciate you meeting on such short notice."

Caldwell replied, "You come highly recommended, Mr. Banner."

"Shall we dispose of the formalities, and go with first names?"

"Yeah, that's fine, Larry," chimed in Driessen.

Caldwell nodded, and continued, "Stephen always spoke well of you."

Banner said, "The same goes for you. Were you as surprised as I was when he left the Agency to become a pastor?"

Driessen answered, "You have no idea."

Caldwell sent another steely stare in Driessen's direction, but he shrugged and smiled slightly in response this time. She answered Banner, "Yes, that decision surprised many of us."

Caldwell went on to offer an overview of CDM, namely, that she and Charlie had left the CIA, and partnered with Sean McEnany, who was an Army Ranger and had considerable experience in corporate and government security and investigative work. She touched on the varied skills and experiences their employees possessed, and mentioned in the most general terms the kinds of cases they had undertaken.

Caldwell naturally left out the difficult circumstances under which she had been forced out at the CIA. She glossed over the fact that her boss at the Agency, Tank Hoard, suggested she and Driessen become independent contractors who could work with greater freedom for the Agency. In addition, it was not pointed out that Hoard put Caldwell and Driessen together with McEnany, a mysterious figure with deep and extensive contacts running inside and outside government, along with unparalleled expertise in communications and other assorted technologies. But all three at the table would understand the concept of "need to know."

As time and the lunch courses passed, it became apparent that Banner liked what he heard. He finally laid out most of the details of his counterfeit wine "dilemma." And then he made clear, "I want a case made against this shit, or these shits, whichever the case may be. I want it done quietly, with nothing linked to me, and nothing coming out until we have an airtight case. Can you handle this?"

Caldwell immediately replied, "We certainly can. The questions are time and resources, and where this takes us, with the international market..."

Banner interjected, "Time? I want quick results. Resources? Not an issue. Yes, this might be an international undertaking. But it seems to me that you have the staff and expertise to make this happen."

"Again, yes, we do. But we also have other clients to consider, and ..."

Banner interrupted. "Would a contract worth $100,000 per month until this is all wrapped up be sufficient?"

Driessen, who had been quiet throughout most of the discussion, suddenly jumped into the conversation. "Larry, that will make it happen."

Over coffee and tea, Banner mentioned, "I'm also thinking about having someone do an analysis on the extent of wine fraud in the global market, the need for the industry to step up with reforms, and improved enforcement among governments. I want to have it ready as a white paper for distribution, and a lobbying and public relations effort right after we get this case wrapped up."

Caldwell said, "I think I know who could undertake that kind of project, and she happens to be married to Stephen Grant."

Banner replied, "That's interesting."

Driessen once more declared, "You have no idea."

After lunch, Caldwell, Driessen and Banner agreed to get together the next morning in Banner's office to sign the contract.

Caldwell and Driessen decided to walk back to their hotel.

Caldwell asked, "Is there a reason that you failed to mention you knew Banner?"

Driessen grunted, "Ah, crap, it's kind of stupid."

"Please, share."

"The Agency sent me to take some wine and poker lessons from him."

"So?"

"It didn't go well."

"Come on, Charlie, just spit it out."

"Fine. Banner cut the lessons short, and told the Agency that I was one of the worst students they ever sent to him."

Caldwell burst out laughing. She grabbed her friend's upper arm as they walked, and continued to laugh.

Driessen finally said, "Enough already. It's not that funny."

She took a deep breath. "Yes, it is. Our crew is going to enjoy hearing this, especially Sean."

"No," Driessen declared with gravity in his voice. "You have to swear not to tell any of them."

"No way, Charlie, this is too good."

"Paige, you know all of the shit I have on you..."

Caldwell stopped laughing, and let go of his arm. "Oh, fine, I won't tell. For someone who tries to act like such a tough son of a bitch, you're a baby sometimes."

Chapter 12

The owners of four wineries had agreed a year earlier to co-host an event on the North Fork of Long Island leading up to the New York City Wine Convention, as well as to establish a joint convention booth.

It was the brainchild of Cathy and Mike Li of Li Vineyard. Evan Byrd from Byrd Nest Vineyards, Willis Slate of Slate Family Winery, and Vince Weathers from Kushner Wines signed on to the effort. The idea was that NYC WineCon would become a vehicle to raise the profiles of their own vineyards, as well as serving as a kind of ambassadorship for North Fork wine in general.

Weathers and his Kushner Wines just seemed to be along for the ride, not really involved in any substantive way.

At a long conference table on the second floor of the main building at Li Vineyard sat Cathy and Mike Li, Evan Byrd and Willis Slate. While never officially appointed, Cathy seemed to naturally take the lead in running the meetings. She looked down at a list on a legal pad, and observed, "I think that's it. It looks like we have everything moving in the right direction. The WineCon booth certainly is all set, and that, of course, is simple compared to the logistics for our pre-convention event. But even that looks good in terms of entertainment, food, lodging, our wines, and perhaps the biggest challenge, making it easy for people to travel out from the city and back." She looked up from the pad, and asked, "Is there anything else?"

Mike shook his head, as did Slate.

But Byrd said, "It would have been nice to have Jason pitching in on this. Nothing more from Weathers, I assume?"

About three years ago, Jason Kushner inexplicably sold his vineyard to Vince Weathers, who had been working at the winery for several years. Kushner also moved his family off Long Island, and cut off all communications with longtime friends in the wine business.

Cathy shrugged her shoulders. "He sent that check a couple of weeks ago to cover his share of the booth, along with the note asking for a final tally of the event costs and that he would cut a check for that as well."

"I don't like him," replied Byrd.

"Yes, we know, Evan," said Willis. "He seems okay to me. Quiet guy, but he seems to get things done."

Byrd appeared as though he wanted to say something, but merely shook his head.

While Cathy, Mike and Willis all knew Jason as a colleague, Byrd and Kushner had been friends. Yet, Kushner avoided answering Byrd's initial questions about the vineyard sale, and then he simply moved away without telling anyone. He failed to reply to Byrd's inquiries, but for one brief telephone conversation. At that time, Kushner merely said, "Thanks for everything, Evan. Take care of yourself."

And that, apparently, was the end of Jason Kushner's friendship with Evan Byrd.

Cathy said, "I don't know what to make of Vince, but for our purposes here, his check has cleared."

Chapter 13

Throughout his adult life, Stephen Grant had dealt with situations that most people couldn't imagine. That included confronting death in a variety of ways, from staring down the Grim Reaper himself, to supporting those facing the final journey home, to personally sending more than a few people into the afterlife.

But even after handling these and other cases of considerable danger, often with great calm and cool, there were still rare, seemingly minor situations that generated some inexplicable discomfort for Grant. This was one of those situations.

Despite reminding himself that there was no reason for it, Stephen was slightly off his game whenever Jennifer Grant, his wife, and Paige Caldwell, his former CIA partner and long-ago lover, were brought together. And Stephen still wrestled with these feelings even though the three together took on some formidable challenges in recent years, including when Paige put her own life on the line for Jennifer.

In fact, while not close friends, Paige and Jennifer had gotten to know each other better. Stephen also came to recognize that Jennifer appreciated the friendship and trust that now existed between Stephen and Paige, while Paige understood Stephen's love and devotion to Jennifer.

These realities, of course, only made Stephen feel worse about his lingering unease.

At the wheel of a silver SUV rental, with Charlie Driessen in the front passenger seat, Paige turned onto a short street in Center Moriches on Long Island's South Shore. At the end of the block was the driveway of the Grants' home, cut into a high row of hedges, and guarded by a light stone column on each side, with an open wrought iron gate.

The Grant home was an upscale compound amidst a largely middle-income suburb. It had been in Jennifer's family for some time. Two acres were bordered on three sides by hedges, with a dock and inlet running along the west side. The water emptied into Moriches Bay to the south. The SUV rolled by an L-shaped, heated, built-in pool with a small waterfall streaming down from a Jacuzzi, a poolside bungalow, and not too far away, an artificial surface putting green and sand trap, and a tennis court.

The driveway ended in a large circle positioned between a tan, 4,200-square-foot, terracotta-roofed, Tuscany-style home, and a three-car garage, with stairs on the side leading up to a second floor.

Driessen looked around as they got out of the SUV, and commented, "Not bad. Where the hell does a pastor get the money for a place like this?"

Caldwell answered, "From Jennifer. You know the deal." Caldwell and Driessen knew that Stephen's father-in-law owned casinos, and that Jennifer, along with two partners, did quite well with her own economics firm.

"Yeah, right."

Caldwell used the iron knocker on the weathered wooden front door.

Stephen welcomed his former CIA colleagues, shaking Charlie's hand and kissing Paige on the cheek.

Dressed in a brown shirt, a tan, button-down sweater, and khakis, Grant fell somewhere between the wide berth of Caldwell's gray, marled-patterned dress and Driessen's traditional rumpled look, this time in the form of a light blue oxford shirt and rather well-worn dark blue pants.

Driessen said, "Nice place, Grant."

"Oh, right, you've never been here. Thanks. Come in."

As he led them to the large kitchen, Stephen asked, "How was the drive from the city?"

Driessen answered, "What do you think? Paige was driving."

Stephen smiled. "So you made good time."

Paige interjected, "Damn right, we did."

They entered the spacious kitchen, where Jennifer and Sean McEnany were waiting.

Sean had arrived about ten minutes earlier. McEnany still looked the part of an Army Ranger, with near-crew-cut blond hair coupled with a muscular, five-foot-ten-inch frame. Even with a dark sports jacket over a white shirt, McEnany's strength was evident. His eyes also signaled alertness and intelligence. And more than anyone in the room, McEnany managed to be the most mysterious and connected, while living a multifaceted, perhaps even divided life. That was saying a great deal in a group like this. Stephen, who moved from the SEALs to the CIA to the Church, managed to experience different aspects of life at different times – for the most part, since his old life tended to pop back up at unexpected times. But McEnany purposefully embraced and lived a kind of duality. He was a family man, living just a few minutes away in Manorville with his wife and three children. He also was an active member at St. Mary's, including serving on the church council. At the same time, however, his work after leaving the Army for CorpSecQuest, a private security firm, was much more than it appeared, given the firm's secret ties to the CIA. For good measure, it was the CIA's Tank Hoard who suggested that McEnany consider attending Grant's church after moving to Long Island. And there was the basement of his very suburban home featuring "workspace" more secure than some military installations.

Jennifer hugged her new guests, with both Paige and Charlie not exactly looking comfortable as she did. That made Stephen smile.

As Jennifer finished preparing dinner, Stephen poured drinks, and light conversation continued.

Jennifer eventually said, "We're about 10 minutes away from dinner. Stephen, do you want to give a quick tour of the house for anyone interested?"

Paige said, "Why don't you boys take the tour, and I'll stay here and talk with Jennifer?"

Stephen spotted the slight smirk on Paige's face. He then looked at Jennifer, who smiled and added, "Wonderful idea."

I'm glad they're both having fun at my expense. Stephen said, "All right, come on, Charlie."

Driessen seemed taken off guard. "Me? Okay, I guess."

Stephen added, "Sean, you coming?"

In his low, raspy voice, McEnany replied, "I've had the tour before, but seeing Charlie trying to look interested during a house tour is worth the replay."

The end of the quick run through the house came in Jennifer's home office. They stepped down into the long room with a shiny, brown-tiled floor, tan walls, and a large window across from the doorway that looked out on the water. At one end of the room was an oversized desk framed by a large, wall bookcase. In the middle of the room sat a deep leather couch facing the desk, with a short bookcase backed up against it.

Most notable, though, was the collection.

Charlie smiled. "I heard about this." He wandered around looking at the extensive sword and dagger collection that adorned two walls, as well as a short-blade, English, 17th-century hanger sword resting atop the short bookcase.

Stephen volunteered, "Jen started collecting these in college. She was an English Lit major undergrad at UNLV. It's a mix of originals going back to the Middle Ages, assorted replicas, as well as some film props that caught her attention."

As Charlie moved his eyes closer to some of the items, he observed, "Well, I know at least two of these have seen some action."

Sean added, "Yes, they have."

Stephen said nothing.

Driessen turned and looked at the man he had worked with years ago at the Agency. He lowered his voice, and asked, "Grant, did it ever occur to you that you have a type?"

Stephen reflexively said, "What do you mean?"

Sean chuckled, and then took a sip of beer from the glass he was carrying.

Charlie laughed as well. "Come on. From what I know, you've had two women in your life over the past – what? – twenty or so years. Not only is each incredibly beautiful, but the first one ranks as the most lethal woman I've ever known, and as for the second, well, you managed to marry an economist who just happens to collect weapons."

Sean joined in, noting, "You're right, Charlie. Talk about living dangerously."

Stephen replied, "'Living dangerously'? What does that mean?"

"What does that mean?" Charlie repeated. "It means that you lucked out that Paige didn't kill you when things ended with her. You better not ever push that luck any further by screwing over Jennifer."

More humorists.

Stephen said, "You know what?"

Sean bit, answering, "What?"

"You're assholes."

Sean and Charlie laughed, as Stephen smiled.

Then Sean feigned outrage. "Pastor Grant, I trust the church council will not have to take issue with your language."

Jennifer appeared in the doorway. "Are you gentlemen ready for dinner?"

Stephen turned, and had one of those moments where he was struck. Jennifer had removed the apron that she had been wearing in the kitchen, and the black and red faux-wrapped dress with a plunging neckline flattered her perfectly. Combined with a warm smile, she radiated a natural beauty.

Jennifer came down into the room, and moved toward Stephen.

"We definitely are," her husband replied.

Charlie said, "Impressive collection, Jennifer,"

"Thank you, Charlie."

"I was just saying to Stephen that he probably had to work hard to find an economist with a sword and dagger collection."

Stephen raised an eyebrow ever so slightly at Charlie.

Jennifer replied, "We sword-wielding economists certainly are rare. But I'm pretty pleased to have found a pastor who was with the CIA. That's pretty exceptional, too."

I love this woman.

She slipped an arm around Stephen's waist, and he did the same in return.

Jennifer then ordered, "Okay, guests to the dining room, and husband to the kitchen to help me serve."

A few minutes later, spread out on the long pine table in the airy dining room was a meal featuring beef stir-fry with steamed white rice, accompanied by Ellis Vineyard's Cabernet Sauvignon.

Compliments flowed to Jennifer for the meal, and eventually Paige turned to the wine. She looked at one of the bottles. "Ellis?"

Stephen nodded, "Yes, Duane Ellis." Before anyone could add comments that couldn't be retracted about Ellis, he added, "I guess you could say that Jen and I have become friends with the former senator."

Charlie said, "I thought you didn't like politicians?"

Stephen smiled, "I also believe in redemption. Let's just say, he's a very different person now."

Paige merely commented, "Interesting." She took another drink of the wine. "I'm not the expert that Stephen is, but I like his wine better than his politics."

Jennifer observed, "Senator Ellis and I used to disagree on just about everything, but like Stephen said, he's not the same man, at least in terms of his views and priorities, that he was when in the Senate."

Paige said, "Speaking of wine and given who's around the table, we can speak freely about Larry Banner." She looked at Stephen, and said, "Thanks for vouching for CDM."

"No need for thanks. Given what he needs, you guys are more than capable of supplying it."

Paige nodded. "I never worked with him, although Charlie did very briefly."

Driessen shifted in his chair, grunted slightly, picked up his glass, and took a big swig of wine.

Paige continued, "Anything more we need to know about him?"

Stephen responded, "Beyond what I already mentioned to you on the phone, just keep in mind that he's a perfectionist. He does not suffer fools well, and likes to be in control." Stephen looked at Charlie, and asked, "Did you find that, Charlie?"

Driessen replied with another small grunt, and by drinking more wine.

Sean watched Charlie with newfound interest.

Stephen added, "Banner also knows his stuff, which is why I'm so shocked he was taken by a counterfeiter. It'll eat at him until this is solved."

Paige said, "That fits with everything else we have on him." She turned to Jennifer, and said, "Banner also wants to get an analysis of the global wine market performed, focused on the reach and effect of counterfeiting, and what's needed from the industry and government. He's looking to have a publication ready to follow up closely after his case is solved, with a PR and lobbying effort. I said that I knew someone who would be ideal. Interested?"

Jennifer said, "Absolutely. My firm could do that. In fact, my partner in California has some experience with the wine business."

Grant watched as Jennifer and Paige exchanged ideas. *Maybe Charlie is right. Do I have a type?* As he picked up his glass, Stephen glanced down the table at Charlie, who moved his eyes from Paige to Jennifer, and back to Stephen. He smirked, pointed his glass at Stephen, and then took a drink.

The conversation between Paige and Jennifer turned back to Stephen. Paige said, "I know I've had a tendency to bring you into things, Stephen, not Jennifer."

He replied, "It's a nice change of pace."

"We still might have to tap some of your expertise. Among the three of us," she glanced at Charlie and Sean, "and our four employees, no one is a true wine expert." She paused ever so briefly, and gave Stephen a look he had seen many times in the past, but few others ever picked up. "So, if it comes up that we need some insights on wine, can we call on you?"

Stephen returned a look of appreciation. With a bit of flair, he sipped the Cabernet Sauvignon, and declared, "Of course, I'd be more than happy to do so." Then he looked at Driessen, and said, "But Charlie, didn't you train with Banner as well many years ago?"

Charlie's eyes narrowed. As he stared at both Stephen and Paige, each began to smile.

Watching all of this, Sean finally asked, "What's the deal?"

Stephen answered, "Yes, Charlie, what's the deal?"

Driessen drained the rest of the wine in his glass. He looked at Sean. "All right, if you must know, and since you're probably the only one who doesn't know" – he glanced at Jennifer, who waved her hands in innocence – "I was sent to Banner for his little course in wine expertise, and it turns out that it was not exactly my strong point."

Charlie looked at Stephen.

Stephen was going to let it stand at that, but apparently Paige could not resist. She said, "Not your strong point? I believe Banner proclaimed you to be one of the worst students the Agency ever sent him. And it wasn't just wine, but poker as well, right? You didn't do so well as a student of poker either."

Sean was not known for displays of emotion, but he laughed heartily at that.

Charlie said, "Paige, remember what we talked about?"

"Oh, Charlie, come on. The cat was out of the bag. Don't blame me." She smiled broadly. "Besides, I couldn't resist, and I know Stephen has become too nice to do this full justice."

As Sean expressed his satisfaction at hearing about Driessen's failure, the laughing continued, with even Charlie finally and reluctantly partaking. At the same time, Jennifer casually moved her hand onto Stephen's and squeezed.

Stephen knew what that meant. As he glanced at Jennifer, the delicate gold cross that hung down from her neck caught his attention as well.

Not a type. Once more, thank you, Lord, for this woman I don't deserve.

Chapter 14

Appearance and reality often stand in conflict.

His black hair, eyebrows and beard were shaggy, all in need of much more than a mere trim. Combined with a wardrobe that rarely ventured beyond denim shirts and pants with work boots, it was an understatement to say that Vince Weathers did not exactly look the part of a vineyard owner on Long Island's North Fork.

Instead, Vince fit the previous role he had played while kicking around the wine business for some 30 years, that is, the valuable employee who had become expert in assorted aspects of the industry, from soil and vines to dollars and cents.

But everyone has weak spots. Weathers lacked "people" skills. He was not about making sales, wine tastings and events, networking, raising money, or generally communicating well. Weathers was a behind-the-scenes guy.

That's why it was such a surprise when Weathers bought Kushner Wines from Jason Kushner. Outside observers had Kushner pegged as the leader and schmoozer, while he relied on Weathers in terms of day-to-day facility operations. Kushner's taking on Weathers as a partner would have made sense to the North Fork winery community. Weathers buying out Kushner, and then Kushner leaving the scene altogether, did not. For good measure, Weathers replaced all of the employees who'd had links to Kushner, and none of the new hires apparently had the people skills that Weathers so evidently lacked.

As he bent over and closely eyed labels spread out under a bright light on a table, Weathers spoke into a cellphone with some irritation. "Yes, it's all been taken care of."

As the person on the other end of the call talked, Weathers straightened up and said, "Sometimes I think you forget who you are talking to, forget my experience."

Weathers listened, and then responded. "Yes, I appreciate that, but I'm not an idiot. You need to calm down. We've been over this time and again. It will take us to a new level. All we need to do is execute."

He once again listened, and then replied, "That's right. Let me know when you hear."

Weathers ended the call, and returned to inspecting the wine labels.

Chapter 15

On this particular Friday, Stephen Grant ate breakfast with Tom Stone and Ron McDermott about an hour earlier than typical. After ordering food and doing their devotional readings, Ron looked at his watch, then at Grant, and said, "So, we have to get up earlier because you have more work to do with Zack being away on his honeymoon?"

Stephen simply replied, "Yes. That's right."

Tom laughed, and added, "Actually, I kind of like getting up earlier. Getting in the shower first, and then out of the house still holds its advantages, even with only three of six kids at home."

Ron asked, "Have you heard from Cara at all?"

Tom answered, "I would hope not. It's her honeymoon."

"Good point," Ron acknowledged. He took a sip of coffee, and then shifted topics. "You're a wine snob, Stephen, have you...?

Stephen interrupted, "Snob?"

"Yes." Ron plowed ahead. "Have you heard of the New York City Wine Convention?"

"WineCon? Sure. Why?"

"A friend of mine serves in a monastery in the Finger Lakes region. The monks have run a winery up there for the past decade or so."

It was Tom's turn to interrupt. "What's up with monks? They make wine, beer, and – what else? – fruitcake. Plus, there are our friends from the North Shore – Grillin' with the Monks. And I think we can all agree, those monks know barbeque."

Ron smirked, and said, "They have a long history in the food and beverage industry. Besides, they've got to fill up the rest of their days when not at Mass or praying."

Tom asked, "Wait, was that a joke?"

Their breakfast orders arrived at the table, along with refills on coffee and iced tea.

As toast was being buttered, syrup poured and sausage cut, Stephen said, "Funny that we're talking about this. A friend is going to be speaking about Christianity and the history of wine at one of the WineCon plenary sessions."

Tom replied, "Hmmm, how widely recognized today is the Church's historical role?"

Stephen said, "Not sure how much those in the wine business know or care, but the Church's role certainly is acknowledged in the histories I had a chance to read recently."

"Why the research?" Tom inquired.

"Duane Ellis is the speaker, and I offered some input as he was exploring the topic."

After swallowing some French toast, Ron broke in, "Senator Duane Ellis?"

"Former senator, yes. Jennifer dealt with him while he was in the Senate. Since his retirement, we've come to know him better, and he's running his family's winery in Napa Valley now."

Ron said, "That's interesting. I wouldn't think that he and Jennifer would have seen eye to eye on, well, just about anything."

"They didn't, but after that near-brush with scandal, let's just say that Ellis has been re-evaluating many things. Anyway, it sounds like he's put together a nice presentation on the Church's history with wine. He's starting with the so-called Dark Ages, and the Church's promotion of wine production given the centrality of the Eucharist, and how the monks proved quite adept at pushing viticulture and winemaking technology ahead. In fact, with donations of land, the Church became the largest wine producer by the Middle Ages. Most of the great vineyards of Europe were created by monasteries, and along the way, winemaking became a business." Stephen became more animated, as he often did on matters of history. "Did you guys know that Dom Pérignon champagne is named for a 17th-century Benedictine monk? Dom Pierre Pérignon was known for improving the quality of grapes and blending wines. There's also considerable evidence that the needs of Communion led to the first vineyards in the New World having Church roots."

Tom said, "Apparently, I can skip Senator Ellis' presentation now."

Stephen smiled in response.

Ron said, "Well, staying with this theme, the reason I asked about WineCon is that the abbey's winemakers will be hosting a tasting at a church in the city during WineCon later this month. I was wondering who might be interested in going?"

Stephen nodded, and said, "Depending on which day and the schedule, you can probably count in Jennifer and me."

Tom added, "Yes, that'll likely work for Maggie and me as well. Tastings and lectures. The wine business all seems so bloody civilized."

Chapter 16

The warehouse stood as one of the larger buildings on Buckeye Road in Goodyear, Arizona. At the same time, though, the non-distinct building blended in with the other low-rise retail and commercial establishments.

Over the front door hung a generic title about wine distributors. Inside, a small, kind-of-dirty office greeted the rare visitor. During a typical week, a couple of vans and trucks might come and go, in addition to the handful of employees. It was all designed not to draw any attention, and it didn't.

Hidden from any straying eyes, a compartmentalized warehouse stretched out beyond the office, with both lighting and temperature specifically controlled. Bottles of wine were stored in the majority of the space, with one area used as a lab for testing, mixing, bottling and labeling counterfeits.

The Arizona desert would not seem like the most convenient location for such an operation. But Jacques Lafleur agreed with Liam that this was to their advantage, and the location worked, given the nearby international airport and the fact that Los Angeles was less than six hours away via Interstate 10. Everything had operated smoothly for the past few years.

Security cameras covered every angle and corner both outside and inside the building. No matter what else was going on, or not, within the building, the front office was manned 24 hours a day. That included 2:30 AM on Saturday morning.

As a converted armored car raced into the parking lot, all of the well-planned security mattered little.

The guard, sitting at a desk facing monitors that showed the feeds from each camera, looked up just in time to see the front of the office implode toward him. He tried to rise from a chair while reaching for his holstered gun, but there simply was not enough time. Flying debris, then the monitors and desk, and finally the steel truck, still speeding forward, slammed into him. By the time the truck had pushed everything through the back of the office into the warehouse and eventually stopped, the guard's chest had been crushed, and the man exhaled for a final time.

Three masked and gloved individuals exited the truck, and moved quickly in specific directions. One entered the lab area, which had been partially destroyed by the ramming of the armored vehicle. He pulled incendiary devices with charges from a backpack, attached them and poured grain alcohol around the room. The other two men did the same throughout the rest of the warehouse, while also shattering a few of the thousands of wine bottles along the way.

Before leaving though, the men returned for the security guard. One of the masked individuals hauled the body up onto a shoulder. Within five minutes of their appearance, the three exited the back of the warehouse, leaving behind nearly everything they came with, including the truck.

The guard's body was dropped in the middle of the back parking lot. One of the masked men reached into a pocket and pulled out a small pin, and attached it to the guard's blood-soaked shirt.

A few seconds later, the three were seated in a dark sedan that had been waiting in the same back lot. Each nodded to the driver, who flipped a switch on the detonator and then slipped the car into drive.

As the vehicle disappeared into the darkness, flames arose and quickly spread throughout the warehouse, fueled by the grain alcohol as well as the alcohol content of the wine. The fire eventually sped its way to the truck and its full gas tank, thereby spectacularly adding to the conflagration.

Chapter 17

It was late Saturday morning, and Jacques Lafleur was sitting at his desk in an airy office that offered a view down on the pool in his Moroccan compound. His encrypted phone buzzed. "Liam, how are you?"

"Bad news, I'm afraid."

"Yes? What is it?"

Liam took a deep breath on the other end of the call. "Goodyear was attacked."

"How bad?"

"Our most experienced and trusted guard, Keith, was killed."

Lafleur shook his head and quickly replied, "Oh, God, no."

Liam continued his report. "Mario arrived on the scene just before the police and fire department. He sent pictures, and is keeping me up to date. But, in effect, the building has burned to the ground. We've lost everything."

He went on to report the very little that was known, namely that in the middle of the charred building sat an armored truck, and that all video evidence would be lost amidst the carnage. Liam chastised himself. "I never should have left the servers on site. I should have had Anton set up a feed to the cloud, at least some kind of backup."

Lafleur finally spoke, "It's easy to say that now, but as we know, there are potential security risks going that route as well."

Liam added, "Given the extent of the fire, we don't have to worry about what the local authorities might find poking around."

"True. Anything else?"

"One odd point that could be nothing."

"Yes?"

"Mario noted an item pinned to Keith's shirt. He said he would not have thought anything about it, but it was shiny clean compared to the blood and dirt on the shirt. Of all things, it was a KGB pin. A shield with a sword coming down the center, and a red star in the middle with the hammer and sickle on it. And across the bottom are the KGB's initials and 'CCCP.'"

Lafleur closed his eyes and leaned back in his chair, and said nothing.

Liam interrupted the silence. "Jacques, are you still there?"

Lafleur opened his eyes, and finally said, "Was Mario able to remove the pin?"

"What? Well, no. The police showed up as he was snapping the pictures."

"Please send me that photo, Liam."

"Of course. Is everything all right? Do you know what this means?"

"I think so."

"Well?"

"It means, or it could mean, that someone I used to know, someone that I thought dead, is anything but dead."

Liam replied, "You don't mean Pudovkin?"

"Who else?"

"But we re-checked that years ago just to be safe. There was nothing to indicate that she somehow survived."

"Yes, I know. But there also was nothing to indicate that she died. And there have been rumors here and there over the years."

"Even if she were alive, why would she do this? Why now, after all of these years?"

"I have no idea." He then paused and rubbed his forehead. Lafleur added, "Who knows, my friend? Even at my age, the female mind often remains a mystery. Perhaps she has held onto feelings of a woman scorned, who now has the ability to take her revenge."

"But you said that you looked for her after the Monaco job."

"And I did. But did I look long enough, hard enough? Did I mourn sufficiently? Ah, I do not know."

"Or, again, this might not be her."

"Perhaps it is not," Lafleur replied, absent any sort of conviction in his voice. "Please, send me the photo. Pass all of this on to Harper and Anton. We will need to speak this afternoon. Set up a conference call."

Lafleur ended the call, got up and walked out on the balcony. He stared out, beyond the pool and grass below, at the Atlantic Ocean.

A few minutes later, Gabrielle entered the room, and joined him on the balcony. She looked at his face, and immediately asked, "What is wrong?"

Lafleur relayed what happened in Arizona. He withheld the information on the KGB pin.

As he spoke, Gabrielle never allowed her eyes to wander from his. She observed, "You think you know who did this, don't you?"

Lafleur turned away from her, directing his gaze back to the blue ocean.

She persisted, "Jacques, who?"

While still looking into the distance, he relented. "Dasha Pudovkin."

In response, Gabrielle whispered, "Shit."

Chapter 18

"Hope I didn't interrupt anything on a Saturday night in Manhattan?" Sean McEnany spoke into his smartphone while leaning back in one of the chairs in the secure basement ops room tucked behind a near-impenetrable door in his Long Island home.

Paige Caldwell listened about 90 miles away. She sat cross-legged on a bed with a laptop open and papers sprawled out around her in an over-priced, under-sized hotel room offering a slim window that caught a narrow glimpse of Times Square.

Caldwell answered, "Don't worry. Nothing that interesting. I'm just reviewing some of the materials that you sent over on suspects and players in counterfeit wine."

"What's Charlie up to?"

"I'm not completely sure, but he mentioned something earlier about a woman he helped get away from Putin about a decade ago. He said that she always was ready to show her appreciation – as he put it 'in weird and wonderful ways' – whenever he was in New York. He also informed me that he was off duty until tomorrow afternoon, at the earliest."

"Paige, apparently Charlie Driessen is getting more action than you are on a Saturday night in the Big Apple. That's just sad."

"First, don't ever compare my love life to Charlie's. Second, who still says the 'Big Apple'? And lastly, you're the one calling me on a Saturday night. What does that say about your life?"

"But when we're done, I'm going upstairs to put the kids to bed, and then who knows what will happen with the wife."

"Sean, you need to shut up, or I'll tell Rachel on you. I liked it a lot more when you talked less. Now, did you call for a reason?"

"I just wanted to give you a heads-up on something strange that I'm adding to my investigation list for this Banner project. A local LEO contact in Arizona gave me a call earlier. It was more or less on a lark. A warehouse burned down early today, and a security guard was killed. Wine was stored in the place."

"Okay, mundane so far."

"The contact sent information my way because the guard was dragged outside the burning building by his killers, and, get this, a KGB pin was attached to his shirt."

"KGB? As in Soviet KGB? He some kind of frustrated communist, or history geek?"

"I don't think so. The body and clothes were covered in blood and soot. But the KGB pin on this dead security guard was perfectly clean, and attached to the middle of the guy's chest. Not where one would normally wear a pin. Also, the assailants drove an armored car into the building, and left that truck to burn with the building."

"That's not so mundane anymore. Any idea what the hell it all means?"

"My contact is clueless. I looked into who owns the building, and it appears to be a dummy corporation, covered very well. Like I said, I'm going to keep digging on this – the owner, business details, and the rest of it."

"Great, thanks, Sean."

"No problem. Have fun doing whatever it is you'll be doing tonight in the city that never sleeps."

"Like I said, I like quiet Sean." She ended the call.

Chapter 19

A charcoal suit with a pencil skirt flirting just above the knees, black high heels, short blond hair, understated makeup, and a broad smile revealing white teeth all fit together perfectly. She was in her late-40s, but looked a decade younger. When she smiled and said, "Please, follow me," it created in the other person a mixture of warmth, ease, appreciation and a willingness to, yes, follow.

At least, that's what Stephen Grant was hit with initially. He wondered if Jennifer felt the same.

With seemingly little effort, the woman pulled open a sizeable glass door to Larry Banner's lower Manhattan office, and announced their arrival. After meeting her less than a minute earlier, it had become clear to Stephen that he had known assorted women just like Banner's executive assistant during his CIA days, both inside the Agency and in other enterprises around the world. Indeed, they were running departments, businesses, and embassies, not to mention assorted missions. He glanced to his side. *As is the case with Jennifer, and for that matter, Paige.*

Banner said to his executive assistant, "Thank you, Holly."

Stephen officially introduced Jennifer and Larry. It was another case, he reflected, of his old life touching his current one. Jennifer briefly presented her firm's background, including some relevant work and a brief take on her own experience and that of her two partners, Yvonne Hudson and Joe McPhee. The give and take between Jennifer and Banner over the task lasted less than a half hour, with the contract and payment essentially agreed to in another three or four minutes.

When Jennifer and Stephen went to leave, Larry moved around his desk, and accompanied the couple to the door. But before opening it, he stopped and turned to Jennifer. "Dr. Grant..."

"Jennifer, Mr. Banner, please," she insisted.

He confirmed that he preferred "Larry," and then added, "Thank you, once again, for coming into the city and meeting on such short notice late on a Monday. I don't like when a wrench is thrown into my schedule just as the week is getting started. But my schedule has been difficult lately. I apologize."

Jennifer said, "I completely understand, and please, do not apologize. I didn't really bring Stephen along for the introduction. He is taking me to dinner, and then we're going to see *The Front Page.*"

"Well, enjoy the evening." Banner looked at Stephen, smiled and then asked Jennifer, "Would you mind if you and I had dinner some time during this project or afterward without your husband?"

Jennifer smiled as well, and raised an eyebrow. "Larry, I don't usually get such invitations, but yes, I'm sure we could do that. That is, if my husband doesn't mind."

Larry interrupted, "Whether he does or doesn't, we need to talk freely about the Stephen Grant I taught. Perhaps I can let you in on a few things you didn't know, and then you can tell me about who this man, this pastor, is today."

Stephen looked at Larry, and said, "You know I'm standing right here?"

Jennifer and Larry looked at Stephen, and then Jennifer turned and said, "Larry, that sounds lovely. Let's do it soon."

Oh, great.

"Absolutely, very soon," agreed Banner.

After leaving Banner's office and heading toward the elevator bank, Stephen said, "You're not only getting well paid for this project, but you're enjoying it on another level, aren't you?"

As they entered the elevator, Jennifer said, "Of course, what's not to like?"

Stephen shook his head, and took her hand as the elevator doors closed.

Chapter 20

Every eye near the dock in Vladivostok seemed drawn to the striking, tall, blond woman. Such a public stance was unusual for her, to say the least. Being out of place did not apparently bother her, though, as she stood watching her 80-foot ocean-faring yacht moving toward open waters.

The scar that Dasha Pudovkin wore across her left cheek would only be visible to those standing within a few feet. But there was no one in such proximity now, as her husband, Pavel Zubov, piloted the departing vessel.

Pudovkin lingered as the yacht journeyed farther away. Her husband had told her not to do exactly what she was now doing. After they kissed, he said, "Now, go, Dasha. I know you want to go with me. But that is not possible this time." He smiled broadly. "It will drive you crazy not being in control, but as we agreed, you are needed here to secure the sale. Besides, this is my specialty. All will go well." He then kissed her again, boarded the large boat, yelled a few orders at the small crew, and was gone.

When the yacht could no longer be seen, Pudovkin finally turned away, and strode to the silver Mercedes S600.

Nearly two days later, under the deep darkness of night in the Pacific Ocean, Zubov positioned the yacht alongside a small Chinese freighter. After predetermined radio communications were made, a powerboat from the freighter approached. In choppy waters, the Chinese crew handed over 30 large silver cases. The exchange was over in less than twenty minutes.

The Chinese freighter continued its journey east. The valuable cargo of 180 bottles of counterfeit wine was destined to bring in nearly eight million dollars. After the wine was properly stowed, Zubov turned his boat west, back toward Vladivostok.

Hours later, the sky started to brighten with the sun just beginning to rise behind the yacht. The seas had calmed, offering one of those moments when the Pacific Ocean lived up to the name that Ferdinand Magellan had given it.

Looking through high-powered binoculars, one of the crew was first to spot the approaching aircraft. He said to Zubov, "Sir, I have one, no, two aircraft approaching."

Zubov had been leaning back leisurely in the center chair on the small bridge. He stood up, and asked, "Approaching? They are coming toward us?"

"They appear to be, yes, sir."

Zubov grabbed the binoculars, and watched for several more seconds. After lowering the glasses, he looked at the radio, and then back out the front window. He whispered, "Shit."

Two Russian-made Mi-35 Hind attack helicopters sped ever closer. Each craft locked onto the yacht with laser-guided missiles.

Zubov finally yelled, "Abandon ship!"

But it was too late. Two missiles screamed forward from each helicopter, striking the target in rapid succession.

The 80-foot yacht, Pavel Zubov and his crew, and 180 bottles of wine were ripped apart and burned.

The helicopters swept by the wreckage. The pilots and their accomplices apparently were satisfied with the results, as each aircraft then banked, turning 180 degrees, and flew back in the direction from where they originated in Russia.

Fifteen minutes later, Dasha Pudovkin's smartphone buzzed, signaling the arrival of a text. It said, "There will be no swimming away from death for him. You should not have stayed hidden." A few hours later, Pudovkin discovered the fate of her husband, his crew and the wine.

Chapter 21

It was Thursday after lunch in the Javits Federal Building in lower Manhattan. Rich Noack and Trent Nguyen had just returned to the conference room they had claimed as their own not long after arriving from D.C.

Much of the FBI's investigation into the murders of Kenneth and Barbara Osborne was spread out on the long table.

Noack reached into his pocket, pulled out some Rolaids, and chewed on two tablets.

Nguyen said, "Perhaps two dirty water dogs from a street cart wasn't the best choice for lunch."

Noack burped silently, and replied, "You can say that again. Might have been the onions and kraut."

"But you had the same thing on Monday. Why?"

"Because they taste damn good, and this is New York. And by the way, you sound like my wife."

As Nguyen shook his head, Eugenio Peraza knocked on the room's open door. The short, dark-haired special agent said, "Mind if I interrupt? I have someone here that you guys should meet."

Noack answered, "No problem. Please, come in."

Following Peraza was a tall, rail thin man with thick gray hair that managed to accentuate a large, protruding forehead. The rest of his face descended into wrinkles, and sagging skin. The man looked very proper, dressed in a white shirt, red and blue striped tie, blue blazer with gold buttons, gray pants with a sharp crease, and shiny black shoes.

Peraza announced, "This is Senior Detective Superintendent Rex Holden with Interpol." Peraza looked at Holden, and then pointed to each man while introducing them: "This is FBI Supervisory Special Agent Rich Noack, and Special Agent Trent Nguyen."

As they shook hands, Holden smiled and enthusiastically said in a thick British accent, "Gentlemen, good to meet you both."

After Noack and Nguyen replied in kind, Noack asked, "Well, why are you visiting the FBI, Detective Holden?"

Peraza chose to interject. "Detective Holden is immersed in investigating counterfeiting, with particular emphasis on vodka and wine."

Holden added, "Indeed, I most certainly am. I understand that you gentlemen are doing much the same?"

Nguyen answered, "Tangentially. We're investigating the murder of a former FBI agent and his wife. We believe that fake wines tie in as motive."

"Yes, I understand. Agent Peraza informed me." Holden paused, looked at Nguyen and then Noack. "I believe we can be of assistance to each other."

Noack responded, "That would be great. How so?"

"It seems of late there has been a rather dramatic step up in violent acts amidst our world of suspected counterfeiters."

"Please, Detective Holden, have a seat, and fill us in."

"Thank you. I am somewhat partial to your American informality. Shall we dispense with titles and such? Call me Rex."

After the men agreed, Nguyen asked, "So, what have you seen, Rex?"

"In your investigation, have you come across Jacques Lafleur?"

As he opened his laptop and hit various keystrokes, Nguyen answered, "Yes, Lafleur. He's former French intelligence, right?"

"That is correct. About 20 years ago, not long after retiring from the DGSE, he pulled off a major wine heist during the Monaco Grand Prix."

"Yes, yes," said Nguyen. "Here's the file." He slid the computer toward Noack.

Holden continued, "Lafleur then disappeared from public for a number of years, building a highly successful counterfeiting and smuggling operation in the shadows. He eventually re-emerged, and no one has been able to get him on anything specific. He is a suspect in various cases, but also is very good at what he does. Lafleur knows how to cover his tracks, if you will, given his own background in intelligence. He also has a savvy team."

As he looked at the computer screen, Noack declared, "That's just wonderful."

"We have suspicions that one of the locations from which he operates is a warehouse near Phoenix. Well, allow me to correct myself. It was a warehouse. Late last week, it was burned to the ground, and a security guard was killed."

Nguyen said, "I assume it was not an accidental fire."

"Most assuredly not. An armored vehicle smashed into the building, the fire was set, and the guard's body dragged outside, with a calling card pinned to his chest."

Nguyen leaned forward. "Calling card?"

"A KGB pin was attached to his shirt."

Noack chimed in, "KGB? What's the deal there?"

"Quite frankly, we were a bit baffled initially. However, earlier this week, one of our informants spotted an individual on the docks in Vladivostok whom many thought dead. Have you heard of Dasha Pudovkin?"

Noack shook his head, and looked over at Nguyen, who said, "No, I don't think so."

Holden seemed a bit pleased. "Pudovkin is former KGB. She was Lafleur's accomplice on the Monaco heist. But she was shot during the heist, and assumed to be dead."

Noack replied, "Assumed?"

"Yes, it seems that her body was never recovered from the Mediterranean."

"Who missed that?" Noack persisted.

"Your CIA apparently ranked among the culprits."

Noack cringed ever so slightly. "So, how does Pudovkin play in?"

"She was seeing off a rather nice yacht captained by one Pavel Zubov. Zubov has operated in the counterfeiting world for some time, and has been both successful and elusive. He certainly gets the work done. At the same time, though, he is not exactly a significant thinker, if you understand my meaning. We have been perplexed as to who was actually pulling his strings for years. Then we received word that Dasha Pudovkin was providing a rather passionate good-bye to Zubov."

Nguyen interrupted, "So, you believe that Pudovkin is behind Zubov?"

"That was our hypothesis."

Noack said, "Was?"

"Wreckage was found nearly two days ago in the Pacific. We are confident it was Zubov's yacht. Completely obliterated."

Silence descended on the room. Nguyen finally observed, "So, you're speculating that some kind of war has broken out between counterfeiters, namely, Lafleur versus Pudovkin after more than two decades."

Holden replied, "It's a possibility. This potential 'war,' as you put it, Trent, might have reached Kenneth Osborne, and he and his wife became casualties."

Noack asked, "Why the war, though?"

Holden smiled crookedly. "Well, leading up to that Monaco theft, Lafleur and Pudovkin were much more than simply partners in crime."

Noack replied, "A woman left behind starts a war among thieves after twenty years?"

Nguyen observed, "It's not like we haven't seen things stranger than that."

Chapter 22

Jennifer and Stephen sat at a shiny wooden table in Buckley's Irish Pub, waiting for their friends to arrive.

The restaurant, situated on Montauk Highway in the middle of Center Moriches, had a long bar running down one side of the space, and tables and booths down the other. Assorted beers were on tap, and the venue offered traditional, hearty pub-style food.

For the Grants, it had become a favorite place for a relaxing dinner or lunch, and a good spot to welcome Cara and Zack Charmichael back from their honeymoon. The newlyweds arrived looking happy, tired, and tanned from their near-two weeks in Cancun.

Soda, iced tea and water were the beverages of choice on this Thursday night. No one apparently was looking for anything stronger that might hamper getting started at work the next day, with Cara staring at a 12-hour shift at the hospital starting at seven the next morning.

While everyone glanced at the menu, Jennifer asked, "So, how was Cancun?"

Cara answered, "It was wonderful. We took advantage of everything the resort had to offer, especially the beach. We did some windsurfing, diving, and ventured out on day trips to explore."

Jennifer replied, "I love Cancun, but it's been a while since I was there." She turned to Stephen, adding, "We've never been there together. We need to go at some point."

Stephen said, "Count me in."

That'll be different from the way I hit the beach last time in Cancun. Stephen recalled moments from a SEAL mission many years before. Coming ashore quietly under the cover of darkness, seeking to rescue Americans held hostage by Marxist guerillas. Ten of the 11 hostages made it home, along with the entire SEAL team. The guerillas were not so lucky. But it was something he replayed on occasion, trying in his mind to will a different outcome for the young American college student who didn't make it.

He returned to the conversation at hand as the waitress approached for their orders.

Having been at Buckley's many times with Stephen, Jennifer and Zack knew that he would be ordering the corn fritters appetizer. However, this was the first time for Cara. Stephen asked her, "Have you had the corn fritters?"

Cara answered, "No. Actually, I've never been here, despite driving by countless times."

Stephen said, "You have to try them."

Zack also advised, "The burgers are very good as well."

Stephen, Zack and Cara chose a variety of hamburgers, with Jennifer going for the fish and chips.

The corn fritters appetizer arrived, and Stephen was glad to see that he had won Cara over as a fan.

During dinner conversation, Stephen mentioned WineCon, that Duane Ellis would be speaking on the history of wine and the Church, and the invitation from Ron for the wine tasting with the Finger Lakes monks.

After swallowing a bite of her burger, Cara responded, "Yes, my dad had mentioned that."

Zack added, "It sounds good to us." He took a sip of water, and continued, "You know, Stephen, since Tom mentioned what Duane Ellis would be speaking on, I've been thinking that we should discuss doing a series of classes at St. Mary's on the sacraments."

Stephen nodded. "I like it. That crosses my mind every time I'm preparing for Communion and Confirmation classes for the kids."

Zack said, "I hate to say it, but I think some of the adults are just as clueless as the kids when it comes to Baptism, Communion, and Absolution in terms of the scriptural basis, why we do what we do, and what each exactly does and means, never mind any of the history of each."

"That also goes for the liturgy in general."

It was evident Zack's enthusiasm was growing, pushing against any fatigue accumulated from the previous two weeks. "How about a series along the lines of 'Why We Do What We Do at St. Mary's'? It could cover the liturgy, the sacraments, the music and hymns we use, prayer, and whatever else we can think of."

"I'd say we're overdue on this. Let's make it happen. You're back at work tomorrow, so we'll lay out a plan then."

Zack smiled, and replied, "Cool."

The meal continued, when Jennifer glanced up at the television hanging from the ceiling. "Stephen, the game's about to start."

"Oh, great."

The Cardinals had made it into the National League Championship Series. At the same time, Tom Stone's Angels were playing in the ALCS. Both New York teams already had been eliminated from the post-season, so the bar-side of Buckley's had few people watching.

"If the Cardinals and Angels make it to the World Series, I'm not sure who will give me a harder time, my wife or Tom."

Cara said, "Oh, don't worry about dad. He's already incredibly nervous. He'll be too much of a wreck if the Angels make it to the Series to give you a problem."

Zack laughed, and said, "I don't know, Cara. The one thing that I've learned about Stephen, Tom and Ron is that they take immense joy in giving each other a hard time."

Jennifer chimed in, "Zack, they thrive on it."

Stephen added, "So says the wife poking her husband about his woeful Reds."

Jennifer laughed, and said, "Oh, poor Stephen."

Chapter 23

Even though it was his own basement, Sean McEnany did not vary in terms of security protocol. He never got sloppy. After a few hours of sleep, he descended the stairs; moved through a portion of the basement featuring a billiards table, a bar and a poker table; and entered a utility room. He went past the house's heating and water units, and pushed aside a set of shelves on wheels, revealing a metal door.

McEnany punched in eight numbers on a keypad to the right of the door, and then leaned his face down to a screen. The retina scan recognized him, and the door clicked open.

Inside the 24x20 room was a long table with two desktop computers, and three wide, thin video screens hanging on the wall.

Resting against another wall stood housing for a small arsenal, including handguns, sniper rifles, and knives, along with night vision goggles and even gas masks.

McEnany sat in one of the office chairs, rolled up to a keyboard, and displayed on the center wall screen his work from the previous night. He slipped on a headset, and made the first of a few calls to Europe that were on his early morning agenda.

Just before nine, McEnany called Paige Caldwell. "Sean, I'm glad you called. Charlie and I are pulling up to the Javits federal building in a cab."

"Anything interesting going on?"

Caldwell got out of the taxi, while Driessen paid the driver. She moved to a spot on the sidewalk, making sure no one else would hear. "Rich Noack got a hold of us yesterday, said he heard we were working on wine counterfeiting and that it could tie in with a murder investigation. So, he wanted to meet."

"How the hell did he hear about what we're working on?"

"I don't know that, yet. What do you have?"

"I'm pretty sure that Noack and Nguyen are working on the murder of Nguyen's old partner, Kenneth Osborne, and his wife, Barbara." McEnany proceeded to tell Caldwell about Osborne's background, the violent deaths, and the fact that he heard that Osborne had been poking around wine counterfeiting before he died.

"That's helpful. Thanks."

McEnany said, "I've got something else, and apparently it involves you and Grant."

"What are you talking about?"

"Do you recall an incident with Jacquoo Lafleur and Dasha Pudovkin?"

"Unfortunately, I do. It was a wine theft in Monaco. Lafleur got away with some rare and expensive bottles, while I shot Pudovkin. One of the ways I used to annoy Stephen was to remind him that he let Lafleur get away, while I killed Pudovkin." She paused, and then said, "Does this have to do with the KGB pin and warehouse in Arizona?"

"It does. Pudovkin's not so dead."

"Shit. I hate when that happens."

McEnany relayed what he had assembled about Lafleur and Pudovkin, which was almost exactly what Interpol's

Rex Holden told Noack and Nguyen, including information on the Lafleur-Pudovkin connection and possible current conflict.

Caldwell replied, "Past relationships. Ugh. Am I right?"

McEnany continued, "Talking about relationships, this is really interesting. After the heist that you and Grant botched..."

"Hey, watch it."

"... not only did Pudovkin disappear for two decades, but Lafleur went dark for about ten years as well. Since he re-emerged, Lafleur has had a unique relationship with his old employer, French intelligence. Apparently, he supplies the DGSE with any terrorism-related information that he might come across in his dealings. In turn, they leave him alone regarding his counterfeit and other less-than-legal business dealings. Well, as long as he swears off counterfeiting any French wines."

"Hmmm, not exactly without precedent."

"Yeah, I know, but he also has had a DGSE operative working on his team for a number of years now."

"Makes sense from the French perspective, to make sure nothing goes wrong."

"Her name is Gabrielle Poyer, and she is in a relationship with Lafleur."

"Does Lafleur know she's French intelligence?"

"Yes."

"Does the DGSE know that she's involved with Lafleur?"

"Apparently."

"Part of her assignment?"

"From what I've dug up, no, it wasn't when she started out. But it developed."

"So, it's a real relationship, and everyone is fine with it?"

"Right."

"How very French."

"Got that right."

Caldwell said, "Okay, Sean, Charlie's getting antsy. There's only so long that he can evaluate everyone who comes too close to me, and still look casual."

Driessen heard that and grunted.

She continued, "Anything else?"

McEnany answered, "Two more. First, Lafleur is attending WineCon, and hosting an event. He's pushing the legit side of his business. Second, there's an Interpol Brit who is focused on counterfeits working with the FBI now. So, don't be surprised if you meet Senior Detective Superintendent Rex Holden today."

"Thanks, Sean, good stuff, as usual."

After ending the call, Driessen said to Caldwell, "Give me the CliffsNotes version before we go upstairs."

Chapter 24

Almost twenty minutes later, as the elevator doors opened, the towering figure of Rich Noack waited to greet Paige Caldwell and Charlie Driessen.

Despite Noack being FBI, and Caldwell and Driessen being former CIA, the rather typical rivalries and differing perspectives rarely came into play. The three actually had seen a good deal of action together, earning mutual respect.

As Noack led them down a hallway, he asked, "How's business?"

Caldwell answered, "We're doing well. As I mentioned on the phone, Charlie and I have been working this counterfeit wine case from here in New York, while the rest of the team in D.C. is seeing to other clients."

Noack replied, "I still haven't forgiven you for luring Jessica away from the Bureau." Jessica West had been an FBI special agent, but left to work for Caldwell, Driessen and McEnany's CDM International Strategies and Security.

Driessen chimed in, "Yeah, your loss, Noack. West is great."

"I know."

Caldwell added, "You were supposed to tell me how I could make it up to you, but I haven't heard anything yet."

"I'm working on it," replied Noack.

When they entered the conference room, not only was Trent Nguyen waiting, but so was Larry Banner.

Training and experience didn't allow Caldwell or Driessen to appear surprised. They greeted Nguyen, and then turned to Banner. The man who hired them said, "It's okay. Agents Noack and Nguyen know that you are working for me."

Driessen said, "You're the boss on this, Larry, but I thought we were keeping that quiet?"

Banner replied, "We still are, Charlie. But when Agent Nguyen contacted me and told me what happened to the Osbornes, and the counterfeit angle, I thought it best to talk with them, though, again, quietly."

Caldwell said, "Sounds good."

Another person entered the room, and shut the door behind him. Noack said, "Ah, this is..."

Caldwell interrupted, "This must be Senior Detective Superintendent Rex Holden, Interpol, correct?"

Holden raised an eyebrow, and replied, "Well, yes. It seems that you have me at a disadvantage. Have we met previously?"

As they shook hands, Caldwell said, "No, we haven't. It's nice to meet you."

Noack smirked.

With final introductions made, each took a seat at the conference room table.

Caldwell said, "So, who is going to share first?"

Noack answered, "As the hosts, we'll kick things off."

He turned the meeting over to Nguyen, who provided the background of the Osborne case. Nguyen continued, "We've been trying to rebuild Osborne's investigation as best we can. But, unfortunately, we just don't know all of his contacts. However, Detective Holden has helped immensely."

Nguyen tossed into the mix everything that Holden had passed along. He then added, "Lastly, this just came up this morning, so we haven't been able to do anything with it yet. Osborne contacted a vineyard owner on the North Fork of Long Island about a longtime vintner who abruptly sold his vineyard, basically cut himself off from friends and associates, and left Long Island. His name is Jason Kushner, and a Vince Weathers was the purchaser. I don't know if those names ring a bell with any of you?"

Banner replied, "I had met Jason a few times at tastings and so on. People who knew him much better were very surprised that he sold Kushner Wines. I know nothing about Weathers."

No one else offered anything on Kushner.

Caldwell jumped into the brief silence. "From what we've dug up so far, it seems like we're on the same page regarding Pudovkin and Lafleur."

Holden rubbed his chin, and commented, "Really?"

"Yes, and perhaps we have a bit more." She looked at Noack and Nguyen. "Were you aware that Lafleur's girlfriend, Gabrielle Poyer, also is DGSE?"

Noack sighed ever so slightly, and glanced at Nguyen. "No, we were not aware."

Holden interjected, "You're saying that Ms. Poyer is French intelligence?"

Caldwell nodded. "And in good standing. Both sides, if you will, know who she works for and who she's sleeping with."

Noack offhandedly added, "That all sounds very French."

Caldwell smiled, and said, "Yeah, I know. Apparently, Lafleur feeds the DGSE information on any terrorist matters he gets a whiff of, and the only real restriction on him seems to be to stay away from counterfeiting any French wines."

Holden asked, "Ms. Caldwell, I have to ask: How did you come across this information?"

She smiled. "Now, now, Detective Holden, I'm not one to kiss and tell."

Noack added, "Paige and Charlie have excellent sources of information. In fact, as Trent and I have often said, they sometimes seem better than the FBI's."

Noack and Nguyen were well aware of the vast skills and networks possessed by Sean McEnany. It also had frustrated them in the past when McEnany had information the FBI lacked.

Caldwell responded, "Thanks, Rich."

"That was part compliment, part lament."

"I know."

Noack turned, and said, "You were smart to hire CDM, Mr. Banner."

"They came highly recommended."

Holden said, "Mr. Banner, I am not clear as to what you hired Ms. Caldwell and Mr. Driessen for exactly."

Banner paused a moment, and then proceeded to answer Holden's question, leaving out his background with the CIA.

"I see. My sympathies on the costly counterfeits. I might be able to assist you in one area."

"How so?"

"I would not be bragging in saying that I have considerable experience in sorting out forgeries in a noteworthy collection, such as you apparently have, and can do so with complete confidentiality."

"I've brought myself up to speed, but I also recognize the need for experience and expertise. I certainly would appreciate your help, Detective Holden. I assume there would be a fee for your services?"

"Please, sir, absolutely not. Rather, I would simply ask that we would be able to more closely examine the forgeries, so as to track down the culprits."

Banner said, "That is exactly what I want to see accomplished."

Holden replied, "Wonderful, might we make arrangements after this meeting?"

"Yes, of course."

Driessen said, "Now that that's settled. Noack, do you also know that Lafleur is coming to New York City, and actually hosting an event at WineCon?"

Holden shook his head, observing in a low voice, "Brazen."

Noack seemed to perk up a bit. "Yes, Charlie, actually we did know that. Unfortunately, as has been the case with Lafleur around the world, we have nothing to arrest him on in the U.S."

Driessen chuckled. "Hey, maybe we can help you out on that, too."

Chapter 25

Once Vince Weathers took possession of Kushner Wines, he transformed the basement in the building housing the fermenters from mundane storage to a laboratory.

The old basement entrances were not just left untouched, but sealed from the inside, with a new entrance concealed in the floor of a file room. Pushing a button on the wall hidden behind a filing cabinet popped open the hatch in the floor. Stairs led down into a lab featuring cutting-edge technology and materials needed to produce masterful replicas of wine labels, corks and bottles, as well as to mix assorted wines to achieve a just-right taste and color that would permit them to be passed off as great and/or rare vintages.

This was not a workspace made for dabbling by one person. Rather, it featured multiple workstations, allowing a team of experts to create a steady stream of fake wines. Weathers had brought together people he had worked with over the years. These were individuals who could be counted on for their varied skills in winemaking and other ventures, and for the fact that their love of money far outdistanced any passion they might have for the wine itself or any allegiance to ethical behavior. This was a small manufacturing facility with well-chosen personnel.

While working for Jason Kushner, Weathers also had been running his own counterfeiting operation – smaller

and in another location. By the time he had gathered
enough damning evidence on Kushner's unwillingness to
come even close to paying his full tax bill for several years,
it neatly coincided with the right time for Weathers to step
up his operations. Kushner meekly acquiesced, sold the
vineyard at a deep discount to Weathers, and left the area
under the threat of being exposed to his family, friends,
colleagues, the larger community, and of course, the IRS.

Weathers and a half-dozen employees were still at work
in the lab late on this Friday afternoon when his
smartphone rang. "Yes?"

It was Liam Casper. "How are things proceeding?"

Weathers answered, "Arizona did real damage."

"Jacques is well aware of that. We all are. We've gone
over this." The frustration in his voice was unmistakable.
"Have you been able to step things up?"

"It's been a real test for my people in China, but they
are proceeding. The pace has quickened, and we're being
careful not to allow for any slip-ups. I like what I'm seeing.
But as we discussed, it will take some time to re-supply.
I'm limited as to what can be done here, at this point, but it
can help."

"We understand, and are going to try to meet some of
the market via what we've got here. But we're concerned. If
I'm reading things right, someone seems to be quietly
stepping in to fill the vacuum."

"I'll let you know when the first shipment is ready."

"Thank you, Vince. Jacques appreciates what you're
doing. Your efforts will be rewarded."

"Thanks, Liam."

Chapter 26

Though it was about 20 miles north of his Manhattan apartment, Larry Banner's brick and stone Georgian colonial set on 14 acres overlooking the Hudson River seemed to reside on another planet.

Banner had sent a black Lincoln Navigator to pick up Rex Holden at his hotel. Holden rode in the front passenger seat, telling the driver he never liked riding in the back. The vehicle stopped at the security gate. The driver punched in four digits on the keypad, and the tall, iron gates slowly opened.

Holden looked around as the vehicle proceeded along a narrow, tree-lined road, which eventually became a circular driveway in front of the sizeable home. When the SUV stopped, Banner, appearing relaxed in jeans, a white shirt and V-neck, gray cashmere sweater, opened the door of the vehicle.

Holden emerged wearing what seemed to be his patented dark blue blazer, along with tan pants and a light blue shirt. Banner shook his hand. He said, "Good to see you, Rex. I appreciate your taking time to perform this assessment of my collection."

Holden smiled, and replied, "Please, Larry, as I explained, this is part of the job. The invitation to stay at your very lovely home for the weekend while I do my work, however, truly is generous."

"I hope work can wait for a bit. I thought I would give you a tour of the grounds and home, show you the wine cellar, and then lunch will be ready. After that, you'll have nearly free run of the place."

"Again, that is most generous. Of course, I will be concentrating on assessing your collection. I have brought various tools of the trade."

"We will make sure that all of your things are delivered to your room, if that works?"

"Yes. Most kind of you."

Banner nodded at the driver who stood waiting nearby.

As Holden's items were taken to a guest room with a view of the river, Banner walked Holden around the grounds, including a stroll out to one of the staircases leading up from a dock far below on the Hudson. Banner pointed out the helipad not too far from the house. Banner said, "Having the helicopter option to avoid traffic and get around quickly has been a godsend."

Holden asked, "What about the neighbors?"

"There have been few complaints. In fact, the only neighbor who did complain became an enthusiastic supporter once I offered to give him a lift on occasion."

Inside the house, Banner moved among assorted rooms, particularly lingering in a few. One was a space across the back of the home featuring a lap pool with large windows looking out on the back lawn and down on the river. Another apparent favorite was a mini-pub with a fully equipped bar and four poker tables. The library featured temperature and humidity-controlled bookcases.

What Banner called the "tasting room" was spacious, offering different types of seating and tables; a walk-in, glass, mini wine cellar; and a small kitchen for accompanying food.

Banner pointed to the glass wine encasement. "I like to have the bottles that we are going to serve brought in from the main cellar before guests arrive."

Holden nodded, and said, "I see. And when can I see the main cellar?"

"Let's go there now."

Banner led Holden across the main floor of the home, through the kitchen, and into an intimate den. As Banner walked by a mahogany desk, he pulled a skeleton key out of his pocket, and inserted it into the mouth of a gargoyle on an oversized fireplace. With the turn of the key, a lock clicking could be heard, and a wall panel next to the fireplace inched open.

Banner turned with a smile on his face.

Holden asked, "Is this what you Americans call 'old school?'"

He shrugged slightly, and replied, "Perhaps. I make sure I always have the key with me. No one else can enter."

Banner fully opened the hidden door, and a staircase was revealed. But it went in the opposite direction than expected.

Holden raised an eyebrow. "Up?"

"Yes. Please, follow me."

At the top of steep but rather wide stairs, Banner opened a large, insulated door, and they stepped into a wine cellar that ran across the top of nearly three-quarters of the home. The ceiling was curved with strips of oak going from one end of the room to the other, with metal support bands running about six feet part in the opposite direction. Each wall was covered with wine racks, but for a heavy, bolted door that led out to a sitting area. The door and outside seating area had not been used in a few years. Several racking peninsulas jetted out into the room. At the far end of the space, a granite-topped island featured a sink. Closer to the entrance stood a long oak table.

Holden whispered, "Lovely."

Banner said, "Thank you."

"Can you really call this a 'cellar' when it's on top of such a large home?"

Banner smiled in response. He then said, "At one time, this was a rooftop hot house. The first owner loved orchids. I ripped it out, and built this."

"It is a shame that you cannot use the outside seating area. I would imagine the view of the river would make for an ideal setting to savor the right vintage."

Banner smiled again. "In fact, while I'm in the city at WineCon this coming week, I have a contractor coming in to completely upgrade that outside area. They are going to expand it, put in a small outdoor kitchen, and build a stone stairway. They are bringing in heavy equipment. It's quite a job, but the contractor is a good friend, and he promises to do it all from the outside. And I can give staff the time off. For good measure, I will not have to deal with any of the noise and mess. By the time I get back, it will be done. Or, at least, that's the promise. Then I'll just refurbish the door. I appreciate when things work efficiently."

"That sounds ideal." As Holden began to look around at particular bottles, he asked, "How large is the collection?

"Just under 1,200 bottles."

"Impressive."

"Let's hope it is still as impressive as I once thought."

"Do not take this the wrong way, Larry, but I am going to enjoy this weekend."

Banner smiled, and answered, "Actually, I completely understand. But first, lunch."

They descended the stairs, and Banner locked the door behind them.

By the end of the weekend, Banner declared his relief that Holden had identified 82 fakes. Holden replied, "That is not insignificant, Larry. I assume you paid a good amount for each of these." The bottles stood on the table in the rooftop wine cellar.

"Rex, I had come to expect far worse. Later, when I tally up what I paid for these and what I assumed they were now worth, I will be angry. Trust me."

"I understand. Well, when might I be able to take these for our investigation?"

"I will have them boxed up and sent to you in a little over a week, if that works, given that the New York City Wine Convention is this week?"

"Of course, that will be fine."

"Good," replied Banner. "Now, before you head back to the city, how does dinner, accompanied, by the way, with a 1952 Ripeau Red Bordeaux, sound?"

Holden answered, "Simply exquisite."

Chapter 27

All 36 guestrooms at The Old Saint Brendan Inn in the middle of Greenport Village were reserved for a pre-New York City Wine Convention event hosted by four of Long Island's North Fork wineries. Half of the rooms showed off views of Shelter Island across the Peconic waters. The inn was full for both Sunday and Monday nights.

At the relative last minute, Paige Caldwell asked Stephen if he and Jennifer would attend the East End gathering. Stephen didn't have to work very hard to convince Jennifer to head east late Sunday afternoon for a day or so of fine wine and food.

Caldwell passed along information the FBI came across regarding Ken Osborne's poking around on Kushner Wines, Jason Kushner and Vince Weathers. Stephen decided not to ask how a room suddenly became available at the inn, or how it wound up being one looking out at the water.

Sunday evening started with two luxury buses taking attendees on a short ride from the inn to Byrd Nest Vineyards. The long driveway carved a path out of the grape vines that ran on each side, leading up a gentle incline from Sound Avenue.

At the top of the small hill stood the vineyard's trademark building. Whenever Stephen drove past, he could never decide whether he liked it or not. It was a large, long farmhouse-style building with yawning windows. It also happened to have a massive turret attached on the east end. Being so close to the water, it seemed inevitable that the turret would serve as a lighthouse lookalike. But as one's eyes climbed, sitting atop the turret instead was a faux bird's nest. A large ring was made to look like interwoven branches and leaves. On the decking inside the nest sat a few tables, a small bar, and a wide railing encircling the area. The railing allowed guests to rest their wine glasses as they looked out on the vineyard, North Fork farms, and the Long Island Sound to the north.

Evan Byrd led the group of nearly 60 around the facility. His professorial tone fit his slight build, round glasses, thinning hair, somewhat unkempt mustache, and tweed jacket. During the tour, Byrd displayed particular pride in his barrels being made of French Oak from Vosges, and seemed ready to defend his position of French Oak being the best aging vessel against any who might disagree. But no one did.

The end of the tour came in a tasting room, featuring a lengthy bar and small circular tables around which people could gather. Wide-ranging discussions among various groups were fueled by wine and hors d'oeuvres.

Dinner followed in a room running across the back of the building. The darkness of the night deprived attendees of the ability to look out on an expansive porch, lawn, gardens, and grape vines.

Cathy Li welcomed everyone with brief remarks. She introduced her fellow vintners who were serving as hosts for these two days. As she went from her husband, Mike, to Evan and then Willis Slate, Li paused briefly upon seeing Vince Weathers enter the room and take an open seat, which happened to be at the same table with Evan Byrd, and Jennifer and Stephen Grant. Li quickly recovered, and introduced Weathers as well.

Stephen took note of Byrd's agitation with the arrival of Weathers. Byrd appeared both surprised and annoyed.

Cathy Li went on to highlight the history of winemaking on the North Fork, noting that it really began in the early 1970s with a single vineyard, subsequently grew to nearly four dozen wine producers, and now received wide recognition for quality. Her closing pitch for the region, and the wines produced by each of the host vineyards, would have put to shame the efforts of most chamber of commerce presidents.

The dinner featured local fare, naturally including a wide range of wines from the hosts. Other than small talk here and there, Stephen was in listening-and-watching mode. To Jennifer's right sat Vince Weathers, to Stephen's left was Evan Byrd, and across the table were two additional couples.

While Stephen savored his oysters Rockefeller appetizer, he listened to Byrd relaying the history of Byrd Nest Vineyards. Weathers said nothing.

With the conversation trailing off some during the main course, Stephen was able to concentrate on the pan-seared Long Island duck with blueberry sauce, accompanied by local roasted potatoes with thyme and rosemary seasoning. He was enjoying the meal.

During his SEAL days, Grant learned a diet designed to meet the physical and mental needs of what was called the "warrior athlete." He also came to understand what could be eaten, if necessary, under the most extreme survival conditions. Stephen never fully shook off those lessons, and carried them into the CIA, where they served him well. But certain Agency assignments also allowed him to nurture a discerning palate for wine, and an appreciation for a wide selection of excellent and sometimes exotic food. As for recent years as a pastor, church potlucks too often tapped into his survivalist SEAL experience, rather than his CIA-developed skills in the culinary arts.

Vince Weathers finally broke his silence while Stephen was dipping a spoon into a coconut tapioca dessert. But Weathers only spoke when asked a pointed question by Byrd.

"Why is Kushner Wines not one of the stops on tomorrow's tour?" queried Byrd.

Weathers took a deep breath. "Too busy."

Byrd's eyes narrowed. "Really? What has you so busy?"

Weathers paused for several seconds, merely staring at Byrd. He finally replied, "Many changes and upgrades."

"That's surprising, given that Jason was always a rather cutting-edge vintner."

"Well," Weathers observed, "that was three years ago, and perhaps he was not as cutting edge as you thought."

Stephen could see that this last comment by Weathers amped up Byrd's anger.

"Since I know this business far better than you ever could, Mr. Weathers, I'm absolutely sure that Jason used the best practices, tools and technology. I also wonder what exactly it is that you are doing there now since you fired the winery's top people, and replaced them with individuals who seem to have far less expertise."

Stephen noted that Weathers remained quite calm.

Weathers said, "Again, three years is a long time, and maybe you should worry about your own staff and vineyard."

Byrd's response quickened. "It's just that I received a call not long ago from a former FBI agent who now owns a restaurant in New York City. He was asking questions about Jason and you, Mr. Weathers."

Weathers failed to respond. Once again, he merely stared at Byrd.

Byrd continued, "Any idea why he would be asking questions?"

"No idea," answered Weathers.

Byrd's anger clearly was growing. "We had an interesting discussion about the problem of counterfeit wine."

Weathers reached for his wine glass. A small amount of liquid remained in the bottom. He finished it, put the glass down, and said, "I hope that talk was fruitful. Wine fakes are a big problem. Now, if you'll excuse me, I have to go."

Weathers briefly nodded at the table in general, and left.

Stephen leaned over to Byrd, and in a low voice, said, "Mr. Byrd, do you have a moment to talk about that former FBI agent?"

It was apparent that Byrd was elsewhere in thought, and still exceedingly annoyed. "What? Oh, yes, but not now. Perhaps tomorrow? I have to say a few words of thanks, and then wrap things up here."

Stephen hesitated, and then said, "Earlier would be better."

As he rose from the table, Byrd said, "Well, I have a room at the Saint Brendan in order to stay on top of things. Tonight, I'll be reviewing the logistics for tomorrow's itinerary." He paused, seemingly trying to refocus, and looked directly at Stephen. "Can you stop by my room around 11:30 tonight? I should have things wrapped up by then. Or, is that too late?"

Stephen replied, "No, that's fine. Thanks."

"Room 408." Byrd then said to everyone at the table, "If you will excuse me."

The two couples across the table quickly re-engaged in a lively exchange they'd been carrying on throughout dinner over whether or not there were any truly great wines produced in the U.S.

Stephen turned to Jennifer, and whispered, "That was interesting."

Jennifer replied, "It certainly was entertaining. It's obvious that Mr. Byrd despises Mr. Weathers, and

Weathers seems to – what's the best word? – tolerate Byrd."

"I agree."

"It's all very *Falcon Crest.*"

Stephen said, "Wow, you went with the eighties nighttime soap opera reference."

Jennifer explained, "Why not? Wineries and intrigue." She paused, looked at her husband's plate, and then asked, "Can I try some of that coconut tapioca?"

"Of course, and by the way, did I tell you how beautiful you look tonight in that red dress?"

She smiled, took a spoonful of his pudding, and casually slipped her left hand onto his right thigh under the table.

Chapter 28

When they returned to the room at the inn, Jennifer said, "It's kind of stuffy in here. Can you crack the sliding glass door?"

Stephen unlocked the door and opened it about six inches. He breathed in deeply, and then turned and sat down in a somewhat comfortable armchair. He leaned his head back, closed his eyes, and said, "After an early start for this morning's services, a few glasses of wine and that food, I admit that I'm ready for sleep, even though it's just ten o-clock. Does that make me a wimp?"

"Stephen, it's Sunday night. You're almost always ready for sleep by ten," Jennifer jabbed, as she moved about the room.

"I guess that's true. So, I am a wimp."

There was no response for a minute or so. Stephen lifted his head, opened his eyes, and said, "Not disputing the wimp comment?"

Jennifer had undressed, and slipped under the sheets of the bed. She laid on her side, with her head leaning on the hand of her bent arm. She still wore earrings, and a string of pearls dangled from her neck. If that wasn't enough, Stephen was pulled in by a seductive smile she kept for him alone.

Jennifer said, "Definitely not a wimp – at least I hope not."

Stephen joined his wife in bed. Cool air moved off the waters, through the open door, across the room and gently touched their bodies.

More than an hour later, Jennifer had her arms around Stephen while nestled into his back. She whispered, "Get out."

"What?"

She pulled her arms back, and gave him a gentle shove. "Go meet Mr. Byrd, get the information you need, and then get your butt back in this bed."

Stephen smiled, and said, "Yes, ma'am."

"Never call me 'ma'am.'"

"Right."

Stephen slipped on a pair of shorts, a polo shirt and sneakers. As he went to leave the room, he stopped and said, "You know, you're right."

"About what?"

"Wine, intrigue, sex. This is like *Falcon Crest*."

Stephen ducked as a pillow flew past his head. He laughed, turned toward the door, and said, "Save my spot."

"Maybe."

As he moved to the elevator, Grant worked to get focused on what he needed to ask Evan Byrd.

Not really much to do other than ask the details of Byrd's conversation with Osborne, and how Weathers seemed to fit in.

The elevator door opened slowly on the second floor. He stepped in, hit the button for the fourth floor, and then waited as the doors eventually closed. The elevator moved so slowly that Grant wasn't sure it was actually ascending.

Nice place, but definitely needs to update the elevator.

The doors finally parted, and he stepped out and turned right. As he saw two men coming toward him, Grant felt something he hadn't in some time. In his SEAL and CIA days, he called it a "red alert." His head and ears felt a kind of tightness, like pressure building up. Trouble usually followed.

As the two men approached, Grant quickly took in details. One was about his size and the other roughly five inches shorter. They were fit and strong. He looked at their faces – in their late twenties or early thirties. The taller man looked Grant in the eyes and smiled, while the other simply kept his gaze straight ahead.

As he moved past them, Grant said, "Excuse me."

The taller man nodded, and said, "Yes, of course."

Were those dark spots on his shirt?

Grant detected a hint of the South in the voice.

As he approached a ninety-degree turn in the hallway, Grant glanced back and saw the two men enter the elevator. He also noted an absence of security cameras on the floor.

Grant moved quickly to Room 408, ignored the "Do Not Disturb" sign on the handle, and knocked loudly.

He heard nothing. Meanwhile, his red alert was still flashing.

Grant knocked again.

He counted off ten seconds in his head, and then reached for the door handle. It clicked open. He pushed the door, and called out, "Mr. Byrd. It's Stephen Grant."

Once the door went beyond a certain point, Grant could see a head tilted back in the room's desk chair. *Lord, please, no.* He moved forward, and quickly saw that it was too late. The eyes stared up devoid of life. His throat had been slit. Grant looked around. *The blood sprayed. The shirt. The elevator. It's slow. Might still be a chance.*

He ran out of the room, sprinted down and around the hallway, and banged through the door to the staircase. Grant partly ran, slid and jumped down the narrow stairs, turning at each floor. When he arrived at the main floor, he plunged through the door, and ran to the front desk.

Pointing to the front doors, he asked the very surprised clerk, "Anyone leave?"

She replied, "Um, no. Two people came out of the elevators and just went that way." She pointed in the other direction.

As he sprinted away, Grant heard her say that there were a few parking spots in the back. He yelled back, "Call 911! Someone's been killed."

He moved past the entrance to the dining room, and went through another door. The kitchen was on his right, and the back exit was straight ahead.

Weapon?

While still moving, Grant reached through the opening where staff dropped off dirty dishes, and grabbed a steak knife.

Grant decided on the element of surprise. He crashed through the exit with the steak knife in hand.

The two men that he passed earlier in the fourth floor hallway were directly in front of him, with their car, less than ten feet away. The car was pointed for easy exit onto a side street. The shorter man just finished lowering himself behind the steering wheel, while the taller was opening the passenger side door.

Grant never stopped.

The taller assailant had begun to turn away from the car toward the sound of the inn door opening. But before he could make the full turn, Grant launched himself into his back. As the target's chest crashed against the side of the car's rooftop, Grant recognized the sound of a rib cracking and air being pushed out of the man's lungs.

Grant recovered his balance, and stepped back. He assumed the man's body would fall to the ground, and had started calculating his options with the driver.

But the first target failed to cooperate. Rather than dropping down, he fell backward toward Grant. The man turned, and landed a fist on Grant's left cheek.

Stephen fell down to the hard, cracked tar. Given the severity of the punch, he was amazed at still being conscious. The taller man approached, and started to reach his right hand around to his back.

Crap. Gun.

Grant not only was surprised at consciousness, but that the steak knife was still in his hand. Before the man could bring the gun around, Grant rose up and drove the knife into his opponent's calf.

The man dropped the gun, and with the knife stuck in his leg, screamed out a string of profanities.

The driver yelled, "Get in the fucking car!"

The taller man stumbled to the open passenger door.

Grant spotted the fallen gun and crawled toward it.

The assailant fell into the car, knife still protruding, and the sedan screeched forward.

Grant reached the handgun, and while lying flat on the ground aimed at the back tire.

Steady.

He fired off a shot, and then two more. The first bullet missed the car completely. The second took out a taillight. And the third lodged in the back bumper. The car was unaffected, turned at the end of the narrow lot, and disappeared.

Grant rolled over onto his back, and looked for cameras anywhere on the building.

Are you kidding? Nothing here either. Where's the guest security?

He lay there for another few seconds, feeling his face throbbing.

Three shots. Not one hit the tire. So much for marksmanship.

Chapter 29

Paige Caldwell said, "What the hell is it with you letting people get away when wine is involved?"

After speaking with the Southold Town police, Stephen was back in his room giving Paige a rundown on the phone as to what happened. One hand held the phone; the other an ice pack to his face.

"Very amusing. Turns out, though, that yours got away back in Monaco, too." Stephen understood, even expected, Paige's needling. But he also was well aware that she knew that it still bothered him that Jacques Lafleur had gotten away many years ago, and that this encounter would trouble him until all those involved were brought to justice.

In her hotel room in New York City, Paige jotted down the information that Stephen relayed, including the discussion at the table between Byrd and Weathers, the descriptions of the two assailants, what he found in terms of Evan Byrd and his room, and the details of the engagement with the two men and their escape.

She asked, "You took three shots?"

"Yes, Paige."

"And they all missed?"

"Apparently."

"Right, and you didn't get the license plate?"

He replied with exasperation in his voice, "Correct."

"You've slipped with this whole pastor thing. Maybe a little more time on the shooting range is in order."

"Paige, I'm a pastor, not..."

She laughed, and then said, "Relax, Stephen. You did what you could."

He reluctantly said, "Maybe."

"And I'm sure the police sketch artist results will make the difference."

Grant repeated, "Maybe."

"I'll pass this information along to Sean and Noack. I don't mind waking up either one, that is, if they haven't already heard. I trust Sean will find out what the local LEOs got from Weathers."

"Have you ever really figured out how he does it, by the way?"

"Does what?"

"You know. Have access to information that no one else seems to have?"

"That's Sean, thankfully. He must be a true wonder on your church council." She switched topics. "I'm sure Sean and Noack will want to talk later this morning. Get a little sleep in the meantime."

Stephen glanced at a clock on a bedside table. In big red numbers, it screamed out 4:14 in the morning. "Sounds good. Thanks."

"Thank you, Stephen. After all, I asked you to go. Apologize to Jennifer, if necessary."

"I'll tell her. Talk to you later."

After he ended the call, Stephen looked at Jennifer sitting cross-legged on the bed. He said, "Paige said to give you her apologies for putting us in this mess."

Jennifer said, "Not necessary." She stood up, walked over to Stephen, kissed him on the forehead, and said, "We've talked about this. You're anything but a typical pastor, and so, I've come to understand that nights like this one might happen on occasion – very rare occasions.

I'll never be comfortable with it because I worry about you. But you will not turn down requests for help. You shouldn't, and I would hope that you wouldn't. I'm here – we're together – in part because of what you, Paige, Charlie, Sean and all of the others stand willing to sacrifice for each other. Like I said, I worry, but I'm also thankful."

"Jen..."

While getting back into bed and under the covers, Jennifer interrupted, "Stephen, it's okay, and we need sleep. Get in bed, and hold me."

He closed his eyes, but his mind would not immediately shutdown as an internal debate persisted on his varied responsibilities. At his core, Grant knew how the debate would turn out, but that outcome did not come without some degree of doubt and conflict. He thought how strange it was that certain aspects of his life had become more complex today than when he was working for the CIA.

Chapter 30

Paige Caldwell and Charlie Driessen stopped at the Jacob K. Javits Convention Center on 11th Avenue on Manhattan's West Side to purchase all-access VIP tickets for the New York City Wine Convention running during the coming week. It also gave them a chance to look the place over.

While exiting through one of the many doors of the glass building, Driessen asked, "What the hell is it with this city and naming things after Jacob Javits – this place and the federal building?"

"That's what they do. Name government buildings after local politicians," replied Paige Caldwell. "Not exactly unique, Charlie."

"Yeah, I get it. But wasn't there anybody else? After all, this is New York City, and Javits was a Republican in a liberal city." Driessen paused, and then added, "Although, he was one of those really liberal Republicans. I'm not sure any of those exist anymore."

"Thank God." Her smartphone rang. "Yes."

"Caldwell?"

"Yes."

"It's Noack. Have any plans right now?"

"That depends. What do you have in mind?"

On the other end of the call, Noack was in the front passenger seat of a black Chevy Suburban pulling away from the other Javits building downtown. Trent Nguyen was at the wheel, and Rex Holden was in the back seat. Noack smiled and shook his head. "Jacques Lafleur just checked in at the Waldorf. Trent, Rex Holden and I are going to call on him, and then head east to pick around the Byrd murder."

"Count Charlie and me in on both, if that works for you?"

"Absolutely. Where are you?"

"Outside the Javits Center on 11th Avenue."

"We'll pick you up in a few minutes."

* * *

Jacques Lafleur and Gabrielle Poyer's 900-square-foot luxury suite at the Waldorf featured a foyer, marble bath, and walk-in closet. The three main rooms – a living room, bedroom and sitting room – offered views of Park Avenue. The suite had classic-style furniture throughout.

The door buzzer rang as the couple just about finished unpacking and began settling in to the spacious accommodations.

Lafleur opened the door, and said, "Yes? Can I help you?"

Noack and Nguyen produced their FBI credentials. Noack said, "Mr. Lafleur, I am Special Agent Richard Noack with the Federal Bureau of Investigation, and this is Special Agent Trent Nguyen."

Lafleur smiled, and smoothly replied, "Very nice to meet you gentlemen, and who else do we have here?"

Noack answered, "This is Senior Detective Superintendent Rex Holden with Interpol. And Ms. Paige Caldwell and Mr. Charles Driessen are consultants."

Lafleur looked at Driessen and then Caldwell. "Consultants? For what?"

Noack replied, "Might we come in and talk?"

"Where are my manners? Of course. I think we will have room for all of you."

As he led the others into the living room, Lafleur called out, "Gabrielle, dear, we have guests."

Poyer emerged from the bedroom, and said, "Wonderful." Lafleur introduced the new arrivals to Gabrielle, getting each name and title right.

Caldwell kept her eyes focused on Lafleur, and he seemed to notice.

Lafleur said, "Please, everyone, sit down." As chairs and a couch were filled, Lafleur remained standing, and continued, "So, Special Agent Noack, what is this all about?"

Caldwell interrupted, "Is there anyone else in the suite?"

Lafleur answered, "No. There is no one else." He turned his attention back to Noack.

Noack said, "I don't really like to play games, so I'll be straightforward. We know who you are, Mr. Lafleur, going back to your career with French intelligence, that infamous theft during the Monaco Grand Prix years ago, and your, let's say, shadowy business dealings since."

As he strolled over to where Poyer was seated, Lafleur laughed and smiled broadly. "Well, I'm flattered that the famous American FBI could think that my life since the DGSE has been so exciting." He placed a hand on Poyer's shoulder. While also was smiling, Gabrielle reached up and laid her hand over his.

Driessen reacted to Lafleur with a chuckle and slight shake of the head. But the other four guests simply watched and listened stoically.

Lafleur continued, "Agent Noack, do not misinterpret that comment. I certainly have lived a wonderful, comfortable, and quite profitable life over the past 20 years or so. And with Gabrielle, how could things not be exciting? But rest assured, I no longer work in the shadows."

It was Nguyen's turn. "Really? But you do, Ms. Poyer, correct? As we understand it, you still work for the DGSE."

Poyer's smile did not fade, but it tightened ever so slightly. "You're amusing, Agent Nguyen."

"That's not an answer, Ms. Poyer."

Most eyes were on Poyer and Nguyen, except for Caldwell's, which were still trained on Lafleur.

A brief silence was broken by Noack, who looked at Lafleur. "We're also sorry to hear about that fire in your warehouse outside of Phoenix. The entire thing sounded rather bizarre. Have any ideas about who might be behind that?"

Lafleur replied, "It's still not clear to me why you are here, Agent Noack?"

Noack said, "Four murders are being investigated."

"I'm very sorry to hear that. But what could that possibly have to do with me?"

"The victims were involved in the wine business."

Lafleur again smiled. "So, you have four people killed, who happen to be involved with wine. And since I am in the same business, you drop by with questions just after I arrive in the country. That sounds strange. Either you are leaving something out, or perhaps better investigative work is needed."

Nguyen jumped in, "One of the victims was a security guard at your warehouse in Arizona."

Lafleur sighed ever so slightly. "Yes. The warehouse in Arizona is, in fact, owned by one of my companies. Although I did not know the man, I was very distressed to learn about his death. I trust law enforcement, including yourselves, will find out who did this, and dole out some appropriate U.S. justice. Perhaps John Wayne style."

Caldwell raised an eyebrow at that last comment.

Lafleur continued, "While less important, of course, I should note that my business also was victimized here, as our warehouse, where some very valuable wines were stored, was entirely destroyed."

Nguyen said, "Of course, Mr. Lafleur. Counterfeits are another factor that might tie together the victims."

Lafleur replied, "Excuse me?"

"Counterfeits. Do you know anything about fake wines?"

"Agent Nguyen, I am a purchaser, seller and collector of fine wines. As such, I deplore counterfeiters. They insert uncertainty into the market, and that's never a good thing."

Paige Caldwell finally broke her silence. "I disagree."

Lafleur looked at her, and said, "Pardon?"

"I disagree with most of what you've told us."

"What do you mean, Ms. Caldwell?"

Caldwell leaned forward in her chair. "Dasha Pudovkin."

Lafleur stared at her, expressionless.

Caldwell continued, "Let's start with the fact that I was there when you stole Sir James Blasingame's wine collection during the Monaco Grand Prix. In fact, I was the one who shot Dasha Pudovkin."

Lafleur's smile finally disappeared, but he said nothing.

Caldwell said, "I thought she was dead, until I very recently learned otherwise. What about you, Mr. Lafleur, or you, Ms. Poyer? Did you know that Ms. Pudovkin was alive?"

Poyer replied, "I'm not sure what any of this has to do with us."

Caldwell smiled, and said, "That's funny. Tell me, does any of this information or recent activity potentially affect your deal?"

Poyer said, "Deal?"

Caldwell glanced at Noack, who nodded. Caldwell then explained, "The agreement between French intelligence and Mr. Lafleur. You know. Lafleur passes on any information he comes across regarding terrorists and other major evildoers, and the French give him a pass on his counterfeiting." She looked at Lafleur. "Well, with the caveat that you don't fake any French labels."

Poyer stood up, and said, "I believe we are done here."

Driessen interjected in a low voice, "Of course we are."

Holden continued to observe in silence.

Noack rose from his chair, with Caldwell, Holden, Nguyen and Driessen following his lead. Everyone stood in silence for several seconds. Noack finally said, "Like I said, I'm not much for playing games. Just so you fully understand the situation, one of the murder victims was a retired FBI agent, and another was his wife."

Lafleur's expression changed. He said, "I am very sorry to hear that, Agent Noack."

"If you're clean regarding these murders, then I expect your help, Mr. Lafleur, in the way that you assist the French. Otherwise ... well, for all our sakes, I hope that is not the case."

Poyer said, "I'll show you out."

After their five guests left and the door was closed, Poyer returned to the living room.

The anger on Lafleur's face was unmistakable. "Where the hell did they get that information?"

"I don't know," answered Poyer. "But I am going to find out."

Chapter 31

They approached the SUV outside the hotel. It was parked in a spot that few could get away with in New York City.

Holden said, "I will not join the journey to Long Island. After this meeting, I have to call my superiors and see how they would like to proceed."

Noack said, "Okay, Rex. Where can we drop you?"

"Not necessary. I will hail a taxi."

"All right. Take care."

Nguyen took on the task of guiding the vehicle toward the Midtown Tunnel and the Long Island Expressway beyond, with Noack riding shotgun. Caldwell sat behind the driver's seat, and Driessen behind Noack.

Caldwell said, "I'm going to give Stephen a call to see if he is still in Greenport. Perhaps he can tag along and provide further details on what happened."

Noack replied, "Makes sense."

After Grant answered, Paige said, "Stephen, are you still in Greenport?"

"Yes. Though at this point, I'm not really sure why. I was waiting for something to break, but it's not like the police are going to call me. So, we're planning to leave shortly. Besides, Jennifer needs to get back to the office."

"I'm with Charlie, Rich Noack and Trent Nguyen. We're leaving the city now, and heading out there. Can you stay around to help us out?" She added, "You can tell Jennifer that we won't keep you out late, and will drop you home after we're done."

She smiled at Driessen, who rolled his eyes.

Grant said, "Hold on."

Caldwell heard nothing from the other side of the call for about 30 seconds.

Then Grant said, "Paige, sounds good. That works. Call me as you get close to town, and I'll let you know where you can meet me."

"Done. Since I'm not driving, it'll probably take us more than two hours to get out there."

Nguyen shook his head.

Grant laughed, and said, "Yes, I'm guessing that our FBI friends have a greater respect for traffic laws than you do."

Caldwell ended the call, and announced, "You heard. Stephen will meet us."

Noack said, "Good."

Nguyen asked, "What was the 'more than two hours' crack?"

"Oh, nothing. I just tend to make drives more efficient than most others."

Driessen chuckled. "'More efficient' – interesting choice of words."

Noack turned some in his seat to see Caldwell more easily. She simply shrugged and smiled at him.

As the SUV crept forward with lanes merging at the entrance to the tunnel, Nguyen asked, "So, what do we make of that meeting?"

Noack said, "Unfortunately, the two of them have training in not giving much away. The only thing that I can say for sure is that we made them uneasy – especially you, Paige."

Caldwell said, "Agreed. I didn't get much clarification on Lafleur or Poyer in terms of the games they play, how far

Lafleur is willing to go, or how much Poyer really knows about what Lafleur does."

Nguyen said, "Once we dropped Pudovkin into the conversation, Poyer more or less took over, and shut us down. My guess is that she knows everything, and if someone is withholding information in that couple, it's her. After all, she's the one that's currently French intel."

Noack replied, "Trust me, Lafleur in no way has forgotten what was drilled into him regarding secrets and misdirection. If I had to guess, I'd say that their relationship is hardly a model of transparency and honesty."

Caldwell interjected, "Transparency and honesty are overrated."

Nguyen laughed. "And you're not married, Paige. I'm just shocked."

She replied, "I learned that lesson from my married colleagues at the CIA."

Chapter 32

After parking the SUV in a small lot in Greenport, Trent Nguyen looked at Paige Caldwell and announced, "An hour and 50 minutes."

"Not bad, but I would have shaved off at least another 10 or 15 minutes," said Caldwell.

Nguyen smiled, and said, "How?"

Charlie Driessen replied, "Don't doubt it, Nguyen. Trust me."

Five minutes later, Rich Noack, Driessen, Caldwell and Nguyen were sitting with Stephen Grant at a table in the Coronet Luncheonette. The small restaurant had stood at the center of the village on the corner of Front and Main Streets since the late forties, and still oozed an old-time feeling. The exterior featured brick, green and white awnings, and a light-up sign saying "Soda" and "Restaurant." The interior décor was unchanged for decades, including soda fountains and shake blenders.

It was coffee all around at the Formica-topped table, but for Grant's iced tea.

Grant was brought up to speed on the meeting with Lafleur and Poyer. He then reported, "After Jen left and while you were on the road, I met with a local police detective, Pat Pavelski. He said they identified the two assailants – Rick Rutherford and Byron Sawchuck." He looked at his phone. "He also passed along their photos to me." Grant handed over his phone, with each person flipping between the two pictures.

Noack said, "Can you send these to me?"

Caldwell added, "Me, too? I'll get them to Sean."

Grant nodded in reply, and texted the photos to each. "Pavelski said it looked like the names were likely fake, too clean and no history beyond the very basics. They were still digging. He also said that they had no hits on any Long Island hospitals for injuries fitting what one of the assailants – it was Sawchuck – received last night before getting away."

Nguyen asked, "Why was the detective so forthcoming with you?"

Grant smiled and answered, "He's a Lutheran, former Navy, and apparently familiar with a few of the incidents in recent years where I landed in the news. So, we had a foundation to build on, you might say."

"Right."

Driessen added, "Pays to be a kick-ass pastor, I guess."

Grant ignored that, took a sip of iced tea, and continued, "Detective Pavelski offered to accompany us to The Old Saint Brendan Inn and Byrd Nest Vineyards." Grant looked at Noack. "And to Kushner Wines if you want to speak with Vince Weathers?"

Noack said, "Yes, on all of the above. That would be appreciated."

"I thought so. He should be here in a few minutes."

Everyone stood when Pavelski approached the table. Grant handled the introductions.

In appearance, Pavelski differed markedly from the others. At five-feet-four inches, he was the shortest. Other than Noack, he also was the heaviest. Streaks of gray in his curly brown hair, full beard and mustache made him look older than his 34 years.

The detective's clothes – black loafers, navy blue pants, and a white button down shirt – did not seem to fit exactly right. The shirt also offered clues as to what Pavelski had for lunch.

The Pavelski style, or lack thereof, stood in stark contrast to the two FBI agents' dark blue suits, bright white shirts, and striped ties; Grant's yellow, long sleeve shirt and khaki pants; and Caldwell's boots, dark jeans, off-white shirt, and window pane print blazer. In fact, Pavelski almost made Driessen's rumpled safari-style shirt and well-worn brown cargo pants look sharp.

Each time he shook one of their hands, Pavelski either said, "How ya doin'?" or "Good to meet ya."

The detective said, "We don't get the feds interested in too much around here, at least in terms of law enforcement. Don't get me started on the whole Plum Island fiasco."

Noack offered, "We appreciate your being willing to work together, and give us your insights."

"Hey, no problem, especially since ya think this might tie in with the murders in the city. Crap, a former FBI agent and his wife." He shook his head. "Sorry to hear about that."

Noack said, "Thanks."

Pavelski said, "Are you guys ready? We can walk over to the inn, then head to Byrd's winery, and after that, try talkin' to Mr. Weathers."

"That works for us, Detective Pavelski," said Nguyen.

"Just so you know, we obviously talked to Weathers already, and his alibi looks good. Of course, that doesn't mean he ain't involved."

Driessen asked, "Do you have anything else on Weathers?"

"Nothin'. Guy's pretty clean. He banged around the wine business for a long time. People around here were pretty surprised when he bought the Kushner operation."

Driessen replied, "What's your gut say about him?"

"That's easy. Seems like an asshole."

More than a half hour later, Grant finished walking through what had happened at the inn the night before, from heading to Byrd's room to his failed attempt at stopping Rutherford and Sawchuck. Caldwell already had heard the basics over the phone, and had passed on the information to Noack and Nguyen. But each of these individuals knew there were benefits to being at the scene, perhaps catching something others missed. That, however, was not the case at The Old Saint Brendan Inn.

Outside the building, Noack said, "It's getting late. Detective Pavelski, does it make sense for us to split into two groups – one heading to the Byrd winery and the other visiting Mr. Weathers?"

Pavelski glanced at his watch. "Almost four. Yeah, makes sense. Since I questioned Weathers last night, it's probably a good idea to leave me out this time. Maybe he'll cough up something different."

Noack said, "I agree." He turned to Nguyen. "Trent, why don't you go with Detective Pavelski and see if you can find anything that links to Osborne, especially based on what Byrd said last night at Pastor Grant's table?"

Nguyen hesitated briefly, and then agreed.

Caldwell chimed in, "I'd like to talk to Weathers. Stephen, why don't you come with us, and Charlie, go with Agent Nguyen?"

Driessen said, "Why the hell should Grant question Weathers while I poke around the victim's crap?"

Caldwell answered, "Because Stephen is better at reading people than you are. You know, it goes back to that poker thing. He was one of the best students, and you one of the worst."

Driessen grunted in response.

Nguyen added, "By the way, poking through the victim's crap is a big part of law enforcement work."

Pavelski echoed, "It sure as hell is."

Driessen said, "I'm sure it is. But I'm not a cop – local or fed."

Caldwell shook her head. "Making friends, Charlie."

Chapter 33

Nguyen and Driessen joined Pavelski in his unmarked, navy blue sedan.

As Pavelski started the car, Nguyen asked, "Your department has been over Byrd's winery and his home, I assume?"

Pavelski replied, "Yeah."

"Is the house near the winery?"

"No. Byrd had a condo almost out to the point in Orient."

"Mind if we go there first, and then to the winery?"

"No problem."

"Byrd have any family?"

"His wife died six years ago. No kids. No siblings. Father dead years ago. Mother is in her nineties, in a nursing home, and unable to communicate. She's been out of it for a number of years, according to the staff."

"Anyone close to him?"

"Some friends. We spoke to them. Well, all but one. He was tight with Jason Kushner. But after Kushner sold the winery, he was out of here. Moved away, and apparently has not been in contact with anybody, including Byrd. That was three years ago, roughly."

Driessen interjected, "So, what happens to Byrd's winery now?"

Pavelski said, "Beats the shit out of me. Not my worry."

The three men rode on in silence.

A few minutes later, Pavelski turned into the condominium complex, parking in front of Byrd's unit. He unlocked the front door. Nguyen and Driessen fanned out, while Pavelski simply lingered.

Driessen settled into poking around the bedroom, while Nguyen took the home office.

As Nguyen was combing through a desktop computer, Driessen called out, "Hey, Nguyen, get in here."

Driessen was sitting on the edge of the bed with a leather-covered book in his hand, and about twenty more of seemingly the same book piled in front of him.

Nguyen asked, "What do you have?"

Driessen smiled triumphantly. "Byrd kept a diary."

Nguyen pulled a chair from the corner over to the side of the bed. "You mean a journal?"

"Whatever you want to call it. From what I can tell, these go back a half-dozen years." He held up the book in his hand. "Looks like he started writing when his wife died." He put that one down, and picked up another. "And continued up to a couple of days ago."

Pavelski wandered in. "Where'd you find them?"

"Cardboard box tucked away in the corner of the closet. It was like he was hiding them. But who the hell from?"

Pavelski shrugged. "Maybe he wanted to keep them really personal. You know, so any guests wouldn't find them and ask questions."

Each journal was marked with a start and end date at the bottom of the back cover.

Nguyen already had taken the latest journal from Driessen, and was flipping through it. "He wrote in this almost every day. Each date marked clearly. Seems like much of it is just details about the winery, daily meetings, and so on." He continued turning pages.

Driessen looked through the first journal. "He was writing the early stuff to his dead wife. Telling her how much he missed her, feeling lonely..."

Nguyen interrupted, "Here it is. Byrd wrote about his call with Osborne."

Driessen said, "Read it."

Nguyen nodded.

I received a call today from a former FBI agent, Kenneth Osborne. He owns the Osborne Tavern in Manhattan, which has one of the best wine lists in the city. I thought he was calling about ordering from Byrd Nest. After all, his place carries a Riesling from Kushner and something from Li's, I think. In fact, Osborne did say he would consider offering our wine. After the call, I sent off a case of our best via a delivery service, so the conversation would be fresh in his mind. We'll see.

However, he was really interested in talking about counterfeits. Osborne had been the victim of fake wines at a recent auction, and he was trying to trace the source. He merely said that someone had recommended me, and that the person told him I could be trusted to keep things confidential. I'm not sure who that could have been.

Osborne told me that among the names that came up during his investigation was Vincent Weathers. He knew nothing else about Weathers other than that a source said Weathers was deep in counterfeiting.

Not surprised. Weathers is bad news. I still cannot fathom how he got Jason to sell, and why Jason cut me off.

I told Osborne what I knew about the sale, what I knew about Weathers' background, the changes Weathers made at the winery, the names I knew of Weathers' employees, and that I didn't trust the bastard at all.

He was appreciative, and said he would get back to me with a decision about our wines.

Driessen said, "That gives us something."

Nguyen flipped through the few remaining entries. "Nothing else."

"Noack, Grant and Caldwell are supposed to be with Weathers now."

They quickly agreed on how to spread the news of their find. Driessen texted an alert to Caldwell and Grant, and Nguyen did the same to Noack. They each also took a picture of the journal entry. Nguyen's went to the FBI, as well as Interpol's Rex Holden. Driessen's went to Sean McEnany.

Chapter 34

While Nguyen and Driessen were reading what Evan Byrd wrote about Vince Weathers, Rich Noack, Paige Caldwell and Stephen Grant were standing in the bright, airy, and expansive foyer of the main building at Kushner Wines. Noack introduced himself, and then Caldwell and Grant as consultants, to Vince Weathers.

Weathers suspiciously acknowledged that Grant had been seated at his table at the Sunday night dinner. He then turned back to Noack, and said, "I've already spoken to the police."

Noack responded, "I know, Mr. Weathers. But I was wondering if you could make a little time for the FBI. You know how it is, sometimes different law enforcement agencies fail to completely share information, turf battles and all."

"No, I don't know how that is, Agent Noack. But I'll answer any of your questions."

Caldwell interrupted, "Would it be possible to walk and talk at the same time, Mr. Weathers? I love a good glass of wine, and appreciate tours of wineries."

Weathers paused, and looked at Caldwell incredulous, "You want me to give you a tour, while you are asking questions to see if I had anything to do with the murder of Evan Byrd?"

Caldwell said, "I wouldn't think you'd mind if you had nothing to do with the murder."

Stephen smiled ever so slightly. *Paige, sometimes you are priceless.*

After a lengthier pause than the first, Weathers said, "I'll give you a tour."

As Weathers led the three around, the conversation ping-ponged back and forth between Weathers answering questions from Noack about his background, purchase of Kushner Wines, and relationship with Evan Byrd, and questions from Caldwell about the facilities, grapes, vines, and the winemaking process. Throughout, Grant listened and watched.

Walking back from a quick look at the vines, both Grant's and Caldwell's phones rumbled. Grant looked at the message from Charlie Driessen: "Osborne was on to Weathers as possible counterfeiter."

Caldwell saw the same message. She looked at Grant, who gave a slight nod.

The last stop from Weathers was in front of a door with a "STAFF" sign hanging on it. He opened the door, and pointed to a desk with three computers and nine screens. "As for my alibi, Agent Noack, I handed over our surveillance files to the police. These run 24/7, and clearly show that I returned from the dinner and worked late on the night that Evan was murdered."

Noack said, "Yes, we'll review that. I'm sure it all checks out. One last question." He pulled out his smartphone. "Do you know either of these two men?" Noack held up the phone, showing Weathers the photos of Rutherford and Sawchuck.

Weathers took his time looking at each, and then said, "No. I do not know these men."

At the same time, Grant and Caldwell were taking in the video screens.

"You're sure?" asked Noack.

"Yes, I am sure. I told Detective Pavelski the same thing."

Noack put the phone in his pocket, and said, "Thank you, Mr...."

Grant interrupted, "Mr. Weathers, the most important part of the tour has been missed."

Weathers looked at Grant and said, "And what would that be, Mr. ... Grant, was it?"

"The tasting."

Caldwell added, "Oh, yes, let's please try the Kushner Wines."

Weathers looked at Grant, Caldwell, and then Noack.

Noack shrugged, glanced at his watch, and said, "I'm just about off duty. That is, if you don't mind, Mr. Weathers."

Weathers paused several more seconds, and then relented. He led them into the tasting room.

Grant spotted the restrooms sign at the other end of the room, toward the back of the building. He said, "Before we get to your wines, however, where is the men's room?"

Weathers sighed, and pointed Grant in the right direction.

"Thank you," said Grant.

Caldwell asked, "While we're waiting for Stephen to return, what can you tell us about wine on the North Fork? I was a bit surprised when I first heard that this was wine country."

Weathers obliged with a perfunctory outline, which lasted about five minutes. A minute later, Grant returned. "Hope I didn't miss anything interesting."

Weathers asked, "Can we get on with this?"

Grant looked around innocently, and said, "Yes, of course."

Weathers explained, "Kushner produces three whites – a Chardonnay, a Riesling, and a distinct blend – and three reds – a Merlot, a Cabernet Sauvignon, and a Cabernet Franc. What would you like to try?"

Grant said, "Well, each, naturally."

Weathers again paused, looking at Grant.

Grant smiled, looked over at Noack and Caldwell, and then said, "Hey, why not?"

Weathers clearly was exasperated, but said, "All right, fine."

As he poured small samples, Weathers spoke about each wine in robotic fashion, noting that the Merlot and Riesling were Kushner's longest produced wines.

While Noack and Caldwell drank slowly, Grant examined each sample, first with the eye, then the nose, and finally, with his mouth. He then spat each sample out into a spittoon at the end of the bar.

After this ritual was repeated six times, Weathers said, "If there is nothing else, I have work to do."

"Of course," said Noack. "I appreciate your time."

They each shook Weathers' hand, with Grant being the last to do so.

As the three started walking away, Weathers asked, "What is your opinion of our wine, Mr. Grant?"

Grant turned, and said, "I thought the Riesling was quite nice, and the Merlot was distinctive. The rest were, well, adequate. By the way, it's not really 'Mr. Grant.' I'm a pastor."

Weathers again paused. "You're a pastor going around with an FBI agent?"

"Yes. Life is strange, isn't it? All kinds of unexpected things pop up."

Chapter 35

Byron Sawchuck listened as his current employer updated the orders for his team over the phone.

A hint of the South could be detected in Sawchuck's voice. He replied, "Yes, our man still keeps an eye on him and his family."

He resumed listening, and then said, "That is unfortunate. But we are ready to take that step. We knew it would be a possibility."

The order was given.

"Yes, once we hang up, I'll tell him it must be done immediately."

The employer moved on to other matters.

Sawchuck answered, "I have no problem with any of that. It is, indeed, a lucrative opportunity. However, I do believe that our costs will be higher than you are assuming."

While listening to the reply, he looked down at the bandages wrapped around his calf. Sawchuck leaned down and pushed on the wound. He grimaced slightly.

"That's fair. I appreciate the adjustment."

As the other person gave further instructions, Sawchuck leaned back in the chair, this time testing the rib fracture. He seemed to be pleased with that result. "No. My wounds will not be a problem."

He leaned forward as more questions came.

"Just let my team take action. This will be tight, but not a problem."

Sawchuck heard the response, and replied "Perfect. Thank you."

The call ended, and Sawchuck looked at Rick Rutherford sitting across the room of the Newark, New Jersey, apartment that served as a safe house.

Rutherford said, "What's going on?"

"A great deal of work, and we will be nicely compensated."

Rutherford said, "Give me the details."

"First, I have to call Benino."

"I didn't think that was going to be avoided."

Sawchuck shrugged, as he hit assorted numbers on the phone's screen. He said, "Get the others in here, and we'll start laying out these other matters. Time is short."

Chapter 36

Stephen Grant had the third row of the Suburban to himself.

While driving west out of Greenport, Trent Nguyen filled in the details from Evan Byrd's journal regarding Ken Osborne's inquiries on Vince Weathers and counterfeiting. Noack, Caldwell and Grant listened.

When Nguyen was finished, Noack said, "I wonder if Osborne was fishing, or if he had something hard to go on."

Nguyen replied, "If Ken was to the point of placing phone calls, he found something to go on."

From the front passenger seat, Noack called to the back, "So, Pastor Grant, what was the deal with the Weathers' wine tasting?"

"Once Charlie texted the news on counterfeits and Weathers, it made sense to me to get tastes of what was produced at Kushner Wines. To compare against possible fakes, if the opportunity comes up."

Noack asked, "Really? Is your palate that good?"

"Like much else, it's a matter of remembering the training."

Driessen chimed in, "I hope we're not straying into pretentious wine bullshit."

Grant quipped, "Charlie, pretense and wine, where do you get such ideas?"

Caldwell said, "Getting back to Weathers, I didn't catch anything out of order at his winery. Rich? Stephen?"

Noack said, "Nothing caught my eye."

Grant inserted, "It struck me that on his reluctant tour, Weathers actually mentioned that the basement in the building with the fermenters was just used for storage. Why mention that at all, especially since he was looking to get rid of us as quickly as possible?"

Grant's question was answered with silence. Noack finally said, "Perhaps a little odd, but I don't see that as a big deal. You're going to have to give us more than that."

"That was a pretty straightforward building – the big room with the fermenters, two offices, and a door to the basement inside and one outside. The doors drew my attention."

Nguyen asked, "What do you mean?"

"There was no lock or security pad."

Noack said, "Maybe they don't lock."

"When I excused myself for the men's room, I ran back out to the building and checked. Each door wouldn't open."

Noack said, "So, there has to be another entrance."

Grant said, "It would seem so."

Noack continued, "Unfortunately, his security cameras must have picked you up."

Before Grant could respond, Caldwell said, "No, they didn't. All of the views on those nine screens were of the side, front, and inside public areas of the main building. They covered nothing beyond that."

Noack said, "Crap. I should have caught that."

Caldwell responded, "You were focused on questioning Weathers. Stephen took advantage of the fact that Mr. Weathers doesn't want anything going on behind the main building to be recorded."

Grant added, "I stuck my head in and quickly scanned both of those offices, but didn't see another entrance to the basement. But there's no other place it could be."

Nguyen finished the point, "And it's hidden for a reason."

They drove for a few minutes in silence. Then Noack asked, "And why did you tell Weathers that you were a pastor?"

Grant said, "I thought it would at least throw him a bit off balance given that he also saw me at the Sunday dinner as well. He might discount the meeting to some degree. After all, why take an FBI agent seriously who has a pastor tagging along, especially if they are seemingly more interested in drinking wine than in digging up facts about a murder?"

Noack replied, "Right. Thanks. I think."

Caldwell smiled as she looked out the window.

Nguyen glanced at the GPS readout, and said, "Pastor Grant, we should be dropping you off in about 30 minutes."

"Thanks."

Caldwell interjected, "I'd get you home in twenty."

Nguyen shook his head.

A little less than a half hour later, the SUV turned on the circle at the end of the Grants' driveway.

Caldwell and Driessen got out of the vehicle to let Grant climb out freely from the third row. As he made his way out, Nguyen and Noack thanked him for his assistance. Noack added, "You remain the most unique pastor around, Stephen."

Once outside the vehicle, Grant came to Noack's open window, reached across and shook Nguyen's hand and then Noack's. He said to Noack, "I'm not sure how unique this pastor is, but you guys are always in my prayers."

They both replied, "Thanks."

As Grant was talking with the two FBI agents, Jennifer opened the front door, and Paige and Charlie wandered over to say hello.

Stephen joined the three at the house door. He lowered his voice, and said, "Paige, I can't be sure, but the Merlot that we tasted at Kushner Wines was very much like a fake I had with Banner."

She replied, "You're telling me that one of Banner's fakes might have come from Weathers?"

"It was strikingly similar. Both were very heavy on the vanilla, more so than in a typical Merlot."

"Thanks, Stephen, we'll handle it."

"Are you going to tell Noack?"

"Sure. But while we have faith in your skills, Stephen, I'm not really sure what the FBI could do with an amateur wine detective talking about a stronger hint of vanilla in a Merlot."

Stephen smirked.

Caldwell and Driessen had started to say good-bye when her phone rang. She answered, "Yes?"

It was Sean McEnany. "Paige, I think I've got Osborne's source."

"Let's hear it."

"I dug a little into Kushner's finances, given his abrupt sale to Weathers. It turns out Jason Kushner, for whatever reason, failed to pay anything close to what he owed the IRS. And it looked like that was the case for a few years running. I originally assumed that was the impetus for the winery fire sale, that he was getting ready to pay. I didn't think much more about it until Charlie sent over Byrd's journal entry. I saw that Osborne carried Kushner's wine."

"So?"

"Poking around, I heard that Osborne had a great reputation for personal relationships with the vintners themselves. If he stocked the wine, he knew the owner personally, at least to some degree, not just some salesperson."

Caldwell now joined in with McEnany. "So, then you're speculating that Weathers, having been Kushner's operations guy for so long, also knew about the tax issues, and forced Kushner to sell and leave town, so to speak."

"Right. And if Kushner wasn't looking to face the IRS, why not quietly feed what he knew about Weathers to a former FBI agent who was burned by counterfeiting?"

Caldwell smiled. "We're assuming that Kushner knew about at least some of Weathers' activities." She paused. "I generally like it, Sean."

McEnany added, "I tracked down where Kushner moved with his wife and teenage daughter. I also have his number, but it keeps going to voicemail."

"Where did he move?"

"Lincoln, Nebraska."

"I'll let Noack know. He'll be able to get agents there. Text me the address and number. Anything else?"

"That's all for now."

"Thanks." She ended the call, and quickly filled in the blanks for Stephen and Charlie, while Jennifer also listened.

Caldwell looked at Charlie. "Noack will just love the fact that Sean gave us all of this."

Charlie laughed and said with some satisfaction, "McEnany's magic does drive them crazy."

As Caldwell and Driessen headed back to the waiting SUV, Stephen slipped his arm around Jennifer's waist. She asked, "Done playing wine sleuth?"

"I hope so. Either way, I need sleep."

They closed the door behind them.

Chapter 37

Dasha Pudovkin's flight touched down just before midnight on Monday at John F. Kennedy International Airport. She texted her arrival as the plane taxied.

After deplaning, Pudovkin followed signs directing international travelers to Customs. The eyes of both men and women seemed irresistibly drawn to at least glance in her direction. The twenty years since the encounter on the yacht failed to diminish her beauty. The simplicity of a white t-shirt with a pullover, loose-fitting gray sweater, faded jeans, and black and gray sneakers actually seemed to magnify her attractiveness. The faded scar on Pudovkin's face, along with hair dyed black, added a hint of mystery to her allure.

However, a severe, humorless facial expression led the same people who had glanced her way to quickly avert their eyes.

Pudovkin, with a passport saying she was Svetlana Yeltsov, smoothly moved through Customs and the baggage claim area. Emerging from the terminal, she paused for only a few seconds before a blue Toyota Highlander pulled up.

A man in his late thirties, dressed in a black leather jacket, black V-neck shirt, and dark gray pants, hopped out of the front passenger seat. "I'll take your luggage, Ms.

Pudovkin." He pointed to his former seat in the SUV. "Please."

Pudovkin slid into the vehicle. The man deposited her luggage and himself in the backseat.

The driver leaned over and exchanged kisses on the cheek with Pudovkin. "Dasha, it is good to see you. I am so sorry about Pavel."

"Thank you, Dmitri."

Dmitri Melikov was a survivor. He arrived in New York purportedly as a young staff member for the Soviet Union's ambassador to the United Nations. More than four decades later, he climbed a few positions in terms of title, but essentially held the same position for Russia. In reality, though, Melikov arrived in New York as a KGB spy, and never left. He survived the fallout from the attempted 1991 coup against Mikhail Gorbachev, as many KGB did, to continue serving in the Federal Counterintelligence Service, later renamed the Federal Security Service, that is, the Federalnaya Sluzbah Bezopasnosti or FSB.

Now in his early sixties, Melikov showed no signs of slowing down. If anything, it was just the opposite. He continued to perform his perfunctory duties with the U.N. delegation; worked all intelligence angles and executed missions for the FSB; was committed to a physical fitness regime that bordered on fanatical; and in recent years, provided off-the-books services to assorted Russian business and criminal elements.

Melikov's horn-rimmed glasses, thinning gray hair, and neat, dark gray suit spoke lifelong bureaucrat. The training, history, and muscularity under that suit spoke to something very different.

As Melikov began weaving his way out of JFK, Pudovkin asked, "Is everything prepared?"

"It is," replied Melikov. "By the way, this is" – he indicated the man in the backseat with a tilt of his head – "Vasily Morozov. He is one of my best."

Chapter 38

It was just before eight on Tuesday morning as the two FBI special agents – a man in a blue suit and a woman in a gray pantsuit – climbed the three small front steps of the yellow ranch house with white trim in Lincoln, Nebraska.

They rang the doorbell and knocked several times. There was no answer, just as had been the case with the calls to the family's three cell numbers and one landline.

There was a car in the driveway, and another parked on the road.

The male agent opened the storm door, and tried the inside door. It was locked. He said, "You take that side and I'll walk around the other."

The two moved around the house, each looking at the windows while walking.

They simultaneously arrived at the back, and saw that the inside backdoor was slightly ajar. They drew their weapons. The male agent led the way. He pulled open the storm door, and called out, "Hello. Mr. Kushner? Mrs. Kushner?"

That was met with silence.

He said to his partner, "I don't like this. Come on."

The two moved into the kitchen. The pan and two pots on the stove had food in them. A spatula and serving spoon sat not far from the burners. There also was an open loaf of bread on the countertop.

The female agent caught a glimpse of the dining room, and said, "Oh, shit."

They entered the room and got a full look at the grim scene.

Jason Kushner's head was tilted to the side. Blood that had run out of the hole in his forehead, as well as from the wound in his chest, had largely dried.

Across the table, his wife's head was face down. Blood had puddled in her plate, and overflowed onto the table.

Their daughter's body was sprawled on the floor next to the table. She apparently had tried to run, as the entry wounds were in the middle of her back and the rear of her head.

The male agent said, "Let's check out the rest of the home."

After it was determined to be clear, they returned their guns to the holsters, and went back to the bodies. The female agent said, "It looks like this happened during last night's dinner."

"I agree. I'll call it in." As he pulled out his phone, he said, "Hell of a thing during my second week in Nebraska." He shook his head, and spoke into the phone. "Yes, this is Special Agent John Smith. We've got a murder scene on our hands at the Kushner home in Lincoln."

Chapter 39

Greeting and briefly chatting with church council members, Pastor Stephen Grant slowly made his way into the conference room/library for the meeting at St. Mary's. Since the new church was built, this had become one of his favorite rooms, with the walls, bookcases, and long conference table all made of cherry wood.

Sitting at the other end of the table was Sean McEnany. The two men nodded and smiled at each other.

Seeing Sean at church increasingly reminded Stephen of how much his former life in the CIA continued to linger in the background of his life today as a pastor. At times, Grant recognized that it was much more than mere lingering or background, but more like intruding. Jennifer reminded him of that recently.

Losing two murderers one day. Trying to help track them down the next. But the following day means a church council meeting. You couldn't make this stuff up.

However, since Paige Caldwell and the CIA showed up at St. Mary's a few years ago asking for his assistance, Grant never really considered the idea of once again cutting himself off completely from that previous life. If Jennifer asked him to do so, Stephen, of course, would. He knew, though, that Jennifer wouldn't make such a demand. Before their marriage, she understood him as a pastor, and how that served as the foundation of his life.

But she also came to grasp that Stephen's experience, skills and sense of duty meant that he was unlikely to turn down a request to help his friends and former colleagues, and to protect the innocent and his country. Of course, Jennifer also had firsthand experience that the sense of duty, or loyalty, flowed in both directions.

Worried but thankful, she said.

But Grant sometimes wondered if he should turn down such requests, a query that had come up more frequently of late.

God, help me, please, to do what's right.

Stephen's thoughts were drawn back to pastoral matters as people took their seats. Once again, he found himself switching gears.

In light of what he had chosen to read for the opening prayer, Stephen reflected on how the faces at this table had not changed much. This wasn't a new concern, by any means, and certainly not exclusive to St. Mary's. He truly appreciated that God blessed this parish with people willing to be active to make things operate smoothly. For good measure, most around the table had become friends. At the same time, though, there were only two new additions to the council over the last few years. It was frustrating for him, as well as for the officers who had served for a lengthy period and often wound up shifting among positions on council. Unfortunately, that frustration sometimes flirted with a less-than-healthy, holier-than-thou attitude. The occasional bitch session would develop among council members complaining that others in the church failed to do enough. The not-so-subtle point was, "They don't do as much as we do." Stephen prayed for wisdom, strength and compassion to suppress such sinful impulses in himself and in others. He tried to lead any such discussions to a more productive place, like suggesting that council members talk more to other congregation members about what the council was doing and that all kinds of help would be greatly appreciated. If the complaining persisted, he also provided some gentle reminders that people were often in different places in life that might not let them be engaged in current activities – perhaps facing illness, taking care of family, or struggling at work. Stephen tried to explain that there were times when life seemed overwhelming, and it was the Church that provided hope, solace, support and strength through Word and Sacrament, and by coming together as the community of believers. He also pointed out that some people simply were not joiners.

Glenn Oliver, the new congregation president, brought the meeting to order precisely at 7:30 PM. He turned to Pastor Grant to kick things off with prayer.

Stephen said, "I'd like to start with a reading from First Corinthians, Chapter 12:

> For just as the body is one and has many members, and all the members of the body, though many, are one body, so it is with Christ. For in one Spirit we were all baptized into one body—Jews or Greeks, slaves or free—and all were made to drink of one Spirit.
>
> For the body does not consist of one member but of many. If the foot should say, "Because I am not a hand, I do not belong to the body," that would not make it any less a part of the body. And if the ear should say, "Because I am not an eye, I do not belong to the body," that would not make it any less a part of the body. If the whole body were an eye, where would be the sense of hearing? If the whole body were an ear, where would be the sense of smell? But as it is, God arranged the members in the body, each one of them, as he chose. If all were a single

member, where would the body be? As it is, there are many parts, yet one body.

The eye cannot say to the hand, "I have no need of you," nor again the head to the feet, "I have no need of you." On the contrary, the parts of the body that seem to be weaker are indispensable, and on those parts of the body that we think less honorable we bestow the greater honor, and our unpresentable parts are treated with greater modesty, which our more presentable parts do not require. But God has so composed the body, giving greater honor to the part that lacked it, that there may be no division in the body, but that the members may have the same care for one another. If one member suffers, all suffer together; if one member is honored, all rejoice together.

Now you are the body of Christ and individually members of it. And God has appointed in the church first apostles, second prophets, third teachers, then miracles, then gifts of healing, helping, administrating, and various kinds of tongues. Are all apostles? Are all prophets? Are all teachers? Do all work miracles? Do all possess gifts of healing? Do all speak with tongues? Do all interpret? But earnestly desire the higher gifts.

And I will show you a still more excellent way.

Grant then bowed his head, and said, "Let us pray. Dear Lord, we thank you for bringing us together this evening. Please guide us in our deliberations, providing wisdom, clarity of thought, understanding, charity and compassion as we try to carry out your will. Help us to work together in a broken, sinful world. Thank you for the many gifts bestowed upon us individually and as a group, and strengthen us to use these to serve You, to serve our St. Mary's family, to serve our community, and to serve the entire body of Christ. We pray this in Jesus' name. Amen."

Everyone around the table replied, "Amen."

According to the meeting schedule, Glenn asked each committee leader and church staff member to provide a quick update on what was going on in their respective arenas. Last up were the two pastors.

Stephen spoke about the church's shut-ins, two families in need of support, a few pieces of correspondence of importance, an upcoming visit by the district president to St. Mary's, a Reformation Day class titled "Who Was Martin Luther, Anyway?" and the latest on youth Communion and Confirmation classes. He then said, "That provides the perfect segue for the focus of what Pastor Zack will tell you. But first, I know most of you have done this already at some point, but let's as a group welcome him back now as a married man. Congratulations, once again, on getting married to Cara. I'm confident in saying that you definitely married up, my friend."

Laughter broke out, along with comments like "Yes, congratulations" and "God bless both of you," and then applause.

While smiling broadly, Zack said, "Thank you very much. And yes, Stephen, I know I married up, and I thank God for it."

Stephen replied, "Same here, by the way."

"Now, as for that segue, Pastor Grant and I have decided to start a series of classes or Bible studies called 'Why We Do What We Do at St. Mary's.' We plan to look at the liturgy, the sacraments, the music and hymns we use, and prayer. This series would run for six months, starting next month, with each topic covered over three evening classes each month. There naturally will be some overlap, but each month we would have a central topic that would focus our instruction, discussion and questions." He paused, and looked around. "That's the quick take. Any questions, thoughts, or suggestions?"

Glenn said, "It sounds great."

Everett Birk's chair creaked loudly as he motioned to speak. The former church council president and current head of the building and grounds committee, whose 300 pounds, flat-top blond hair, and thin beard and mustache seemed at odds with his gentle voice, asked, "What night and time are you considering?"

Zack answered, "Three Thursday nights. We were thinking 8:00. That would allow people to have dinner at home, get other things done, and we could offer some kind of dessert and coffee. At the same time, we'd try not to run too late – maybe 9:30ish."

Birk said, "Smart. If you want people to show up, give them food."

Stephen could see Nicole, who led the education committee, getting ready to say something. Nicole was a friend of Jennifer's, and one of those rare people in life who truly baffled Stephen. That was no small feat considering that during his SEAL and CIA days he had to get into the heads of all kinds of people, including terrorists, spies, military leaders and politicians. Nicole was perky and liked to talk, but to Stephen, it was her name changes that epitomized what he saw as unpredictable. As far as he could tell, she was happy with her husband and their two children, but a few years ago she dropped her married name of Foreman and went back to Freeman, her maiden name. This predictably stirred unfortunate gossip. When asked about it, she simply giggled, and said that she just liked the sound of "Freeman" better. Her husband and kids just shrugged. That lasted a couple of years, and then she went with a hyphenated Freeman-Foreman.

Now, when he saw her, Stephen's mind inevitably wandered to a question: Could Nicole Freeman-Foreman really sound better to her?

Zack said, "Yes, Nicole?"

"I'm glad we're doing this. I've gotten a few questions recently from a friend, and I'm not really sure how to answer them."

Stephen asked, "Like what?"

"She goes to the South Fork Community Bible Church, and gets kind of confrontational with me about Communion, baptizing babies, and the crucifix in our church. She says Communion is just symbolic, that we shouldn't baptize children before they can decide for themselves if they believe or not, and that her church has no crucifixes because they celebrate a risen Jesus."

Stephen replied, "Those are not unusual statements from some of our Christian brothers and sisters, Nicole, nor are they new. Unfortunately, they rest on different interpretations of Holy Scripture. This is, in part, why we are doing these classes."

Nicole said, "That's good, I guess. But what do I tell her in the meantime? I know she's going to bring them up again when I see her later this week."

"Well," Stephen began, "you can give her the straightforward answers to start off. Matthew, Mark and Luke are clear on what Jesus said about the Lord's Supper. In Matthew, for example, it says, 'Now as they were eating, Jesus took bread, and after blessing it broke it and gave it to the disciples, and said, "Take, eat; this is my body." And he took a cup, and when he had given thanks he gave it to them, saying, "Drink of it, all of you, for this is my blood of the covenant, which is poured out for many for the forgiveness of sins."' And then Paul wrote in First Corinthians, 'The cup of blessing that we bless, is it not a participation in the blood of Christ? The bread that we break, is it not a participation in the body of Christ?

Because there is one bread, we who are many are one body, for we all partake of the one bread.' It's clear that both bread and His body, and both wine and His blood are present. It's not mere symbolism."

"Okay. I'd like to point her to those, if I could."

"It's in Matthew 26. I believe verses ... 26 to 28?" He looked to Zack for help.

Zack said, "Yes, right."

"And it's 1 Corinthians, chapter 10, verses 16 to 17." Stephen continued, "As for Baptism, Peter is clear in Acts that Baptism is for all." He pulled out *The Lutheran Study Bible* that was among the materials he brought into the room and spread out on the table. As he flipped through, Stephen said, "I want to get this right. It's Acts 2, verses 38 and 39." He read: "And Peter said to them, 'Repent and be baptized every one of you in the name of Jesus Christ for the forgiveness of your sins, and you will receive the gift of the Holy Spirit. For the promise is for you and for your children and for all who are far off, everyone whom the Lord our God calls to himself.'"

Stephen looked around the table, and recognized in various expressions that a good number either had forgotten or never heard this. *Hence, the classes.*

Nicole clearly was engaged. Her short black hair was bouncing back and forth; her green eyes brightened; and her smile widened. "Thank you, so much. And what about the crucifix?"

It was Zack's turn. He said, "Of course, there's nothing wrong with using a cross or a crucifix. You see them both in Lutheran churches. But a crucifix is a powerful reminder of Jesus' suffering and atonement for all of our sins, that is, for our salvation. It reminds the Christian that Jesus has conquered sin and, yes, death, as we know that He rose from the dead. I've always thought that the crucifix serves as a much clearer reminder of what Jesus has done for each of us."

Stephen added, "I agree with Zack. The only thing that I would add is that the crucifix also serves as a reminder of the confidence we have in Christ. There can be much suffering in this life, and of course, we all die. The crucifix reminds us that God became man, suffered – indeed, suffered beyond anything we can imagine – and died. He experienced what His children experience, what we experience, and it shows us the way to love, forgiveness, redemption, salvation, and eternal life."

Nicole was silent now, as was everyone else in the room. She finally said, "Thank you, Pastor Zack, Pastor Grant. I don't think I could communicate it the way you have, but I'll try."

Stephen added, "Those are just first takes for a bigger conversation, Nicole. My other suggestion is to please invite your friend to our classes. Tell her no pressure, but that she's more than welcome. And as Everett pointed out, let her know there will be desserts."

She smiled, and said, "I will."

Chapter 40

"Too much vanilla," mumbled Charlie Driessen.

Paige Caldwell smiled and said, "What did you say, Charlie?"

"We're heading back to Kushner Wines in the middle of the night, and one of the reasons is that Grant essentially said there was too much vanilla in a wine. And Banner bought into that."

Caldwell jabbed, "As you know, Stephen was Banner's best student."

Driessen grunted. "And there's the hidden basement door theory."

It was after 11:00 on Tuesday night. Caldwell was behind the wheel heading east, with the headlights of the silver SUV cutting into the darkness on the Long Island Expressway. The two were dressed in black shirts and cargo-style pants.

Caldwell rolled her eyes, and said, "Oh, right, and what about Kushner and his family being murdered, and Byrd's journal entry about Osborne's inquiries on Weathers? I think we're on firmer ground than 'too much vanilla.'"

"Yeah, I got it."

"What's eating at you? I know it's not Stephen's points. You trust him as much as I do."

Charlie looked at her. "Well, almost as much as you do."

"Charlie."

"I don't know. Wine ain't in my wheelhouse."

"Really?"

Driessen ignored her sarcasm, and said, "I'm spinning my wheels on this. You should have brought along one of the others. I think Dicce and Lucena are wine drinkers."

Lis Dicce and Phil Lucena, along with Chase Axelrod and Jessica West, worked for Caldwell, Driessen and McEnany's firm.

"I think we make assignments based on a bit more than beverage choices."

"The only reason Grant's involved seems to be because he's a wine drinker."

"Not exactly. He's closer to a wine expert."

"Give me a break."

They drove in silence for several more minutes.

Driessen asked, "Did you tell Noack what we're doing?"

"On the phone with him, Nguyen and Holden, I mentioned that we would be heading back to Kushner Wines late tonight. I offered some details, but they didn't respond."

"Ah, yes, they want deniability, but also any information we get."

"You know how it's played, Charlie."

Forty minutes later, Caldwell parked the SUV in a dark spot on a narrow road running along the west boundary of Kushner Wines.

They checked their handguns. Caldwell slipped her Glock 20 into a holster strapped to her right thigh, and Driessen holstered a Glock 21 on his belt. He also slipped on a black backpack. Inside was what Driessen called his "Break Any Damn Lock Toolkit."

As they moved through the grape vines, Driessen said, "Nice of Weathers to not have any security cameras behind the main building."

As she led the way, Caldwell merely replied, "Right."

They approached the edge of the vines, stopped and squatted. It was about 30 yards to their goal – the building housing the fermenters.

Both scanned the area. There was no one to be seen.

Driessen said, "Low lighting and no security around. I like this, too. I think."

The two moved silently to the building.

Driessen started to slip off the backpack as he approached one of the entrances. He paused, and whispered, "Shit."

Caldwell turned from her scanning. "What is it?"

He pulled his gun out, and pointed. "No need for the tools to bypass security. The door's open."

Caldwell pulled out her Glock. "Shall we?"

Driessen led the way into the dark building.

They spent several minutes scouting out the main floor of the building, including the two small offices. Caldwell found a hidden button on the wall behind a filing cabinet. She stuck her head outside the office door, and saw Driessen approaching. "Hey, come here. I think I found Stephen's secret entry to the basement."

As Driessen entered the doorway, he immediately spotted a tiny red light on the floor in the middle of the room. He reached for Caldwell's shoulder, but it was too late. Her finger touched the button behind the filing cabinet.

Driessen grabbed Caldwell by the collar and pulled her.

"What the hell?" she yelled.

"Get out!"

Driessen pushed her ahead of him, and they ran toward the exit.

The fuse delay allowed them to almost reach the door when the incendiary instruments ignited in the office. A combination of devices strapped across the floor and ceiling of the basement unleashed immediate destruction coupled with an intense inferno.

Caldwell had moved outside the building, and Driessen was just a step away when the floor erupted with force and flame.

Driessen pushed off with his last step on solid floor and started to dive ahead. This effort, though, became magnified by the rising energy, flames and heat from beneath. He was launched farther than otherwise would have been possible, eventually landing on his left shoulder on the dirt parking lot. Driessen then tumbled, rolled and slid.

Caldwell ran and dropped to his side. "Charlie!"

He groaned, and declared, "Shit."

"What hurts?" She looked up and down his body.

His groan turned into a shout of pain. He clenched his teeth, and said, "Is it possible to separate your shoulder, and break the same damn arm?"

"Unfortunately, yes. Left side only?"

"Not sure ... think so."

Caldwell saw a protrusion under the sleeve on his left arm, between the wrist and elbow. She told him, "This is going to hurt."

She ripped the shirt sleeve fully open where it had been torn by the explosion.

Driessen screamed out in pain. "What the hell are you doing?"

"Shut up, you baby. I told you it would hurt." Caldwell saw that bone had come through the skin. She continued, "Compound fracture. But it looks like it'll be all right until the ambulance gets here. If that's all you wind up with, you'll be damn lucky." She pulled out her smartphone to call 911.

"Sure as hell don't feel lucky." He turned his head slightly, and as blood dripped, he spat out a tooth.

By the time Caldwell finished the call, the fire was raging in full, with the building crumbling and fermenters melting.

Paige was still kneeling on the ground. As more sounds of pain came from Driessen, she gently took his right hand.

She stared into the fire. "Maybe Weathers isn't our guy."

Caldwell looked back to Driessen. "Looks like you saved our lives, Charlie. I guess it was a good decision that you came along on this one."

Driessen managed a small smile, and said, "You're welcome."

Chapter 41

As dawn was breaking, Vince Weathers turned out to be the final person Detective Pat Pavelski questioned on site. The fire laid waste to the Kushner Wines' fermenter building, and nearly took the lives of Paige Caldwell and Charlie Driessen.

Pavelski went through a series of questions as the two looked over the smoldering remains. By the time they entered Weathers' office in the main building, the conversation turned in a different direction.

Looking at each other across the desk, Weathers and Pavelski could have been mistaken for brothers, both with shaggy hair and beards.

Pavelski closed his notebook, and slipped it into the inside pocket of his brown sports jacket. "All right, Mr. Weathers, that's all I got, for now. But I remind you, once more, this was meant for you. Please call me if you think of anyone pissed off enough to do this, or who would gain from it."

Weathers replied, "Of course. But I have some obvious questions that need answers. What were Mr. Driessen and Ms. Caldwell doing in the middle of the night in my vineyard? Were they behind this, and it just blew up in their faces? Caldwell visited me with the FBI yesterday. She was introduced as a 'consultant' by Agent Noack. Is this some kind of game being played by the FBI, some kind of government harassment? I don't like any of this, and I want to know what you are doing about it, Detective?"

Pavelski sighed. "Yeah, I got a lot of unanswered questions, too. I talked to Caldwell, and she wasn't exactly straight with me. Quite frankly, I don't think those guys and the FBI are your problem. But if it turns out that this is some kind of Fed bullshit, I'll be pretty pissed, too. I'm headin' to the hospital to talk with Driessen. I'm also gonna grill Caldwell again. I'll keep you up to date."

Weathers stood up from behind the desk, and Pavelski rose with him. They shook hands, and Weathers said, "Thank you, Detective. I appreciate your effort. Now, I have to get back to the clean-up process."

After walking Pavelski out of the building, Weathers went back to his office, closed the door and returned to the desk.

He picked up the phone.

Jacques Lafleur grabbed his smartphone on the nightstand in the bedroom of his suite at the Waldorf Astoria. He paused before answering to see the time on the screen. "Yes?"

Weathers said, "Jacques?"

"Yes. Who is this?"

"It's Vince Weathers."

Lafleur sat up in bed. "Judging by the time and how infrequently we talk directly, I am guessing that this is not good news."

"It's not. My fermenter building, with the lab in the basement, was burned down."

"Shit! This is ridiculous. Another fire. What the hell happened?"

"They broke in, set explosives and incendiaries, and torched the place."

Lafleur threw off the covers, turned and sat on the side of the bed. Gabrielle had woken up when he first cursed, and now rested on her elbow.

Lafleur said, "Give me more."

Weathers relayed some details, while leaving out others, including the roles played by Caldwell and Driessen.

Lafleur asked, "Who? Do we know?"

"The police have no clue."

"And you? Do you suspect someone?"

Weathers answered, "I got word yesterday that Dasha Pudovkin landed in New York City on Monday night."

Lafleur's head and shoulders slumped. "I see. Let me know if you learn anything else. We will start working on this on our end as well. Liam and Harper will touch base on production and so on. We'll get through this."

"Yes, of course."

After the call ended, Gabrielle asked, "What has happened?"

Lafleur repeated the story, and noted that the police were clueless. He added, "Weathers said that Dasha arrived in New York on Monday night."

"We have to stop that woman."

Chapter 42

Caldwell stood at Driessen's bedside in the emergency room. He refused any pain killers, and made his disgust known that the torn ligaments in his shoulder and the compound fracture would both require surgery, not to mention weeks of awkward recovery.

Caldwell said, "This is getting ridiculous, Charlie."

"What?" he grimaced.

"You and hospitals. D.C., California, and now this on Long Island. I think you've lost more than a step. Maybe it's time for you to stay in the van from now on."

"You know what, Paige?"

"What?"

"Go to hell."

Caldwell laughed.

A nurse and orderly showed up. The nurse announced, "Time for surgery, Mr. Driessen."

Caldwell leaned in and whispered, "I'll call to make sure all went well. But I'm out of here. I leave Detective Pavelski to you after surgery. Give him a song and dance. Well, as best you can."

He grunted.

Caldwell squeezed his right hand, stepped back, and said to the nurse and orderly, "Take him away, and take care of him."

The nurse smiled, and said, "We most certainly will."

Caldwell exited the small hospital, and climbed into the SUV. She pulled her smartphone out, but then spotted Detective Pavelski walking toward the building.

She said to herself, "That was close."

Caldwell started the engine, and drove away. After a few minutes, she pulled into the parking lot of a small beach on the Long Island Sound.

She picked up the smartphone sitting on the passenger seat, and made a secure call.

Sean McEnany answered, "Yes."

"It's Paige."

"How are you and Charlie?"

"I'm fine. They took Charlie into surgery a little while ago. They've got to operate on both the arm and the shoulder."

"He's going to be more of a pain in the ass than usual for a few weeks. Are you waiting at the hospital?"

"No, I'm parked at a beach outside of town. I'm trying to avoid the police. I brushed off Detective Pavelski in the midst of the chaos at Kushner Wines. But he wants to know why Charlie and I were there. I'm not sure how much I can get away with in his case."

"Understand. I have some additional information. Dasha Pudovkin landed in New York City, at Kennedy Airport, on Monday night. She's using the name Svetlana Yeltsov."

"I know I shouldn't ask, but how the hell did you find that out?" The truth was that McEnany was slowly becoming more forthcoming with both Paige and Charlie as to his sources, or at least some of them.

"There's a Russian, former KGB and current FSB, who owes me. He let me know that she arrived, but he won't spill anything else. So, unfortunately, I don't know exactly where she is, at this point. This guy's cover is at the U.N. But that's not just for his FSB work. He's also been taking on some freelance work from various non-governmental

Russian clients. I think he's trying to build up a retirement nest egg. But he made a big mistake a few years ago, and I caught wind of it. I lent him a hand, and let's just say that his debt is ongoing until he leaves the country. But, of course, he's selective in what he gives me. You know, just enough that he thinks it will keep me happy."

Caldwell said, "And to think, you run this vast network from the basement of a suburban home on Long Island."

McEnany said, "Hey, there have been stranger things in the history of espionage, like 35mm film in a pumpkin on a farm."

"True. Anything else?"

"Not right now."

"All right. I'm going to drive back to the city. I'll also touch base with Banner and Noack. Thanks."

Chapter 43

While passing by store after store, and the multiple chain and fast food restaurants that populated Riverhead, Caldwell weaved the SUV through the two westbound lanes of traffic. As she turned to enter the eastern start of the Long Island Expressway, her smartphone rang.

"Yes."

"The police are looking for you," declared the FBI's Rich Noack.

"Things didn't go exactly as planned last night."

"Yes, I know. I just got off the phone with Detective Pavelski. I'm putting you on speaker. Trent and Rex Holden are with me."

"I'll do the same. I don't want any further trouble with New York police. This is a hands-free state."

Caldwell went on to provide the details of what had happened at the Kushner Wines' vineyard.

When she paused, Noack asked, "So, Driessen's going to be all right?"

"Yes. I'll call the hospital in a few hours to make sure the surgery went as planned. The trick will be keeping him civil during the recovery. I also left him to deal with Detective Pavelski."

"I imagine that when Driessen comes out of surgery, he'll be as displeased with that arrangement as Pavelski. I ran some interference with the detective for you, by the way."

"Thanks, I appreciate that. Meanwhile, in addition to Weathers' winery being targeted, McEnany learned that Dasha Pudovkin arrived in New York under an alias on Monday night."

Caldwell next heard the British accent of Interpol's Rex Holden. "Yes. We heard that last night as well."

Caldwell merely responded, "Okay."

It was Trent Nguyen's turn. "Even more interesting were the two calls I received within the last hour or so. First, a friend of mine at the DGSE made contact. She said that Poyer was willing to provide critical information, but only if we agreed to abide by the deal that the French have with Lafleur. I got a thumbs up, and called her back."

Caldwell interrupted, "How the hell did you get the FBI bureaucracy to make such a quick decision?"

Noack said, "Because I approved it. It's my ass on the line."

Nguyen continued, "My friend said that Poyer would be calling. Within a few minutes, that was the second call."

"So," asked Caldwell, "did she actually give you anything?"

Nguyen said, "If we can believe her, she gave us everything."

Caldwell replied, "Meaning?"

"Gabrielle verified nearly everything we hit them with during our meeting on Monday. She went on to tell me that Weathers is a key supplier to Lafleur's counterfeiting operation."

Caldwell restated what she had just heard. "Lafleur and Weathers work together."

Nguyen said, "Right."

Caldwell continued, "Okay. That would line up with the attack in Arizona and last night's fire."

Noack jumped in, "It would."

Caldwell continued, "But what about the attack that killed Pudovkin's husband?"

Nguyen answered, "Poyer swore that was not Lafleur."

Caldwell said, "Yeah, like you said, if we can believe her."

Holden agreed, "You are quite correct, Ms. Caldwell. She certainly is not going to volunteer that her lover, who, by the way, provides her with a lifestyle beyond what your typical French government salary would supply, is a murderer."

Nguyen added, "She's going to give us just what is to her advantage."

Caldwell asked, "But what about the murders of Evan Byrd, Jason Kushner, and the rest of the Kushner family? How do those fit into this?"

Holden said, "They certainly fit, as you say, in terms of the links to Osborne's inquiries, and to Weathers and his link to Lafleur."

Noack responded, "Hmmm, perhaps."

Holden continued, "I would have to say more than perhaps, Rich. All of this strengthens my view that this is a war between Lafleur and Pudovkin. We simply now know that Weathers is in bed with Lafleur's group. Poyer naturally wants the focus exclusively on Pudovkin, as does the DGSE, since Lafleur has provided them, presumably, with good information."

Noack offhandedly proclaimed, "Sometimes this international espionage shit gives me a headache."

Caldwell ignored that comment, and said, "Do you know where Pudovkin is?"

Noack replied, "No. And obviously you don't either."

"No. Sean considers his source very reliable, but at the same time, this person only provides as much information as deemed advantageous."

Nguyen said, "Just like Gabrielle Poyer."

Holden added, "At the risk of being obvious, it appears to be to the advantage of everyone to find Ms. Pudovkin."

Caldwell said, "Just as obvious, the New York City WineCon has put all of these people in the same place at the same time. Based on the assessment laid out here, it serves the purposes of Dasha Pudovkin."

Nguyen said, "Gabrielle Poyer agrees, and she is looking for our help in protecting Lafleur, especially at the event he is hosting tomorrow night on the *U.S.S. Intrepid.*"

"Now that's ballsy," observed Caldwell.

Noack said, "Yeah, it is. And I don't think I'm going to be able to sell additional protection from the Bureau beyond Trent, another agent, and me."

Holden interrupted, "Hopefully, you may count me in as well. However, I am receiving flak, if you will, from the home office."

"Thanks, Rex." Noack added, "Hell, I hope I still have my current job after I tell the powers that be what I agreed to regarding Lafleur."

Caldwell said, "Right, good luck with that. Obviously, Charlie's down, but I could bring in the rest of my CDM people."

Noack replied, "That would be much appreciated, Paige."

"No problem, though I will have to bill you."

Noack chuckled, and said, "Now, now, no double dipping. I think this should be covered under your contract with Mr. Banner."

Caldwell smiled, and said, "Fair enough."

Chapter 44

After the hour-and-twenty-minute ride on the Long Island Railroad from the Ronkonkoma station into Penn Station, the group of seven decided to walk across 34th Street.

It was a cloudy, cool Wednesday evening in October, with a breeze coming off the Hudson River. The four clergy members – Stephen Grant, Zack Charmichael, Ron McDermott and Tom Stone – wore their collars under overcoats. The seasonal fall dresses worn by Jennifer Grant, Maggie Stone and Cara Charmichael were hidden by coats that varied in colors, fabrics and style.

Rather than entering the Javits Center for the opening night gala of the New York City WineCon, their ultimate destination was a different event. It was related to WineCon, but far more low-key and of a different character.

They entered the High Line across from the Javits Center at 34th and 11th Avenue just after 6:30. The plan was for a leisurely stroll along this park on a reclaimed, out-of-use elevated railroad track. The 1.45-mile High Line ran above 22 city blocks, and through and up against assorted buildings. Along the way, High Line park visitors were treated to a wide range of perennials, grasses, shrubs, trees, artwork, lighting, sitting areas and seasonally-changing vistas.

Stephen, Jennifer and Ron led the way.

Jennifer slipped her arm through Stephen's and leaned gently into her husband. She said, "I love this walk. It's such an original park."

Stephen said, "It really offers a completely different perspective on the city. And the story of it being transformed from an abandoned, overgrown train line into an urban oasis is fascinating."

Ron asked, "Did you know that this High Line actually is based on one in Paris – the Promenade Plantée?"

Jennifer answered, "I didn't."

Stephen knew it, with firsthand knowledge thanks to a meeting on the Paris park when he was with the CIA. He stayed silent on that bit of the past.

Ron continued, "It opened in 1993, I believe, and until the High Line opened in 2009, the Promenade Plantée was the only park built on an elevated railway."

Jennifer asked, "Why the interest in the Paris version, Ron?"

"When I took a vacation to Paris, I explored nearly all of the city. A park on an old elevated train track made an impression. That's part of the reason why I like this so much as well."

Stephen smiled. "Ron, you are a man of many and varied interests."

A few paces behind were Cara and Zack walking hand-in-hand, and more or less in their own just-married bubble. Their conversation focused on whether or not they could ever live in a city like New York, and each seemed surprised to learn that the other would be open to the possibility.

Immediately following were Tom and Maggie Stone, arm in arm. Cara's parents eavesdropped on the conversation between their daughter and son-in-law, and smiled as Cara and Zack expressed mutual surprise upon discovering something new about the other.

Tom whispered, "Do I surprise you anymore?"

Maggie said in a similarly hushed tone, "After six children and over 30 years of marriage, normally, no. But then there was your decision the other night to not watch the Angels. For you, that was crazy unpredictable."

Tom chuckled. "I told you that I decided not to watch because they lost the two previous games. I tried to break the bad luck; maybe by not watching, they'd win."

"Do you know how ridiculous that sounds? When did my Anglican priest husband suddenly become superstitious, and talk himself into not watching a playoff game in an effort to change his team's luck?"

He smiled. "Yeah, I know. It's stupid."

"So, yes, that surprised me."

"But it worked."

Maggie gave him a good-natured glare.

They walked a few more steps, and Maggie asked, "Do I surprise you?"

Tom stopped, allowing the others to drift ahead. He looked into Maggie's blue eyes and said, "I wake up every day, look at you either lying next to me, or see you already downstairs keeping the madness of our home at bay, and yes, I'm surprised. I'm surprised at being so fortunate to be married to you."

Maggie smiled, and said, "Now, there you did it."

"What?"

"You really did surprise me."

They kissed briefly, and then turned to catch up with the rest of their group.

On the left, they approached the Church of the Guardian Angel. The rear of the building backed up against the High Line. They exited the park at 20th Street, and backtracked along 10th Avenue to the church at 21st Street.

As they approached the Southern Sicilian Romanesque-style brick church, a voice from behind called out, "Jennifer! Stephen!"

They turned to see former Senator Duane Ellis and his wife, Janice, crossing Tenth Avenue. Stephen and Jennifer hugged their friends from California, and then made introductions.

Jennifer asked, "What are you doing here, Duane? As a WineCon panelist, I assumed you would be at the Javits Center opening tonight."

He said, "Given that I'm speaking on the Church's role in the history of wine, I thought it prudent to come here tonight, to find out what the monks from the Finger Lakes Monastery have to say about winemaking, and to get a taste of what they've produced. Besides, I hit my quota of glitzy opening night galas a long time ago."

Jennifer smiled, and replied, "I understand that."

Ron asked, "Do you know Abbott Michael Quinn?"

"I have not met him," answered Duane.

"He's a longtime friend. I'd be happy to introduce the two of you."

"Thank you. I appreciate it."

Noticing a few others entering the church, Ron said, "Shall we go in?"

As the expanded group started to move toward the church doors, a man in a blue sport coat seemed to appear from out of nowhere. He said, "Excuse me, Senator Ellis, and Pastor and Mrs. Grant, might I have a brief moment?"

Stephen replied, "Yes?"

"Thank you. I wanted to introduce myself. I am Senior Detective Superintendent Rex Holden with Interpol."

Stephen replied, "Right. Good to meet you. I understand you're working with the FBI, and have helped Larry Banner."

Holden shook hands with Stephen and then Jennifer. He smiled. "Yes, that is correct. You are well informed. I know of your work as well, Pastor Grant. I am sorry about what happened in Greenport, but I think we are closing in." He turned to Duane Ellis, and said, "Senator, we have met previously."

As they also shook hands, Ellis said, "Forgive me. When was that?"

Holden replied, "Oh, it was several years ago. I briefed your California congressional delegation on international counterfeiting issues, and our group was given a tour of several wineries in your state."

Ellis said, "I apologize for not recalling that."

"Please, I completely understand. My one briefing of American lawmakers naturally stayed with me, but I can only imagine how many briefings you received during your years in Congress."

Ellis said, "Well, thank you for your fight against counterfeiting."

Holden introduced himself to the rest of the group, and he then walked away and entered the church.

Duane maneuvered himself so as to speak privately with Jennifer and Stephen. He whispered, "Before going in, can I get a word?"

After the others, including Janice Ellis, entered the building, Jennifer said, "What is it, Duane?"

He looked at Stephen, and said, "I've come to understand that your CIA background has kept you in touch with certain parties."

"Yes. Why?"

"It's likely nothing. But I just told a little lie. I actually do remember Mr. Holden. As he mentioned, it was a number of years ago that he was with a group that gave us a briefing, and they received a tour of a few California wineries, including our vineyard. As you know, I wasn't involved with the business then. However, I recall a very basic background check was run on Holden and his group. Everything checked out, I assume. But my chief of staff did come to me with an unusual occurrence. He let me know that we received a rather cryptic message from the CIA that there were questions about Holden and his contacts."

Ellis appeared finished.

Stephen said, "And?"

Ellis shrugged. "Sorry, but that's it. The CIA did not give us anymore, and did not advise us to un-invite him. Given the unique CIA communication, I could not help but watch him more closely than anyone else in that group. And quite frankly, there was nothing out of the ordinary."

Stephen said, "Okay, Duane, thanks for the heads up." He looked at Jennifer, and then back to Duane. "We'll pass this along."

Duane smiled, and said, "Shall we head in?"

Stephen said, "Jen, why don't you go in with Duane? I'll be right behind you; just have to make a call."

Stephen moved across West 21st Street to a spot where he would not be overheard. He pulled out his smartphone, and scrolled to a certain contact. "Hello, Sean. It's Stephen. I have some information."

Chapter 45

In the Church of the Guardian Angel, the monks from the Finger Lakes led a prayer, spoke about daily life at their monastery and vineyard, and discussed their wines. At the same time, thirteen blocks to the north at 34th Street and 11th Avenue, it seemed like all of the remaining wine lovers in Manhattan – dressed in the very best suits, gowns and little black dresses – circulated throughout the exhibit halls of the Javits Center.

The opening gala of the New York City Wine Convention featured welcoming remarks by key organizers – a publisher of a leading wine magazine and website, a billionaire wine collector and city resident, and the owner of one of the city's oldest and most celebrated restaurants. That was followed by two musical acts. A brief, rather angsty performance by a folk trio earned polite applause, along with whispered comments wondering how they were hired for the event. The mood of the attendees then ratcheted up with the sounds of Call Us Men, whose recent resurgence saw the onetime nineties "boy band" regaining some of the popularity they had achieved two decades earlier.

The live bands were followed by a DJ playing a wide array of music that allowed some attendees to dance, while most circulated, drinking and talking wine, and sampling some of the finest foods in the city.

In a short, black lace, V-neck Tadashi Shoji dress, Paige Caldwell gracefully moved about the gala accompanied by a handsome, six-foot-three-inch African-American man. Chase Axelrod donned an ocean blue Calvin Klein suit, a light blue shirt and striped tie. He was one of the CDM International Strategies and Security personnel that Caldwell had promised Agent Noack.

"You're always quiet, Chase, but particularly so tonight," observed Caldwell.

"Give me a ballgame over a wine festival," he replied.

"I understand, but you have to adapt, or pretend to do so, in our business."

"Right."

Caldwell spotted their client, Larry Banner, talking with four individuals, and not looking particularly pleased.

She whispered to Axelrod, "Stay here. I have a feeling that our client might need a little help."

Banner was silently listening to master sommelier Colin Wiggs, and Pearson Gerards, the wine-tasting columnist, gushing over the details of the evening when Banner opened the 1929 Merlot – or what they thought was a 1929 Merlot. They had captured the attention and imagination of the billionaire collector who was one of the organizers of NYC WineCon, along with the man's wife.

The billionaire turned to Banner, and said, "Larry, that's a magnificent find. And to think how the wine held up so well after all it went through, including being in the clutches of Hitler. Were you as impressed as Wiggs by the taste?"

That's when Caldwell inserted herself into the group. She smiled, and said, "I apologize for interrupting." She squeezed between Wiggs and Banner, slipped her arm around Banner and gave him a kiss on the cheek. "But I must pull Larry away for a moment." She looked directly at Banner, and said, "Bill is leaving, and you still haven't met him."

Banner's poker experience allowed him to adapt to Caldwell's fiction without any overt sign of surprise or discomfort. "Well, we cannot have that, dear." He looked at the small group, and said, "Forgive me, but I promised that I would finally meet Paige's law partner."

As Caldwell directed him away from the group, the billionaire couple, the columnist and the sommelier acquiesced.

Banner whispered, "Thank you, Paige."

"I had a feeling you needed an out."

Banner tensed, and said, "I really want this counterfeiter nailed, so I can stop trying to avoid conversations like that one, and just generally be more at ease. That damn article on the opening and tasting of that shit has made things so much worse."

They stopped in front of Axelrod. After Caldwell introduced the two, Banner turned back to Paige and asked, "When are we going to nail Weathers?"

"Hopefully soon. But the circumstances have changed."

"Yes, I know. But Stephen seemed pretty sure that the ..." Banner looked around, and further lowered his voice. "He was pretty sure that my counterfeit tasted almost exactly like the wine he had at Weathers' place. And based on what he described to me, I tend to agree with him."

Caldwell said, "I understand. But there, unfortunately, is more to consider now, given the murders."

Banner looked around. The billionaire couple, the columnist and the sommelier were nowhere to be seen. He said, "Yes, of course. I apologize. Keep me up to date. I'm staying in the city during WineCon."

Caldwell said, "We will."

Banner went in one direction. Caldwell and Axelrod headed in another, and eventually made it to the North Fork wineries area. All four wineries – Li Vineyard, Byrd Nest Vineyards, Kushner Wines, and the Slate Family Winery – had impressive displays. Caldwell introduced herself and Axelrod to Cathy and Mike Li. She started to explain that Stephen Grant was a friend, and that he had relayed the conversation he and Cathy had about counterfeit wines.

Mike Li interrupted, "Yes, and you're one of the individuals who was present when Vince Weathers' building went up last night."

Caldwell hesitated for a moment, and said, "Yes."

Mike continued, "The North Fork basically is a small town. If you're plugged in, there isn't too much that remains a secret. I happen to play in a band with Detective Pavelski."

Caldwell said, "I see. I'm very sorry about Evan Byrd and the Kushners."

The Li's both nodded, with Cathy saying, "Thank you."

Axelrod glanced around at the other three booths, and asked, "I assume Weathers is not here?"

Cathy said, "He is not. In fact, no one from the other vineyards is."

"What do you mean?"

Cathy was visibly annoyed as she responded. "Members of our staff, our Li Vineyard people, are actually manning each booth. No one showed up from Byrd Nest." She paused briefly. "I understand that. And there's no one from Kushner here either. Weathers has been absent throughout this process, and I get what happened last night. But even Willis Slate isn't here. I called him, and he just said that he couldn't make it or send anyone. That was it. So, we're stuck. We're promoting not just our own vineyard here, but the North Fork as wine country, and no one else shows up." She then cursed in Mandarin.

Axelrod replied, also in Mandarin, saying, "I, too, am sorry for your losses and troubles."

Cathy Li was surprised, and continued speaking in Mandarin to Axelrod. "You speak Mandarin. I learned it mainly from my grandfather. Have you spent time in China?"

His answer continued the Mandarin exchange. "Yes. I've spent time in many places around the world. I have a certain expertise in languages, and it tends to open doors." In addition to English and Mandarin, Axelrod spoke German, French, Russian, Spanish and Japanese.

Cathy Li looked at Caldwell and Mike, and returned to English. "I apologize. I'm always surprised when I come across someone else in the U.S. who speaks Mandarin."

Mike only spoke English. Caldwell also had rudimentary skills in Arabic.

Caldwell said, "No need to apologize. Chase has a real expertise in languages. It opens doors."

Cathy smiled and replied, "Yes, Mr. Axelrod said as much."

With a glance at Axelrod, Caldwell added, "And Chase is so chatty anyway." She then looked at Mike. "Can I ask a couple of questions?"

"Sure."

"Stephen mentioned that you're doing work on counterfeits in the industry?"

"That's right. That part of our business has kind of taken off over the past year."

"Via that work, combined with your North Fork contacts, is there anything that you've heard or seen regarding counterfeiting?"

Mike glanced at his wife, and then answered with another question. "What do you mean, exactly? I've primarily been working with vintners on ways that they can protect against being victims of counterfeiting."

Caldwell said, "More along the lines of any counterfeiting specifically being done on the North Fork?"

He again looked at his wife. Cathy gave him a slight nod.

Mike indicated that Caldwell and Axelrod should follow him into the corner of the Li display, away from the ears of others. "I've had some suspicions about Weathers."

Caldwell asked, "Based on what?"

"Once he took over the Kushner winery, he cleaned out the entire staff, and brought in new people."

Axelrod shrugged. "What's unusual about that? You bring in your own people."

"Yes. But I've quietly poked around some, and Weathers' people seem to be a shady lot."

"Meaning?" pushed Axelrod.

"The ones I was able to check on have records. Nothing particularly big. But it adds up." As Caldwell and Axelrod glanced at each other doubtfully, Mike Li continued, "I know, believe me. But there's more. And this is perhaps most interesting, but also, I have to acknowledge, still pretty flimsy. Each vineyard obviously keeps track of their production and sales, and we collect the data regionally for various purposes, like for promotional material. Since Weathers took over, production at Kushner wines has dropped markedly, at least on paper. By those numbers, they should have harvested a fraction of their grapes, including for a period before Weathers bought out Kushner. But at the same time, as far as I or Cathy can tell – and she's on top of this kind of thing – there's never been a drop off in production activity. The numbers make no sense."

Caldwell said, "So, where's the wine? That's the question, correct?"

Mike replied, "Right. Listen, I'm a lawyer, and I know none of this would stand up in court, if you will. Geez, it wouldn't get you through the doors of the courtroom. But..." His comments trailed off.

Caldwell merely said, "I get it."

Mike Li appeared uncomfortable, like a lawyer who just broke some kind of lawyer-client privilege. He merely nodded in response.

Caldwell looked at the various bottles displayed at the Li booth. "Before we move on, what's your best vintage?"

Cathy quickly replied, "Our Riesling won an award at..."

Caldwell interrupted, "Perfect. Sold. Can you send a case to my office in D.C.?"

For the first time during the conversation, Cathy truly flashed her sunny smile, and answered, "Of course, we can. Thank you, Paige."

Chapter 46

After placing her order with Cathy Li, Paige Caldwell and Chase Axelrod grabbed a couple of chairs away from the WineCon activities. Caldwell pulled out her smartphone.

Sean McEnany answered from the fortress-like office deep in his basement.

"Sean, Chase and I just engaged in an interesting conversation with our client, as well as another with a couple that owns one of the North Fork wineries."

"Okay, what do you have for me?

"First, can you do some digging on this couple – Cathy and Michael Li? They own Li Vineyard."

"Will do."

"Also, Willis Slate is the owner of the Slate Family Winery. Let's do a rundown on him as well."

"All right. So, at this point, we're looking, in one way or another, at the owners of all four of these East End wineries in the mix."

Caldwell said, "Yes. Questions keep popping up, so let's look at the entire field."

"There's another tidbit to look into that I received from Stephen in a call just a short time ago."

"What's that?"

McEnany relayed the incident explained by Senator Ellis regarding the cryptic CIA notification about Interpol's

Rex Holden. McEnany added, "As the former senator told Stephen, it's likely nothing, but I'm doing a little digging there as well, just to make sure."

"Are you in contact with Tank to get the specifics on what the Agency was worried about?"

"Yes, but he hasn't gotten back to me yet."

"Okay. Thanks, Sean."

* * *

While Caldwell and McEnany were talking, another pertinent phone call was taking place between New York City and eastern Long Island.

Dasha Pudovkin sat at a small, round table in a spacious apartment on Central Park West. She looked down at the general darkness of the park, and across at the many lights from Manhattan apartment and office buildings.

Her right hand held a smartphone to her ear, while she stirred sugar into a cup of coffee with the left. "This is an unscheduled call from you at an unusual time. It must not be good news."

"We have taken another hit."

She sighed. "Do not waste my time. What does that mean?"

"The building housing my lab has been destroyed."

In response to the news from Vince Weathers, Dasha Pudovkin declared, in Russian, "Son of a bitch!"

Weathers added, "It was part explosion, part fire. It incinerated nearly everything."

Pudovkin said, "He is continuing the attacks."

"How can you be sure?"

"Trust me. I know."

"What's next then?"

Pudovkin took a sip of the coffee. "Don't worry about that. You focus on how best to fix our supply issues. I will take care of Jacques Lafleur."

"What are you going to do?"

"Just stay away from Lafleur's WineCon event."

"You know me, Dasha, it's about keeping a low profile."

"I do. And that's why you are my best supplier."

*   *   *

After the call with Dasha Pudovkin ended, Vince Weathers said, "She's primed."

Willis Slate sat behind a desk in his office at Slate Family Winery, looking across at Weathers. Slate said, "These are dangerous games. It seems like there would be a more direct way of getting this done."

"If more is needed, so be it. But everybody loves a war among thieves, from cops to those left to pick up the business."

Chapter 47

The clock hanging on the faded, dirty, yellow kitchen wall ticked past midnight. Byron Sawchuck and Rick Rutherford had been on the phone with their employer for nearly an hour.

Before the call, Sawchuck and Rutherford had gone over their plan several times, understanding that the man they worked for demanded a certain exactness. The two men assured each other that everything was covered, and then they contacted the client.

After explaining the plan, they successfully answered each question tossed their way.

Sawchuck started wrapping things up. "Given the information and tools we have, I don't see any of this being a problem. Barring any unforeseen issues, we estimate getting in and out in an hour-and-a-half."

The voice emanating from the speaker of the smartphone resting in the middle of the table said, "Indeed. Good."

Rutherford added, "Also, time is on our side. When we reach the storage facility in Plattsburg, no one will have a clue."

The voice replied, "Excellent. I will await the confirmation when all is finished."

Sawchuck said, "Works for us."

The call was ended.

Rutherford shook his head, and said, "You know, when I started thinking about this, I wondered how the hell we'd get it done. But then this incredible gift was dropped in our laps."

Sawchuck nodded. "My mother used to say that sometimes things are just meant to be. It might turn out that our easiest heist also happens to be the most lucrative."

Rutherford said, "There's a part of me that wants to cut him out." He pointed at the phone.

Sawchuck replied, "I understand the impulse. But definitely not in this case. Compared to what he has to do, we've got the easiest part of the deal. Besides, that's shortsighted. He's always been a reliable, profitable source for work."

Rutherford nodded. "Yeah, you're right."

Chapter 48

Thursday morning brought the arrival of raw, wet autumn weather.

The high for the day in the New York metropolitan area was predicted to be 46 degrees. That's where the temperature stood outside the Grants' home at 7:15 in the morning. Heading west, the high slightly dropped, as would temperatures over the rest of the day. Combined with a moderate, steady rain that had already started and the occasional wind gust, it promised to be a dismal day.

Before heading to St. Mary's, Stephen stuck his head into Jennifer's home office to see her behind the desk. She wore a gray sweatshirt sporting a portrait of William Shakespeare and a Cardinals hat. She looked up from her computer, and smiled. "Heading out?"

"I am." He looked out the window at the rain, and added, "These are the days that you particularly love your home office."

"Most certainly. Barring any interruptions, I should be able to finish up my draft of this analysis of the wine market and counterfeiting for Larry, and get it off to Yvonne and Joe for their thoughts and edits."

"I'll leave you to it. My plan is still to head into the city later tonight for the WineCon event on the *Intrepid*. Are you sure you don't want to go?"

"No. I've got work to get back to after the Larry thing is done. And I think I'd be a distraction. After all, Paige called last night asking if you're going for a very specific reason." She got up from the desk and walked over to him. "Please be careful tonight."

"I will."

Stephen kissed her, and then headed for the office door, while Jennifer returned to her desk. Over his shoulder, he said, "I love you."

"You, too," she answered.

As he moved away from the office, he called out, "By the way, can I drive the new Jeep?"

"You know the answer to that."

Jennifer's beloved red Thunderbird convertible was wrecked the one time Stephen drove it. While she understood that it was a life-and-death situation, Jennifer still enjoyed making her husband feel guilty about the loss. So, since she replaced it with a new Mojave Sand-colored, four-door Jeep Wrangler, Stephen had not been given clearance to take the wheel.

Stephen laughed, and as he approached the front door, he said, "Can't blame a guy for trying. Bye."

Ten minutes later, he pulled his red Chevy Tahoe into the parking lot at St. Mary's Lutheran Church. Stephen was the first to arrive for the day, which was exactly how he wanted it. His sermon for the weekend was almost done, and he hoped to put the finishing touches on it before anyone else arrived.

Stephen was at his desk within a few minutes. He liked his office. It was a bit more spacious and upscale than what many pastors had, and he understood how good he had it at St. Mary's.

Two walls were dominated by floor-to-ceiling bookcases filled mainly with theology and history tomes, along with some historical fiction. Behind his desk was a bay window bordered by more bookcases. The fourth wall, in which the door was carved, featured an antique wardrobe housing assorted pastoral clothing. Half the room focused around Grant's desk, while the other half was a bit more welcoming, with a couch, armchair, and a stand with a small television. In front of the chair and couch sat an oak coffee table. That table also doubled as a gun cabinet, with a 10 mm Glock 20, a Taurus PT-25, and a Harris M-89 sniper rifle. Grant found it convenient to keep such items under lock and key in his office for when he would go practice shooting at a local sportsmen's club. But that was only half of the truth. As a matter of straightforward security, it had proven wise to have the items inside this coffee table.

Grant opened his old-school schedule book. The rest of the morning featured a quick staff meeting on nearly everything for the coming weekend, from bulletins to music, and then time with Zack to finalize the details of the Reformation Day "Who Was Martin Luther, Anyway?" class. Stephen then had lunch scheduled with Glenn Oliver, council president, and an afternoon including a Divine Service at a nursing home, a hospital visit, and a stop to see an elderly parishioner who was having a difficult time adjusting to lost independence after surgery. If all went smoothly – always a big "if" – he would grab a train to get him into the city with a little time to spare.

Grant pushed aside the schedule book, and opened his MacBook Pro to finish up the sermon. As his mind wandered, though, he sat back and turned his office chair to look out the window. This was a rather common practice when facing the occasional sermon block. But this time around, it wasn't about, for example, being unable to find the right words, getting a point clear in his head, or struggling with how to best communicate to the congregation. Instead, Grant found himself distracted by something that he usually did not dwell on all that much – the past.

I'm trying to keep my schedule on track in order to get to an aircraft carrier and help provide security for a thief who escaped when I was with the Agency.

He chuckled to himself.

Catching a ride on an aircraft carrier wasn't unusual. Not just with the SEALs, but even a few times with the Agency. But that was different business. Yet, it still bugs me that Lafleur got away 20 years ago. What's up with that? I know parishioners who can't let go of anything – whether it's their own sins, or where others fall short. Even after receiving forgiveness for something, they still feel guilty, and can't let it go. It's even worse when they won't move on from what others did. That bugs me. Yet, here I am doing the same thing, and this happened freaking two decades ago.

Grant knew why the Lafleur situation, along with a few others, more or less stuck in his craw. He had always been relentless in demanding or pursuing justice. That impulse did not, necessarily, conflict with God's forgiveness in Christ Jesus.

But forgiveness requires confession, right? How about acknowledging and being sorry for sin, rather than making a career out of, at the very least, ripping people off with wine thefts and fakes? And who knows what else? The Lord's forgiveness is an undeserved, unfathomable gift, but it's not a license to sin. And God's forgiveness does not necessarily wipe away the earthly consequences of our earthly actions.

He shook his head, and turned back to his computer. *Come on, finish the sermon, Grant.*

Chapter 49

It was just after ten in the morning when the office phone rang. She answered, "Hello. Jennifer Grant."

"Jennifer, it's Sean." The raspy voice of Sean McEnany was unmistakable.

"Sean, how are you?"

"Things are busy. And you?"

"Actually, your timing was perfect. I just finished up the first draft of my report for Larry Banner on the wine market and counterfeits."

"Perfect. That's what I'm calling about. Can I pick your brain?"

"How can I help?"

"Can you give a very quick overview of the hotspots around the world for producing counterfeit wine?"

She laughed. "That's a pretty broad question."

"I understand. But I'm just looking for the highlights that might point me in the right direction."

"Okay. Much of the wine counterfeiting phenomenon had been rather localized, or at least national in nature. What I mean by that is that the fakes were made and sold in the same geographic area. For example, fake wines auctioned in the U.S. – such as in New York, L.A. or D.C. – were made domestically. Of course, that doesn't mean the fakes weren't rip-offs of French or German wines. In fact, that tends to work better. Odds are that it's easier to pass off a fake German wine in L.A. than it is in Germany."

Jennifer seemed to be getting caught up in talking about her work, while on the other end of the call, Sean listened. He did not create his own global empire of information by talking. Rather, he did so by listening, along with mastering the skills of knowing what information was of value, identifying which sources had valuable information and what motivated each, and being able to determine when individuals were or were not being honest.

Jennifer continued, "But that's changed in recent years. It's become more international. As is the case in so many areas of counterfeiting, China has taken on a big role. The number of wine drinkers in China has exploded in recent years along with the growth in middle and upper income earners. Going hand in hand has been a dramatic increase in Chinese wine counterfeiting for both the domestic and international markets." She added, "I'm not sure why people are surprised that counterfeits and intellectual property violations persist in China. After all, it's still a communist nation that dabbles in markets as a low-cost manufacturer."

Sean simply replied with a slight chuckle, saying, "Right."

"Wine counterfeiting in China is now a sizeable underground industry – although again in China, not too far underground. French wines are a major import in China, and therefore, French vintages have become a big counterfeiting target. It's certainly not limited to the French, but one respected estimate pegged the counterfeiting rate at 50 percent. So, for every legitimate bottle of French wine, there is a fake. That's well above the estimated global wine counterfeiting rate of about 20 percent. And the Chinese have become very good at producing, if you can call it that, high-quality fakes. In a sense, the Chinese have industrialized counterfeit wines, and those fakes are being exported."

Sean asked, "Who are the other nations that are big players in counterfeiting?"

"You have to understand that nailing down the counterfeit wine market, by its very nature, is hard to do. But many say that, along with China, it's the U.S."

"Okay," Sean replied. "Switching gears a bit, in terms of the local market, do you have any numbers on production for individual wineries?"

"Actually, yes. One of my partners created a database on sales by individual wineries in California, and then built it out to cover all of the major U.S. wine regions."

"That's handy."

"Well, it is for those in the industry primarily," observed Jennifer.

"Can you tell me how sales have fared in recent years for Byrd Nest Vineyards, Slate Family Winery, Kushner Wines, and Li Vineyard?"

As she pulled up the file on her computer, she said, "Ah, the North Fork wineries in the mix."

"Yes."

"Just give me a second..."

Sean waited patiently.

Jennifer said, "Here we are. I'll send you the numbers, but Li and Byrd Nest have experienced solid growth – actually running a bit above the industry trend of late." She paused while scanning the Excel sheet. "Quite a different story, for Kushner. Their numbers are down markedly. Slate also is off, but not as steeply as Kushner."

"Don't you love when data helps tell a story?"

"Sean. I'm an economist. Of course, I do. So, this has been helpful?"

"Very much so. I'll look for the files, and thanks."

Chapter 50

Stephen Grant's life experiences were, to say the least, quite diverse. He grew up and attended college in Middle America; journeyed around the world with the Navy SEALs and then the CIA; returned to the heartland to study theology; and landed in a parish on Long Island. Even given this wide and varied background, a situation occasionally struck him as somewhat incongruous. That was the case strolling about the hangar deck of the Intrepid Museum early on Thursday evening.

Given his Navy background, there was a level of comfort Grant felt on warships, including aircraft carriers, even after so many years of being away. The *Intrepid* had hit the seas in 1943 during World War II, saw its final action in the Vietnam War, and was decommissioned in 1974. It opened as a museum at Pier 86 in New York City in 1982. Grant wasn't old enough to have seen any action aboard this particular carrier, but there was an obvious familiarity.

Meanwhile, with the CIA, he had seen assorted extremes of humanity up close, including the interests and pursuits of individuals who had earned significant wealth, as well as those who acquired wealth without earning it.

That was the case with Monaco and Lafleur.

So, a major wine-tasting celebration was not completely foreign. But the conversations, bars and buffets were discordant with the ship, the assorted aircraft on display, their histories and the men who served.

Walking next to Grant was Paige Caldwell. She asked, "I hope I'm not pushing things with Jennifer?"

Grant shifted his gaze from a blue-and-gray TBM-3E Avenger bomber, and said, "I'm sorry, what was that?"

She said, "Jennifer. Is she okay that we drafted you for another night?"

Grant smiled, "She's not doing cartwheels, by any means."

"Not because of our history?" She smiled mischievously.

Grant's clergy collar suddenly felt a little tight. A twinge of guilt ambushed him for noticing how Paige looked in a shimmering blue dress that left one shoulder bare. "Of course not. She understands my getting some requests to help out now and then, but at the same time, she worries."

"Good."

"Good?"

"Of course. Spouses should worry about each other. Right?" She smiled at him, once again. "Relax, Stephen. You look good, even in that collar. I look good. And that's the end of it, as it was many years ago."

She has a way of laying things out.

Paige continued, "So, what were you thinking about?"

He looked at her quizzically.

"I can still tell when your mind is not fully on matters at hand. Don't tell me you were reminiscing? That would be sad. Pondering the past was never for you."

It's disconcerting how well she knew me, and apparently how little I've changed.

Grant said, "Guilty as charged. Kind of. I've known aircraft carriers quite well, and I've known – well, we've known – events like this. But put them together, and it's a little odd."

"Really? Hmmm." She shrugged slightly.

Grant also knew Paige well enough that her reaction signaled disinterest. She never saw an upside in such reflections, deeming them largely a waste of time. *Apparently, I'm not the only one who hasn't changed.*

Paige lowered her voice further. "Let's continue circulating and getting our focus right. It's a big event given that we only have nine of our own people covering it."

In addition to Stephen and Paige, Rich Noack, Trent Nguyen and Eugenio Peraza from the FBI were in attendance. And from Caldwell's firm, Chase Axelrod, Jessica West, Phil Lucena and Lis Dicce circulated throughout the large hanger deck.

Before arriving, they had established a pattern and schedule of how each group would move. Caldwell and Grant were paired together, as were Lucena and West, and Axelrod and Dicce. The three couples looked natural as they casually walked amidst the several hundred in attendance.

Meanwhile, Noack, Nguyen and Peraza looked more like law enforcement present for security purposes, which is exactly what they were.

Caldwell and Grant moved slowly around a small group of people, when Paige bumped into the billionaire organizer and funder of NYC WineCon and his wife. He smiled, and said, "Well, we meet again. Where is Larry?"

Paige said, "Oh, he's around here. I've lost track of him again."

The man asked, "And who is this?"

Paige replied, "This is Stephen Grant. He's my pastor. I'm hoping that he'll do the wedding if I can ever get Larry to pop the question."

The man said, "Really?"

She quickly added, "I don't mean to be rude, but we're trying to catch up to a friend. Good seeing both of you once again."

Several steps away, Caldwell laughed. "Banner will just love that."

Grant shook his head. "You still amuse yourself."

"Yes, I do."

After a few more steps, however, the sea of people seemed to part, and standing in front of Grant and Caldwell were Jacques Lafleur and Gabrielle Poyer.

For Grant, it was one of those moments where time seemed to slow.

Well.

Lafleur spoke first. "I recognize the face. Indeed, I do not believe that I will ever forget it from our last meeting. And given what I've heard, I am not surprised by the collar." He held out his hand. "Hello, Stephen Grant. It has been quite some time."

Grant looked into the man's eyes, then down to the extended hand, and back to the eyes. He reached out, and shook the hand. "Jacques Lafleur. You have not changed very much, have you?"

Lafleur replied, "Ah, we all change."

Grant said, "But perhaps not as much as we like to think."

Lafleur smiled broadly. "It's apparent that you have." He lowered his voice, and moved in closer to Grant. "After all, the last time we met you were shooting at me, and now look at you, a pastor, and here to, in some way, help protect me. That is a significant change, correct?"

"In some ways."

"Of course it is."

Grant could not resist adding, "But I still value justice."

Lafleur laughed. "Ah, yes. I remember. You still appreciate John Wayne. But you are no longer in the justice business, correct? You are in the forgiveness business."

"Funny you should say that. I was thinking about this very matter earlier today."

"Is that right?"

"Yes. I was reflecting on how forgiveness of our sins is tied to being sorry for and confessing those sins."

Lafleur raised an eyebrow.

Grant continued, "God's forgiveness does not eliminate the worldly consequences of our actions. To put it plainly, God will forgive you, but that doesn't mean there's no jail time."

Lafleur replied, "I see. Well, thankfully, the statute of limitations on what brought us together ran out long ago."

It was Grant's turn to lean in closer to Lafleur. "You're technically correct. But it does not wipe away the stain of you going from the DGSE to being a thief – high end perhaps – but a thief nonetheless."

Lafleur turned to Paige and said, "Ms. Caldwell, you did bring Pastor Grant to help protect me, right?"

She shrugged, and said, "That was my assumption, but you know how picky about right and wrong some of these men of God can get. And throw in the fact that this one was a SEAL and used to be with the CIA. So, who the hell knows?"

She gave Stephen the knowing glance that he had seen many times before when they were partnered at the CIA.

Grant smiled to himself. *Thanks, Paige. Keep him guessing.*

Chapter 51

With one partner in an East End hospital and the other onboard the *U.S.S. Intrepid*, Sean McEnany remained in his basement office. He had been working phones and the Internet for hours to get more information on a rather lengthy list of people. The frustration was clear on his face.

He looked down from the information spread across three large screens on the wall to a legal pad. He had written down the name of each person being researched.

The names of Cathy and Mike Li had lines through them, as did Jason Kushner. Those were the people that McEnany finished looking into, and was satisfied that they were "clean," as he said out loud to himself. That left the names of people he was still researching or wrestling with – Willis Slate, Vincent Weathers, Jacques Lafleur, Gabrielle Poyer, Dasha Pudovkin, Rick Rutherford, Byron Sawchuck, and Rex Holden.

He looked up from the list, and whispered in exasperation, "Shit."

But then a phone that received calls from just one person rang. He picked it up, and said, "Yes."

The call came from an office in the headquarters of the CIA in Langley, Virginia. Tank Hoard said, "It's hard to tell when you're pissed off, Sean, but you sound more irritated than normal."

"I'm not getting anything of substance on a long list of names."

"Well, I've got information that will help."

"Good. Let's hear it."

"You asked about what Senator Ellis said about Interpol's Holden. It seems that Holden popped up on the Agency's radar because of who he came in contact with. The guy's name was Elmer Danford, but of late his preferred moniker is Byron Sawchuck."

"Crap."

"Sawchuck was a cop in Atlanta. He rose to detective, but apparently became far too focused on how much the criminals he was investigating were making, as opposed to concentrating on how to lock them up. He eventually got pushed out the door, and then suddenly started showing up with some not-so-nice people internationally as a hired gun, heist man, and whatever else might need to be done. The Agency was keeping an eye on him when Holden stepped into the picture. At first, the Agency thought Holden was just doing his own Interpol thing. But then it was becoming pretty clear that Holden was interested in earning some extra cash as well. But he's far more skilled at hiding that fact than Sawchuck ever was. Interpol apparently has no clue."

"So, the Agency did what about Holden?"

"The decision was made to keep watching him, thinking that he might be valuable in the future."

"I hate that shit, Tank."

"Not my call, Sean. I'm passing along what I just learned. At the same time, you know how this works, so don't get all self-righteous."

"Yeah, I get it. What else?"

"This is where it might be getting even uglier. The Agency has been tracking a couple of accounts that Holden controls. Activity in those accounts has stepped up notably in the past two-plus years. Much more revenue coming in the door, along with some significant payments going out the door. The source of the revenue seems to be the same, given the regular timing. But as to who that is, they haven't figured that out yet."

"Send me what you have on the accounts, and I'll see what I can dig up."

"Right. But as for where recent payments have gone, the Agency has been keeping tabs on Holden's phone calls. Plus, a phone bill under a pseudonym actually was paid for out of one of his secret accounts."

"Wait. He paid the phone bill out of a secret bank account?"

"They always slip up somehow. I guess he figured no one could track the bank or phone account back to him, so why not? Unfortunately, no one here has rolled up their sleeves on the Holden file in a few weeks."

"Of course."

"I just did, however, for the past couple of hours. Each of the recent large payments occur shortly after Holden finished a call. Nothing trackable there, unfortunately, except one call. It lasted less than five seconds. Probably realized he called the wrong phone, a traceable number. That phone number is registered to Byron Sawchuck. The call and bank transfer occurred on the day that Evan Byrd was murdered."

"Son of a bitch."

"There's more. Another big transfer was made last night, after a call."

"So, what the hell is that all about?"

"Don't know. That's all I have."

"Thanks, Tank. This has been invaluable. If anything else comes up, let me know."

"You got it."

After ending the call, McEnany pushed back, rested his elbows on the arms of the chair, and had his hands form a pyramid in front of his face. He finally picked up another phone and dialed a number.

Paige Caldwell answered. "Good timing, Sean. We just finished an interesting conversation with Jacques Lafleur and Gabrielle Poyer. Hold on, let me find a spot on this aircraft carrier where we can talk." She indicated to Stephen to follow. Caldwell stepped outside the carrier on a platform leading to a staircase and elevator. The rain from earlier in the day had moved away, and the wind died down to an occasional cold breeze. She asked, "What's up?"

Sean replied, "Hoard passed on some significant information."

"Should I get Stephen to listen as well?"

"Sure."

Paige said to Stephen, "Come here. Sean's got information that we should both hear."

Grant leaned his ear close to Paige's phone. Her head touched his as they listened.

Could it get more awkward? Jen trusts me. She'd get it. Ugh.

Sean relayed the information that Hoard had shared. At the conclusion, he asked, "So, what the hell do you guys think?"

Stephen was just about to say that he didn't have a clue when Larry Banner emerged through the doors of the carrier.

Grant walked to Banner. Caldwell moved to catch up with the phone still in her ear. She said, "I'll call you right back."

Grant said, "Larry, Holden stayed at your house, right?"

Banner seemed a bit surprised. "Rex Holden, the Interpol gentleman? Yes. He assessed my entire collection this past weekend. He stayed as my guest. Nice fellow."

Grant asked, "You're staying at the apartment for the week, I assume?"

"Yes, with WineCon, I am. Plus, I've got construction being done on the house, so it worked out that I did not have to deal with the noise, and so on."

"What work are you having done?"

"I'm finally upgrading and expanding the sitting area outside the wine cellar, adding a staircase. It's a good deal of work."

"Does Holden know about this?"

"Holden? Well, yes, I mentioned it when I was giving him a tour of the place. Why the hell are you...?" Banner's look of bewilderment suddenly transformed into sternness. "No. You cannot be serious. That fucking Brit is involved in this?"

Caldwell shared much of what they knew. The possibility that Holden might be targeting Banner's collection simply went unsaid among the three. All Caldwell added was, "This could be nothing. And even if it is something, we have no idea when it might occur."

Banner clearly was struggling to control his anger. "I understand that, Paige. But I want your team up to the house now. There is no one there."

Caldwell took a deep breath.

Promise to Lafleur and the FBI, and now this. Grant looked at Caldwell, and then leaned in to Banner "Part of Paige's team has to stay here. They made promises to the FBI. I'll go with Paige up to your place, and make sure everything is all right. Does that sound good?"

Banner paused before responding. "Good, Stephen. Thank you."

Grant turned to Caldwell. "Good?"

"Yes. Of course. We can get up there pretty quick if we leave now."

Banner interrupted, "We'll take my helicopter."

Caldwell said, "That's not necessary, Larry."

"Yes, it is, Paige."

Grant clearly saw Banner's determination. *The client's always right.*

"All right," Caldwell replied. "Let me just update the team quickly."

Banner nodded. Grant stayed with him.

Knowing the pattern and schedule they'd established, Caldwell found Noack quickly despite the large gathering. "Rich, do you know where Rex Holden is?"

"I haven't seen him since yesterday. He was annoyed that the home office was pulling him away from what we're doing. That's why he's not here tonight. Why?"

Caldwell rapidly explained to him what the reality was on Holden, and the concern about Banner being a target.

As he listened, Noack periodically cursed. When Caldwell wrapped up, Noack said, "There are few things I hate more than law enforcement gone bad. But then add in that this little shit deceived us." He gritted his teeth. "We have freaking Lafleur, now Holden, and this Sawchuck asshole. What is it with these law-enforcement traitors?"

Caldwell added that she and Grant were about to accompany Banner to his home north of the city.

Noack said, "Makes sense. Why don't you take two more of your people, and leave this to Nguyen, Peraza, and myself, and whoever you keep here?"

"I still think Pudovkin is a threat here. I'll take one more of my team with me and leave the others with you."

"Fair enough," agreed Noack.

Chapter 52

The last two vehicles from Carleeni Construction exited the front gate of Larry Banner's 14-acre estate on the Hudson River. They drove up the long single lane road, made a couple of turns, and then moved past two large dark blue vans in the parking lot of a Dunkin' Donuts.

Sitting in the passenger seat in one of the blue vans, Byron Sawchuck watched as the vehicles disappeared. "They sure do work late. But that works to our advantage." He looked at Rick Rutherford behind the wheel, and said, "Let's go." He turned to the van parked in the next space, and gave a thumbs up to the driver, Paulie Benino. In the van with Benino were the other two team members.

The vans pulled into a dark corner of the parking lot. The two men with Benino jumped out, and quickly peeled long covers off the sides of each van to reveal "Carleeni Construction" signage.

A few minutes later, Rutherford guided the first van up to the front gate of the Banner home, reached out and punched in the supplied security code.

The gates opened, and the vans moved through and proceeded toward the large brick and stone Georgian colonial. The vans circled around to the back of the house, where two vehicles needed for the job were waiting, courtesy of the actual Carleeni Construction.

The first was a straight boom, which allowed workers to move up and down to the patio sitting area that was under reconstruction outside the unique rooftop wine cellar. The second was a telehandler with a telescopic boom and pallet forks attached, allowing construction materials to be easily moved up and down. It just happened to be ideal for moving pallets with empty wine cases up to the roof, and then bringing them back down and sliding them into the two vans.

Rutherford and Sawchuck rode the straight boom up to the roof, and stepped onto the patio that was the focus of the work. They walked over to the door leading to the wine.

Rutherford dropped a large canvas bag on the floor, and closely inspected the door. "Holden was right. This is an old, heavy door. Blowing it would have put too much of the wine at risk."

Rutherford bent down, unzipped the bag, pulled out a formidable reciprocating saw, and snapped on a long blade. He skillfully worked the device so the blade eventually found its way through the wood. After that, guiding the saw through the wood seemed relatively easy.

While Rutherford was effectively carving a new door into the old door, Sawchuck turned to see the first of four pallets being deposited a few feet away via the telehandler. The neatly stacked empty wine cases waited on the pallets. He looked back to Rutherford's progress, then glanced at his watch. He smiled.

Behind them, as the telehandler was being withdrawn, the straight boom was being lowered as well.

A couple of minutes later, Sawchuck's attention was drawn away from Rutherford's near completion of the door. He turned and saw no additional activity. "What the hell?"

He took a step away from Rutherford's work, but then stopped upon hearing the noise of the straight boom once again rising. Surprise on his face quickly transformed into irritation when he saw who was on the rising platform. "What are you doing here?"

Rex Holden, dressed in his usual blue blazer, along with a red and blue striped tie, white shirt and crisply creased gray pants, looked strikingly out of place amidst the construction equipment and materials.

When the platform stopped, Holden stepped onto the rooftop patio area. "Our plans have changed."

Rutherford glanced over his shoulder, paused briefly at seeing Holden, shook his head, and then got back to completing the task at hand.

Sawchuck asked, "What's changed?"

Holden replied, "I have a plane waiting at Stewart Airport. We will be taking our goods directly there, and flying out of the country. Everything has been cleared."

Sawchuck said, "That's not what we're being paid for. What the hell is going on?"

"We have no choice."

Sawchuck took a few steps forward. His face was inches from Holden's. "I don't care how much you're paying us. I asked a question and I expect an answer. What the hell is going on?"

"Yes. Of course. A friend at the CIA just let me know that certain inquiries have been made, and I am afraid that pieces are being put together. Therefore, I need to get out of the country. That would be best for you and your men as well. So, I made arrangements for each of you. I hope you appreciate that. I also thought we would be able to continue our lucrative work together. Well, after matters calm down, that is."

Sawchuck had been closely watching Holden's eyes, and continued to do so. Finally, he said, "Shit. How much time do we have?"

"There is little reason to think that they know we are here. However, it is always best to be prudent. Therefore, stepping up the pace would be a wise precaution."

The saw went silent. Holden and Sawchuck turned to see Rutherford kick the door twice. The second blow sent a large, carved-out portion crashing onto the wine cellar's oak floor.

Rutherford declared, "Bingo! We're in."

Holden smiled, and said, "Jolly good."

Sawchuck shouted, "We need to pick up the pace, boys!"

Holden stepped into the long, barrel-shaped room, looked around, and declared, "We have to make this worthwhile, gentlemen."

From below, Paulie Benino called up to Sawchuck, "Byron, do you need me up there?"

Sawchuck hesitated. "No, Paulie. Stick with the plan, and keep watch." He added that the two other team members should get up top quickly, suggesting, "Bring a couple of rifles up, too."

Benino continued walking around the area with a semiautomatic rifle in hand.

Chapter 53

Roughly 20 blocks north of the *Intrepid*, Larry Banner walked next to a short, bald man in a tan uniform, with Grant, Caldwell and Phil Lucena trailing a couple of strides behind.

Lucena, who also came to Caldwell's firm courtesy of the CIA, was deceptive. His smile, unrelenting politeness, neatly cut brown hair, and five-foot-six-inch stockiness did anything but reflect his various abilities, including hand-to-hand combat skills few could match. For good measure, he recently shaved off his beard, which made him look very young. Lucena also did not look terribly comfortable in the expensive black suit he was wearing for the *Intrepid* event.

They walked onto a brightly lit helicopter pad, and approached an idling white and blue, 8-seat Agusta helicopter. Banner said to the man, "Johnny, thank you, once again, for having her ready so quickly."

"Not a problem, Mr. Banner."

"Like I said, I'll most likely be back tonight. However, I am not 100 percent sure. I, of course, will call in my plan."

Johnny smiled. "I'll be here."

After shaking hands, Johnny, along with the pilot/mechanic who had readied the aircraft, retreated into the darkness surrounding the pad.

The four entered the copter and strapped in.

Caldwell sat in the front seat next to Banner, who was in the pilot's spot. She said, "We really could have handled this on our own. After all, this is part of the reason you hired us."

"I want to know as soon as possible if there is something happening at my home."

The helicopter lifted into the air, and Banner gently turned the craft to the north. At a typical cruising speed, the flight would take less than ten minutes, tracking along the Hudson River.

Grant looked out at the city lights in a seat behind the pilot. *Now there's something you never get tired of.* His thoughts quickly shifted. "Not that I'm expecting trouble, but just in case, are we adequately armed?"

Caldwell said, "What is it with you and guns, Pastor Grant?" She turned and smiled. "I'm good. Phil?"

"Yes. Thanks." Lucena was seated next to Grant.

Banner said, "Stephen, as the Agency teaches: Be prepared."

Caldwell interrupted, "That's the Boy Scouts."

"I think it's the CIA, too." Banner directed his comments back to Grant. "Stephen, behind the rows of seats, there is a small door on the wall."

Grant unbuckled, and went to the back. "Right."

"Slide the panel open, and punch in 2-9-1-9 on the keypad."

Grant did so, and a large concealed compartment slid open. "Larry, you are prepared."

Inside were two semi-automatic rifles, and two Glock 17s, along with accompanying magazines. For good measure, there was rappelling equipment, including nylon ropes, knives, gloves and harnesses. Grant grabbed a Glock and two magazines. He closed the compartment, took his black sports jacket off, returned to his seat, inspected the gun, loaded a magazine, and slipped the weapon in between his pants and shirt at the small of his back.

He looked over to see Lucena watching. "Phil?"

"Oh, I apologize, Stephen. It's just that it strikes me as odd seeing you doing this, that is, with your collar on."

"Yeah. I know."

Banner announced, "We're a few minutes out."

Caldwell requested, "Larry, can you come in higher than normal and make a pass, just in case we do see something that's not right, and we have to make adjustments?"

He nodded.

Chapter 54

The first pallet was nearly filled as Sawchuck, Rutherford, and the two assistants rapidly loaded, sealed, and moved each case. Inside the rooftop wine cellar, Holden helped, but mainly directed the crew to which bottles should be moved out.

In the distance over the dark waters of the Hudson River, Benino spotted the lights of a helicopter. It continued on its path, and disappeared from his line of vision behind trees to the north.

The first pallet was filled and secured. Sawchuck and the two assistants stepped into the straight boom, and lowered themselves to the ground. Sawchuck walked over to the telehandler. He maneuvered the vehicle and its arm, grabbing the filled pallet. He raised the pallet slightly, pulled it away from the house, lowered it, and turned the valuable bottles of wine toward one of the vans. The assistants moved next to the cargo as it was slipped into the van. One of the men signaled that all looked good. Sawchuck lowered the pallet. The van rocked slightly. The arm was withdrawn, and then turned to the next pallet stacked with empty wine cases. Sawchuck deposited that on the rooftop area. The three men re-ascended, and were back casing up and moving wine in a few minutes.

Benino was the first to respond to the growing sound of the helicopter blades. He looked up into the sky.

Banner's helicopter emerged from the side of his Georgian colonial that faced away from the river. It moved sideways, and then hovered. Both sliding side doors were open. On the side facing the robbery below, Phil Lucena hung in a harness halfway down an 80-foot nylon rope, with his Glock 22 drawn. On a second rope hanging down from the other side of the aircraft, Stephen Grant had a Glock 17 in his hand.

Still in her blue dress, Paige Caldwell was on one knee at the door aiming a rifle down on Holden's crew.

Larry Banner flipped on a speaker, and announced, "You are robbing my home, and I do not appreciate it. Please stop what you are doing. Discard any weapons, and lay flat on the ground."

Inside the rooftop wine room, Holden sighed, and then said, "Well, that is terribly unfortunate."

Sawchuck said, "Shit."

On the ground, Benino whispered, "That's bullshit." With apparently little thought, he raised his rifle, pulled the trigger, and sent a spray of bullets skyward. That unleashed havoc.

Most of Benino's shots flew wild, but two struck the helicopter. Banner wavered at the controls, and Caldwell nearly lost her balance. She demanded, "Steady, Larry."

Lucena returned fire at Benino, who moved to take cover next to one of the vans.

One of Sawchuck's men grabbed a nearby rifle on the patio area, and started to raise the weapon.

Caldwell trained her rifle on the man, and fired off one shot. It landed in his chest, and he fell to the broken tiled floor.

Inside the wine cellar, Rutherford pulled a handgun out of the holster in his back. He looked at Sawchuck, and asked, "Weapon?"

Sawchuck shook his head in response.

Holden said, "Byron, here." He held out a SIG-Sauer P226 handgun. He added, "They, so to speak, have the high ground. Is it worth it?"

Sawchuck raised an eyebrow, and then took the gun.

Outside, Lucena and Grant began slow descents.

Benino came out from behind his cover to fire shots at Lucena and Grant. Lucena paused his drop and returned fire.

That put Grant ahead of Lucena in moving downward. He was just 15 feet above the rooftop target when Sawchuck's other team member came through the sawed-open door. He was moving for the other rifle resting just a few feet away. Behind him emerged Rutherford looking to provide cover fire.

One from the hotel in Greenport.

Grant tried to steady the Glock at Rutherford, and squeezed off a string of shots, with the last two finding their target. One slug entered Rutherford's shoulder and the other his chest.

Lucena accelerated his descent, practically going into freefall. He landed before Grant, and unclipped his harness as he rolled forward toward the thief who was raising the other rifle. Lucena hurled his body at the man, who dropped the rifle, trying to protect himself from the assault. He managed to knock Lucena's gun away, and the two were immediately in a kind of life-and-death bear-hug struggle.

* * *

Grant landed and moved against the wall next to the door. Sawchuck climbed over the dead Rutherford to get out the door, leading with the SIG.

As Sawchuck's hand holding the gun emerged from the door, Grant came down hard with the butt of the Glock. The SIG fell to the floor, and Grant started to bring the gun back around at his opponent. But as he came the rest of the way through the door, Sawchuck grabbed Grant's wrist. The two men wrestled for control of the gun, with Sawchuck pushing into Grant, who fell back.

Round two with Sawchuck.

Now on his side, Grant bore the force of Sawchuck's body as it crashed on top of him. He never loosened the grip on the gun.

Let go of the gun, and you're dead. Lord, help.

* * *

After Sawchuck went through the door, Holden pulled out his phone, and hit a contact on the screen. He said, "They're here, unfortunately. It might not turn out in our favor. If you do not hear from me again in a few minutes, then all I can promise is holding off until the morning. You will have that much time from me." Holden ended the call, and turned to the bottles behind him. He scanned briefly, pulled a bottle off the rack, picked up an opener, and began to remove the cork.

* * *

At the side of the helicopter, Caldwell had the rifle trained on the edge of the van as Benino again emerged to take more shots. But before he could move his rifle into position, Caldwell pulled the trigger. The shot entered just above Benino's left eye. He was dead just when his body hit the dirt and gravel.

* * *

Holden sat down and poured a glass of the wine. He eyed the liquid, and then breathed the bouquet in deeply.

* * *

Lucena worked to separate himself from his opponent,
trying to free his hands. But the other man seemed to
understand that any such freedom of movement would put
him at a disadvantage. Lucena finally gained leverage with
the two bodies. He managed with a driving knee to push
his opponent's body over his. The man landed flat on his
back, but also next to Lucena's Glock. As he reached for the
gun, Lucena pulled out a knife that he had shoved into his
suit pocket on the helicopter. The thief began to lift the
gun, but then his hand fell back to the ground. His fingers
opened and dropped the gun. The knife that Lucena had
shoved into his opponent's neck ended the brawl.

* * *

Holden took in a mouthful of the wine. The vintage
bathed every taste bud. He paused, and then swallowed.
There was a smile of satisfaction on his face.

* * *

Sawchuck seized the advantage on top of Grant. He put
his second hand on Grant's right wrist, and started to pull
the arm back. Grant knew that his opponent would not
have to bring the arm back too far in order to gain full
control.

But with a clear look, Sawchuck stared quizzically at
the white square in Grant's black collar. Grant didn't miss
the ever-so-brief moment of hesitation and slight loosening
of the grip. He turned his body in the direction he was
being pulled, and smashed his left fist into Sawchuck's eye.

That allowed Grant to pull his right hand free. He
swiftly moved the Glock under Sawchuck's chin, and said,
"You can either stand down, or I pull this trigger. I'd rather

not, but I will if I have to, Mr. Sawchuck, or should I say, Elmer Danford, former and long disgraced Atlanta cop?"

Sawchuck gritted his teeth, put his hands into the air, and moved off of Grant, who popped up while continuing to point the gun at his opponent. He looked over and saw Lucena checking the stabbed man for a pulse. "Phil?"

"I'm fine. He's dead."

Lucena moved to the man who was shot by Caldwell. "Him, too."

Grant looked back at Sawchuck. "You, through the door."

The helicopter continued to hover with Caldwell pointing the rifle down on the scene.

"Yeah, yeah." Sawchuck added, "What's with the priest get up?"

Apparently, it paid off wearing the collar tonight.

Grant merely said, "Move."

After Sawchuck went through the door, with his hands still up, Grant leaned in, Glock at the ready. He scanned, and came into the room. Lucena followed, confirming that Rutherford also was dead.

The three stopped, and stared at Rex Holden, seated at a table taking another drink of wine.

Sawchuck snarled, "Thanks for your help."

Holden replied, "Best to understand when and when not to fight." He looked at Grant, and said, "I am not armed, Pastor Grant. I gave my weapon to Mr. Sawchuck."

Lucena moved forward, made Holden stand, searched him, and finding nothing, shoved him back into the seat. Holden immediately took another drink.

Lucena stepped out of the door, and gave a thumbs up to Caldwell, who was watching from above. The helicopter began to move toward the pad on the lawn between the house and the river. Lucena came back inside, and saw that Sawchuck had been put in a chair in the middle of the room. Grant was standing across the table from Holden.

Grant asked the apostate Interpol officer, "Why?"

Holden smiled sadly. "On the most basic level, for the same reason as Mr. Sawchuck there. Money is a very nice thing. However, I suspect his tastes run in another, less-expensive direction. So, in a certain sense, he is more of a mystery than I am."

Grant said, "You two deserve each other."

Holden looked at Grant. "Perhaps. But to answer you clearly: Because of this." He held up the very rare and incredibly expensive bottle of Bordeaux, and then poured himself another glass.

Holden hesitated, pulled over another glass, and looked up once again at Grant with the silent question. Stephen Grant briefly, and almost completely, returned to the man who served the CIA many years before.

I'll probably never have another chance in my life to sample a $200,000-plus wine.

Grant nodded.

Holden smiled with far less sadness, and poured the wine.

With the Glock still in hand, Grant picked up the glass. Holden raised his own in salute. Stephen eyed the color and clarity, and breathed in the aromas. He then took more than a mere sip, moved the liquid around his mouth and swallowed. "Impressive."

Holden declared, "Worth the money."

Caldwell came into the room first, now with her own gun in hand, followed by Banner. Taking in the scene, she looked at Grant, shook her head and smiled. "Some things do not change."

Grant didn't like that comment, and felt a flash of guilt over his drink of Bordeaux. He put the glass down.

Upon entering, Banner's head swiveled around, trying to take in the entire scene. Seeing Holden sitting at the table taking a drink, he froze. Banner's eyes focused on the bottle. His shoulders sagged. "Not the '47 Bordeaux."

Chapter 55

Paige Caldwell called Chase Axelrod, and updated him on what had occurred at Larry Banner's home. When she finished, Axelrod said, "The event here is not far from wrapping up. Nearly half of the guests have already left."

Caldwell replied, "Wasn't the idea to get Lafleur and Poyer out of there by now?"

"Yes, but Lafleur waved off his own people, not to mention Noack and the FBI, insisting on staying. He's going to make some kind of announcement to a select group, and also wants to stay to the end."

"Noack must be so pleased."

"Right, especially at having the FBI jerked around by a thief. I told Noack that we would follow Lafleur, Poyer and their team back to the hotel. He was fine with that, saying that once we heard from you – and if everything basically looked okay here – he, Nguyen and Peraza would move out. I imagine that they'll head your way now."

"Okay, we'll talk later."

Axelrod slipped the phone back into his suit jacket. Fifteen minutes later, Noack's FBI trio were off the ship, and in an SUV heading north to Larry Banner's home.

Meanwhile, Axelrod approached Lafleur and Poyer, and said, "It's long overdue to leave."

Lafleur glanced at his watch. "Not quite yet. I'm going to make my announcement, then we will see."

Axelrod reminded, "This was not the way it was supposed to go."

Poyer interjected, "I know, but thank you. We will not be much longer."

Axelrod sighed. "Our team will be ready to follow you over to the Waldorf."

Poyer said, "Thank you."

Axelrod turned and eventually found Jessica West at the main exit of the hangar deck. Given the event, the slim, six-foot tall, blond-haired, blue-eyed West had put aside her usual conservative attire and hair-in-a-bun in favor of a black, sequined dress. Her hair hung down long and free.

Axelrod asked, "We're ready for when this guy is finally good to go?"

West nodded. "Lis is ready out front." She shook her head. "She's great, but it still amazes me how much Lis can talk. I don't know how her husband gets a word in at all."

Axelrod said, "You assume that he wants to get in a word."

West smiled, and said, "Of course you would say that. I imagine that when you and Sean get together to watch a game, nothing is missed since neither of you say anything." Axelrod was brought into CDM from one of Sean McEnany's other shadowy, CIA-linked enterprises.

Axelrod observed, "Normally that would be true, but he's getting a bit more talkative lately. Kind of annoying. He should save that for his wife and kids."

West laughed. "Oh, right, the chatty Sean McEnany."

The two quickly returned to the business at hand.

West said, "I'll look around outside and make sure everything is still clear for getting these two out of here."

"Good."

On the other side of the hangar deck, Lafleur was drawing together a group of guests. He began speaking about a new global wine distribution enterprise that he was launching, and wanted this group to be the first to hear about it. As he continued to cover some general details, one couple that had been looking at the TBM-3E Avenger bomber moved around the group and closer to Lafleur and Poyer. It was Dasha Pudovkin and Vasily Morozov. Pudovkin's hair was still dyed jet black, and her make-up not only made the cheek scar disappear but also darkened the eyes and lips. Lafleur's security apparently had not been up to seeing through the subtle shift in Pudovkin's looks.

As Pudovkin and Morozov began their move, so did two of the bartenders, leaving their stations behind.

Four of the six bar areas suddenly erupted in explosions. The effects were brutal, bloody and, eventually for 11 people, deadly. At the same time, each bomb, hidden by the bartenders on Pudovkin's hired team, was far less damaging than it could have been. While the bombs certainly created chaos and deadly diversions, their primary purpose was to allow Dasha Pudovkin to enact her revenge, first by killing Gabrielle Poyer in front of Jacques Lafleur, and then killing Lafleur himself.

In the midst of the destruction, Chase Axelrod found himself knocked to the floor of the aircraft carrier, but conscious, aware, and able to act.

While everyone else was looking for an escape route, Poyer focused in on the two figures coming toward her and Lafleur. She called out, "Jacques, look out!"

Both Pudovkin and Morozov brandished GSh-18 handguns. Morozov led the way, and was met by Poyer, who expertly executed a spinning roundhouse that took out his left leg. He fell hard.

Lafleur went for the other figure. He dove at the hand holding the gun, grabbed it, and the two crashed to the floor. They seemed to freeze when their eyes met.

Lafleur said, "Dasha?"

She hissed in his ear, "Darling, have you missed me?"

He continued to look into her eyes.

She added, "Apparently not."

"Dasha, please, I..."

She kneed him in the groin, pulled the gun away, and sprang to her feet. "Shut up, you pig. You had my husband murdered, and now I will kill you."

Lafleur managed to reply, "What? Dasha, that's not true. I would never do that, never to you."

While Pudovkin hesitated, Morozov had recovered from his fall, and turned his gun on Poyer. But by then she had removed a Heckler & Koch P30SK from a well-hidden holster, and fired two shots into Morozov's chest.

The sound of gunfire managed to create even more panic amidst the smoke, blood and death.

Pudovkin started to turn her gun toward Poyer. But Chase Axelrod's voice cut through the noise. "Don't even think about. Drop the gun."

Perhaps it was the smoke that had irritated his eyes, or the impact of the explosive force he had absorbed earlier, but Axelrod failed to react before Pudovkin turned and fired a shot. The round tore through flesh on the left side of his chest. Axelrod fell back to the floor.

Poyer trained her weapon on Pudovkin, but Dasha immediately rolled forward. Poyer's shot missed. Pudovkin's return fire went astray as well. Dasha turned the gun back toward Lafleur, who now was sitting up. She aimed, but hesitated. Dasha then quickly spun back toward Poyer, and pulled the trigger. The slug landed in Poyer's right calf, and she dropped to the floor next to Lafleur.

Pudovkin took the opportunity to flee. As she emerged from the smoke, her two accomplices, who had been posing as bartenders, were waiting exactly where they were supposed to be. One held open an elevator. She declared, "We need to get out now. It has all gone to hell."

As the elevator door closed, Axelrod staggered forward with his Glock in one hand, a smartphone in the other, and blood escaping from the flesh wound on the side of his chest. He was talking to West. "They entered the elevator. Heading down to you."

She replied, "Okay, Lis is with me."

Axelrod moved toward a staircase, and said, "Do they really think they can shoot their way out? Are they that stupid?"

He went through a door, down two steps, and then stopped. "What if they're not going down? What if they're heading up to the flight deck?"

West said, "What?" She looked at the blinking numbers above the elevator door. "Shit. That's what they're doing. They're on the flight deck."

Axelrod ended the call, turned, and worked to move up the staircase.

On the outside deck, Pudovkin and her accomplices were heading toward the stern of the *Intrepid* and the Space Shuttle Pavilion housing the *Enterprise*.

Axelrod emerged on the flight deck, located Pudovkin's group, and started moving in that direction. As he attempted to jog, he gritted his teeth in pain.

Spotting him, the fake bartenders pulled out handguns and fired.

Axelrod fell to the deck, sucked in air, steadied his gun and returned fire.

Pudovkin joined in the shooting.

Axelrod trained his gun on one of the bartenders, and pulled the trigger.

After three shots, his target fell.

More bullets flew in Axelrod's direction, some ricocheting off the flight deck around him. He fired back with no success.

Another volley of fire, however, suddenly came from a new angle. To the left of Pudovkin, it was West and Dicce coming forth from another set of stairs.

The remaining bartender turned his shots in that direction, while Pudovkin continued firing at Axelrod.

West lowered herself to one knee. Her second shot landed in the thigh of the bartender. He dropped his gun, and toppled sideways.

Pudovkin quickly picked up the weapon. With a gun in each hand and arms spread out, she fired in each direction, at Axelrod and at West and Dicce. One of her rounds caught West's upper left arm. The former FBI special agent declared, "Son of a bitch!"

Dicce paused and asked, "Are you all right?"

West grimaced, and answered, "It's okay. Not bad."

Pudovkin ceased firing, kicked off her heels, and ran toward the stern of the ship.

Dicce moved forward to check on Pudovkin's two assistants lying on the flight deck.

Back on his feet, Axelrod stumbled after Pudovkin. Moving alongside the shuttle pavilion, he wasn't gaining any ground.

Still in full stride, Pudovkin tossed the two guns over the side. She then slowed, grabbed the railing, and launched herself over it, following the weapons down into the dark waters. After the long drop, she hit the Hudson feet first.

With two people onboard, a high-speed boat arrived as Pudovkin's head emerged from below. One man helped her onto the boat, while Dmitri Melikov stood ready at the controls.

Dmitri called out, "Where's Vasily and the others?"

She answered, "Didn't make it."

"Shit."

Pudovkin ordered, "Move, Dmitri!"

Looking down from the flight deck, Axelrod aimed his Glock, and pulled the trigger. But to no avail. He watched as the boat gained speed on the water. He then pulled out his phone, hit a number, and said, "She's in the boat moving away from us."

The reply came, "Got them." The call ended.

Axelrod was joined by West. They glanced at each other's wounds.

West said, "You okay?"

"Yeah, how about you?"

"Fine," she replied.

Dmitri guided the boat away from the *Intrepid*, and continued to accelerate.

After getting to more open waters on the river, the sound of the boat's engine drowned out the helicopter sweeping down from above.

Watching from the *Intrepid*, West asked, "You called Paige?"

Axelrod replied, "Right after the bombs went off."

The doors on each side of Larry Banner's white and blue Agusta helicopter once again were open. Paige Caldwell held a rifle on one side of the craft, and Stephen Grant wielded a second semi-automatic rifle on the other. Banner was at the controls, while Phil Lucena remained back at Banner's home with the local police, waiting for Noack's FBI team to arrive.

Caldwell called to Banner, "Keep them on my side, Larry."

He gave a thumbs up.

As she raised the rifle, Caldwell declared, "Okay, warning shot time."

She fired off five rounds in front of and to the side of the streaking boat.

That earned the attention of Pudovkin and Melikov. Dmitri whispered to himself, "You've got to be kidding."

Having lost her dress after the long plunge into the Hudson, Dasha was left in bra and panties, looking more like a joy rider in a bikini out for a spin, rather than a killer trying to escape. That look morphed into something out of a James Bond movie when she demanded a gun from the other man. She turned skyward, and launched return fire. Dmitri kept his hands on the wheel of the speedboat, while Pudovkin and the other team member continued firing.

As bullets rose toward the helicopter, Grant leaned back, and declared, "I've had enough of the shooting at the good guys in the helicopter."

Caldwell said, "Me, too."

She leaned forward, and squeezed off several shots.

Additional projectiles rose into the air in response.

Banner worked the controls to keep the helicopter steady, while more pings rang out from the craft's exterior.

Dmitri apparently decided it was time for evasive maneuvers. He called out a warning to the others, and then turned the wheel to the left, while also decelerating.

Banner could only respond by banking. That gave Grant his first direct look at the boat. He raised the rifle, and tried to get focused on the man firing at them. Grant released ten rapid shots. Two hit his target, and the man slipped to the deck of the boat.

One down.

Caldwell called out, "Nice. Just like old times."

He cringed slightly. *Too much like old times?*

Banner swept the helicopter back into position above the boat. Pudovkin increased the accuracy of her shooting, as one shot cracked the window in front of Banner, and a second barely missed Caldwell, entering the roof above her head.

Caldwell whispered, "Enough of this shit."

She zeroed in on the helmsman, and fired off several shots. One caught Dmitri in the shoulder, and his body slammed forward. His grip on the wheel kept him from falling. "Damn it, Dasha, this is no good."

Pudovkin ignored him, and continued to fire skyward.

Grant called out to no one in particular, "Why doesn't she stop, give up?"

Banner replied, "I don't know, but she's chewing up this helicopter. Either she stops, one of you stop her, or I have to veer off. She's going to hit something that will send us into this river, and perhaps kill us."

Grant started to say, "Paige, should we pull back, and let...?"

More shots came from below.

As her former partner spoke, Caldwell was repositioning her rifle. Grant's question was cut off by a single shot fired by Caldwell.

The projectile entered Dasha Pudovkin's forehead and exited the back of her head. Her body was pushed back by the force of the shot, and she tumbled over the side of the still speeding boat, into the Hudson River.

Caldwell declared without a trace of emotion, "No chance of surviving that time."

Grant sat back. He hung his head slightly, and said, "No, Paige, not this time." He was pulling himself back from the grip of his old work.

Dmitri Melikov stared at the spot where Dasha Pudovkin went over the side into the dark, murky waters. He turned back and gradually slowed the boat, raising the one arm he could into the air, signaling his surrender.

Banner slowed the helicopter, and hovered as the boat came to a stop.

Grant stared down on the scene.

Lord, help us, forgive us. Forgive me. What a bloody night.

He reflected that here was another case of Stephen Grant, the pastor, asking for forgiveness for doing what he used to do, more or less, as a SEAL or with the CIA. He again struggled with whether or not this particular plea for forgiveness was real or the result of misplaced guilt.

Grant continued to watch the boat below. He stared at the unmoving body and the man with a bleeding shoulder, who was now sitting quietly in one of the boat's chairs. Grant listened to Banner's radio call explaining to authorities what was happening.

Okay, Lord, I'll keep praying for guidance. While I'm not clear on the details in these instances, I still know that I need your forgiveness. And please watch over those back on the Intrepid.

Chapter 56

Rich Noack, Trent Nguyen and Eugenio Peraza stood shoulder to shoulder, motionless, each staring ahead, as the straight boom lifted them higher. The machine stopped, and they stepped onto the patio area.

A local police detective came forward, introduced himself, and shook hands with each FBI special agent. He then said, "He's inside, like you requested on the call."

Noack said, "Thank you, Detective. We'll take it from here."

"Excuse me?"

"You and your men can leave us. We will take it from here. If you could wait with Sawchuck until the rest of our people arrive, that would be greatly appreciated. Of course, we'll touch base a little later on to make sure we haven't missed anything, and get all of your notes and so on."

The detective became indignant. "You're fucking kidding me, right?"

Noack took a step closer, and replied, "No, I'm not kidding. Again, thank you for your fine work."

Peraza looked slightly uncomfortable. Nguyen simply stared at the doorway leading into the rooftop wine cellar.

"Shit, you fucking feds," declared the detective. He called out, "We're out of here, boys. Now!"

Two uniformed officers and another plain clothes detective emerged through the doorway, joining the detective who had made his displeasure clear to all.

Nguyen moved past them without looking at their faces. He stepped around Rutherford's body, and through the doorway. Lucena was standing behind the seated Rex Holden.

Out on the patio, Noack said, "Peraza, why don't you head down with them? The rest of our team should be here soon."

"Yeah, okay," he answered, looking still more uncomfortable.

Back inside, Lucena nodded at Nguyen, and said, "I'll leave you to it." He exited the room, nodded at Noack as well, and then joined Peraza and the cops on the boom. The police loudly complained on the way down.

Noack entered the room to find Nguyen silently staring at Holden.

Holden finally said, "Gentlemen."

Nguyen moved forward. Noack stayed where he was. Nguyen stopped next to Holden, and stared down at him.

Holden shifted in his seat. Nguyen still said nothing.

The disgraced Interpol agent looked up. "I truly am sorry about Agent Osborne and his wife."

Nguyen reached inside his jacket, and pulled out his Glock.

Holden said, "Now, now, gentlemen. We know that this is not how things are done. I have valuable information to exchange."

Nguyen looked at Noack, who nodded in reply, and moved toward the door.

Holden's cool British tone evaporated. "Wait, where the hell are you going?"

Noack exited the room without looking back.

Nguyen pulled a chair over, and sat down just a few feet away from Holden. The Glock was in his hand and resting on his right thigh. And then he spoke, asking, "Do you know that Ken Osborne was my first partner and a friend? Of course, you knew that because you also violated our trust presenting yourself as something much more than the traitorous, murderous piece of trash that you really are."

All of Holden's years of training with Interpol and the calmness necessary to fool everyone around him were stripped away. His hands trembled, as did his voice. "I-I know. And again, I-I am very sorry."

"You are sorry. I'm just supposed to accept this?"

"Listen, I-I never liked that part of this. It was not my call. It really wasn't. That was Weathers."

"Weathers?"

"Yes, yes, when it comes to what I did in the counterfeiting markets, I've worked with Vince Weathers the entire time. I-I helped with financing, steering investigations elsewhere, and providing information. But the ugliness, that was not me. In fact, I didn't want to know about that. Weathers controlled all of that. He ordered the burning of Lafleur's warehouse in Arizona. He ordered the attack on Pudovkin's husband. He provided the wines to both of them, but wanted them at each other's throat, while he ... I mean ,,, we took over their markets. He also destroyed that building at his own winery to throw focus elsewhere. And he, unfortunately, had Agent Osborne and his wife killed. Osborne was getting too close. That was all Weathers, not me. I didn't want to know."

"How nice for you. But you obviously did know. You knew about all of it. You benefited from all of it. You let it all happen. You were intimately aware and complicit in all of it."

Holden lowered his head, and broke into sobs.

Nguyen said, "And why should I believe any of this?"

Holden looked up directly at Nguyen. He struggled to clear his throat. His hands shook more, and he quickly shoved them under his armpits. He spoke barely above a whisper. "That is not who I am, or I was. I could not go that far. I wouldn't."

"Keep telling yourself those lies. But all of the blood is on your hands as well."

Holden lowered his head, once again.

"Did you tell Weathers?"

Holden whispered, "I called him, and said I would not give him up until tomorrow morning. As far as I know, he is out east, probably at his winery. He will flee. He may already have."

Nguyen raised the gun, and stood up.

Holden closed his eyes.

Nguyen slipped the gun back into his holster. He paused, drew his arm back, and backhanded Holden across the face.

Holden fell out of the chair. He didn't try to get up. Instead, he turned his face into the oak floor, and wept.

Nguyen stepped outside, and said to Noack, "We need to get Weathers, immediately."

"I'll call Detective Pavelski."

Nguyen replied, "No, call Sean McEnany."

Chapter 57

Vince Weathers' anger had contorted his face for nearly two-and-a-half hours now. He cursed as he cleaned out what he needed to take from his home, and destroyed anything else of value. He spewed more curses into the air while driving to Kushner Wines, and as he entered the building in the post-midnight darkness.

He opened his office door, and flipped on the light switch.

A raspy voice declared, "Vince Weathers, you have a choice."

"What the hell?" Vince reflexively responded upon seeing a muscular man with very short blond hair casually sitting at his desk.

Sean McEnany had a large amount of money and incriminating records spread across Weathers' desk.

Weathers looked at the open wall safe, and back at McEnany. "Who the fuck are you, and what're you doing here?"

McEnany ignored the first question. "What am I doing here? Holden gave you up."

"Holden. I don't know who that is."

"Sure, Vince. Hey, you're not listening. Never mind all of this. It's over. Don't you want to know about the choice?"

"What?" Weathers started looking around the room.

"It's just us, Vince, for now."

"How did you get in here?"

"Vince, try to focus. I'm not a big talker, so I'm going to quickly lay out the choice. You can die right here, or you can die after going through the justice system for all of the people you had murdered, including a former federal agent. For good measure, there's all of this" – he indicated the material spread out on the desk – "and who knows what else in your computers." McEnany took a deep breath, and added, "So, which is it going to be? Quite frankly, I'm fine either way."

Weathers smiled. "You're alone?"

"Yes, Vince, I am alone."

Weathers moved his right hand to grab the gun holstered in the small of his back. But before he could pull the weapon out, Sean McEnany, in one smooth, quick action, sprang up from the chair, pulled his Glock 22 from its holster, pointed the weapon, and fired off three shots into Weathers' chest.

McEnany walked around the desk. He kicked away the gun on the floor, and watched life drain from the eyes of Vince Weathers.

McEnany placed his gun back in its holster, and pulled out a smartphone. "Detective Pavelski, do you have Mr. Slate in custody?"

He listened to the response. "Good. Unfortunately, Weathers was not as compliant. I had to shoot him. You should get over to the Kushner winery immediately."

Pavelski responded, McEnany thanked him, and then sat back down in the desk chair.

He hit another number on his phone. "Honey, did I wake you?"

His wife, Rachel, assured him that he did not. She was waiting up for him.

McEnany said, "That's all right. Go to sleep. I've got more work, unfortunately. I'll be out probably the entire night. But I'll bring breakfast in for you and the kids."

Rachel spoke, and Sean replied, "Right, I almost forgot. Pumpkin picking tomorrow afternoon with the church youth group. I'll increase the caffeine intake. It'll work."

He listened again, and said, "I love you, too. Good night."

The next call was to Rich Noack. McEnany explained what happened, closing out by saying, "Tell Nguyen, I gave Weathers a clear choice. This is what he chose."

Another call to Paige Caldwell went much the same way. McEnany ended that conversation, slipped the phone into his jacket pocket, and leaned back in the chair.

Chapter 58

The sun was just coming up and visiting hours were far off, but Sean McEnany made his way into Charlie Driessen's hospital room nonetheless.

Driessen was asleep in a sitting-up position, with a massive cast engulfing his left arm and shoulder.

McEnany sat down in a high back chair next to the bed, and announced, "You look like shit."

Driessen's eyes bolted open. "What the hell?" He looked around, with his eyes settling on McEnany.

Sean repeated, "You look like shit."

"Yeah, I know. What the hell are you doing here?"

"Well, I'll bring you up to speed on what's happened, but first, I thought you might like something non-hospital for breakfast."

McEnany pulled the tray table to Driessen, and placed a small paper bag on it. He pulled out a sandwich wrapped in tin foil, a container of orange juice and a cup of coffee. "A local deli was open, and the breakfast specials looked pretty good."

Driessen brightened, as McEnany unwrapped the sandwich.

McEnany said, "Two eggs fried, bacon, sausage, salt, pepper and ketchup."

"I take back every crappy thing I've ever said to you." He grabbed half of the cut sandwich with his free, unharmed right hand.

"No, you don't, but you're welcome nonetheless."

Driessen took a big bite, and as he chewed, said, "Didn't you get one?"

"No, I'm heading home shortly, and I promised Rachel that I'd bring in breakfast."

Driessen nodded as he swallowed, and then dove back into the sandwich.

"You've been out of the loop, and missed a hell of a time last night, Charlie."

"I caught the TV reports about the *Intrepid*." He sadly shook his head. "All of our people okay?"

"Absent a superficial bullet wound here and there, yes."

Driessen eyed Sean closely, and then said, "Good. Then open that orange juice for me, and let's hear all about it." Driessen simply ate and listened to McEnany, only speaking when Holden's true colors were revealed, declaring, "That son-of-a-bitch Brit."

As Sean finished, Charlie asked, "How the hell did Holden know? Who tipped him off?"

"Good question. I spoke to Tank. He's got some concerns about one or two people at the Agency that might have been deflecting or burying things."

After swallowing a swig of coffee, Driessen simply shook his head and said, "Shit."

Chapter 59

The room used to brief the press in the federal building was deemed too large or too small depending upon what was being announced, and how many in the press cared to show up.

In this case, it was overflowing as representatives from the FBI and local police spoke and answered questions about what had happened the previous night on the *Intrepid*, on the Hudson River, in Westchester County, and on Long Island's North Fork.

Supervisory Special Agent Rich Noack did most of the talking, including giving credit to the various police departments involved, the Bureau's intellectual property theft team, and Larry Banner's efforts as a private citizen who was a victim but one who took action. Banner stood behind Noack, along with Trent Nguyen, Eugenio Peraza, other FBI staff, and various local LEOs.

In the back of the room, Stephen Grant stood next to Paige Caldwell.

Paige said, "Larry got what he wanted. Justice and salvaging his reputation."

Grant added, "I'd say that after his own press conference next week with the results from Jennifer's study, he will have seized a leadership role in the battle against wine counterfeiting, and his reputation will be enhanced beyond what it was before. He played his cards well, and it paid off. The Agency will love it, too."

Paige nodded, and then said, "Are you heading home?"

Stephen said, "Yes, I think I'll head out now."

"I'll walk with you." As they moved toward the elevators, Paige added, "And what about you and helping to fight the bad guys?"

Stephen replied, "Meaning?"

They entered the empty elevator and the doors closed.

Paige answered, "You were uncomfortable last night."

"I'm a pastor, not a CIA operative, or part of a private outfit for hire. How am I supposed to feel?"

"You tell me."

They were silent for a few seconds. The doors opened, and they stepped out and started toward the front doors.

Paige continued, "Seems to me that you felt guilty."

It's annoying how well she can still read me.

"Perhaps."

"Stephen, what the hell do you have to feel guilty about? You did what had to be done, and as far as I can tell, you did nothing wrong."

"I don't know."

"You've become a bit namby-pamby."

Stephen smiled and chuckled. "Thanks, Paige."

They exited into the cool morning air and bright sunshine. Grant was still in his pastoral garb from the previous day, though with the collar open, while Paige had borrowed basic black FBI sweats. Paige said, "What I mean is, you like this. Acknowledge it. Hell, embrace it. Answer a question: Does it still bother you that Jacques Lafleur never paid for that wine heist, not to mention everything he's done since?"

"Of course it does."

"Yeah, I know it does. Listen, I've actually come to better understand your pastor thing. I get you and Jennifer. But at the same time, stop pretending that these times when I disrupt, or the CIA disrupts, your daily life are unwelcome. Stop thinking you should somehow push it away, or feel bad about it. Aren't you supposed to see a purpose in things that others don't?"

"But..."

"I'm not done," Paige interrupted. "And from what I can tell, Jennifer understands you – all of you – better than you think. She might not be thrilled with some of this, as you mentioned, but she loves you." Paige paused briefly, and then continued. "She better. Love creates understanding and, yes, sacrifice. I've seen you sacrifice for your wife, your friends, colleagues, and for me. I see her willing to do that as well."

Stephen continued to listen and process, not saying anything.

Paige took a deep breath of the October air, raised her face to the sun, and closed her eyes. While still in that position, she advised, "Here's an idea. Think of these occasional adventures as an unusual, adrenaline-filled hobby. I'm sure there are pastors who like to jump out of planes, or take part in some kind of extreme sports."

He laughed a little, and said, "This is my crazy hobby?"

She looked at him. "Don't be a wise ass. It's more than that. When you're needed, you willingly try to do some additional good beyond the church stuff. Maybe I'm wrong, but I'm thinking God is okay with this."

Paige Caldwell just mentioned God. Wow.

Stephen said, "Thanks, Paige. You're a good friend."

They hugged, and kissed each other's cheek.

Stephen stepped back, and asked, "So, what's next for you?"

"Check out of the hotel, grab the SUV, and get out east to the hospital. Hopefully, I can get Charlie back to his place in D.C. over the next couple of days."

"That'll be interesting."

"And you?"

"I'm going to train it home."

Paige smiled. "Really? When is your next train?"

Stephen glanced at his watch. "Not sure. There aren't many heading east at this time of the morning."

"And then it's over an hour ride to your stop?"

"More like an hour and forty minutes."

"Come on, get in a cab with me. You can gather Charlie's stuff at the hotel. I'll check out of both rooms, and still get you home before the Long Island Railroad could."

"I have no doubt. Sounds good."

Chapter 60

The FBI's Trent Nguyen saw Jacques Lafleur and Gabrielle Poyer off at the airport on Saturday morning.

Beyond talk about how Poyer's leg felt and some innocuous chit-chat, the couple had said little to each other since the events of Thursday night. That continued on the flight to Morocco.

It was dark and late in the night when they arrived at the massive seaside villa in Casablanca.

Gabrielle proclaimed that she was tired, and immediately went to bed. Meanwhile, Jacques went about minor tasks involved with returning home.

Forty-five minutes later, Jacques joined Gabrielle in bed. Her eyes were closed and her back to his side of the bed, but he slipped his arm around her.

He said, "I am sorry, Gabrielle."

She said nothing.

Jacques continued, "Are we all right?"

She asked, "Did you still love her?"

He hesitated, and finally said, "Yes."

"For the entire time I was here?"

"No. I thought she was dead."

"But did you love her memory?"

"Yes, I did."

They were quiet again for a few minutes.

Jacques eventually added, "But I also have loved you since we met, Gabrielle. You must believe that."

She nodded.

Then he said, "We've certainly acted like it, but never explicitly said it over the years. Do you love me, Gabrielle, or is this still work for you, enjoyable, but still work?"

"It took time, but I grew to love you."

"And now?"

She paused, and then answered, "Yes, I still do."

Gingerly, so as to not reinjure her leg wound, Gabrielle slowly and carefully turned back to him, and they kissed deeply. The rest of the night was dedicated to cautious, gentle love making.

The next day would bring Liam and Harper Casper, and Anton Lange, to the house, beginning the process of repairing Lafleur's counterfeit wine business, looking at how to expand given the losses of Dasha Pudovkin and Vince Weathers, and more planning on the cover of legitimate wine distribution.

If Paige Caldwell and Rich Noack had been watching and listening, they would have agreed, "It was all very French."

Chapter 61

After the Words of Institution, Pastor Stephen Grant lowered the cup, and placed it on the white linen covering the altar table. Looking down, he caught a glimpse of himself in the shine and reflective light of the red wine.

From sin tied to wine to wine serving as a means of God's grace, offering forgiveness, life and salvation. What man does; what God does. Quite a journey in recent days.

It was the third Divine Service of the weekend in which Grant had served as celebrant, and these kinds of thoughts had moved in and out of his head throughout.

A few minutes later, as he moved down the Communion rail, he felt little bits of joy as he was able to declare "The body of Christ" and "The blood of Christ" to people he had not seen in church for some time. That included those new to the railing at St. Mary's, as was the case now at Sunday's late service with Duane and Janice Ellis.

*   *   *

Three hours later, seated at the long pine table in the Grants' dining room, a small assembly of people at various stages of exhaustion had just about finished up lunch. The food selections included three types of smaller sandwiches – ham, brie and apple; roasted beef with herbed goat cheese; and lamb burgers with blue cheese and basil mayonnaise.

Sunday afternoons were at least periods of decompression for Stephen, Zack Charmichael, Tom Stone, and Ron McDermott. But Grant felt particularly drained after the happenings over the previous week. Working on his second glass of Ellis Vineyard's Cabernet Sauvignon added some appreciated relaxation.

Jennifer Grant and Maggie Stone knew the Sunday rituals of their husbands. And while Cara Charmichael was new to being married to a pastor, she was more than familiar with the Sunday routine, having learned from watching her parents.

The last two at the table were Duane and Janice Ellis.

All of the sandwiches had been eaten, and the conversation that covered much of what happened during the previous days continued. No one seemed quite ready for the pear-cranberry hand pies for dessert.

Instead, Stephen brought another bottle of wine to the table, and refreshed a few glasses. He said, "Duane, this is the last bottle you sent. Thanks again, it's delicious."

"I'll send another case," Duane replied.

Stephen laughed. "No, I wasn't fishing for more. Your gift was quite generous."

"Consider it payment for inviting Janice and me to stay over tonight."

Jennifer said, "We're so happy you decided to say yes. Stephen might fall asleep on us later, after services this morning and wine in the afternoon, but we'll find something to keep ourselves entertained tonight."

Tom volunteered, "World Series starts tonight."

Jennifer said, "How could I forget that?" She looked at Duane and Janice, "Are you fans?"

Duane replied, "While a senator, I learned to become a fan of all of the sports teams that play in California. So, yes, I'd like to see the Angels win."

Tom brightened and said, "I'm a longtime Angels fan, originally from California." He then added, "But Dr. Grant is a Cardinals fan."

Jennifer smiled, and said, "Guilty as charged."

Janice Ellis good naturedly asked, "Can we still stay?"

Stephen inserted, "I'm certainly okay with it, but my wife is pretty passionate about the Cardinals."

Jennifer said to Janice and Duane, "Oh, ignore him. His Reds are stuck rebuilding ... again."

The conversation eventually came back around to wine. Ron McDermott asked, "Duane, do you enjoy being a vintner? Any regrets on leaving the Senate?"

"None whatsoever. My life..." – he looked at Janice and continued – "our life has been so much better, and I feel as though I'm actually producing something, rather than playing politics that seem to never make a positive difference, or sometimes even make matters worse. I've learned quite a bit since leaving government, with the help of Jennifer and Stephen."

Tom said, "I get that you learned about economics from Jennifer, but what the heck did Stephen teach you?"

Amidst a few laughs, Stephen replied, "Thanks, buddy."

Tom said, "You're welcome."

Duane explained, "At the risk of getting serious once again, Stephen helped guide me back to the faith, back to church."

Stephen said, "Not me. That's the work of the Holy Spirit."

Duane added, "Well, thanks for what you did. I also felt blessed – I think that's the right word – that St. Mary's used our wine for Communion. It added an even deeper layer of meaning to our work."

Stephen said, "Let's see if we can continue doing that."

Ron added, "Duane, I'd like to see if St. Luke's might get our Communion wine from you as well."

Tom joined in, "Same for St. Bart's."

Duane smiled, placed his hand on his wife's, and said, "Thank you, I'll make sure it happens." He added, "Maybe we can even save your churches a little money."

Tom smiled, and added, "St. Bart's budget committee would appreciate that."

Maggie said, "Tom, please."

Stephen took a sip of wine, and looked at the people seated around the table, stopping to focus on his wife. *This is where I belong. St. Mary's is home. Jennifer is home – whatever might come of my ... hobbies? That sounds ridiculous. Whatever might come when I'm asked for help.*

Stephen said, "I'm glad we got together to do this, especially after all that happened over the past week or so. I don't know about the rest of you, but I needed perspective. I got that at church this weekend, and here among friends."

Tom said, "Church as community."

Zack declared, "As Jesus said 'I am the true vine, and my Father is the vinedresser. Every branch in me that does not bear fruit he prunes that it may bear more fruit. Already you are clean because of the word that I have spoken to you. Abide in me, and I in you. As the branch cannot bear fruit by itself, unless it abides in the vine, neither can you, unless you abide in me. I am the vine; you are the branches.'"

He looked around a bit sheepishly.

Everyone raised a glass in response.

Tom Stone winked, and added, "My son-in-law, the show off."

That generated laughs, while at the same time, Pastor Stephen Grant gave Pastor Zack Charmichael a nod of approval.

Acknowledgements

Once again, thanks to my bride, Beth. Her edits and insights have been invaluable and are appreciated – even though she might think I get a bit temperamental as a writer. I also thank my two sons, David and Jonathan, for making me proud, and keeping me grounded.

The Reverend Brian Noack, a good friend, once again came through when I asked about various theological details.

Naturally, any shortcomings in my books are completely my own responsibility.

Finally, I appreciate the generosity of those who have used their treasure and time to purchase and read these thrillers. As long as someone keeps reading, I'll keep writing. God bless.

Ray Keating
September 2016

About the Author

This is Ray Keating's sixth novel featuring Stephen Grant. The first was *Warrior Monk: A Pastor Stephen Grant Novel*, followed by *Root of All Evil? A Pastor Stephen Grant Novel*; *An Advent for Religious Liberty: A Pastor Stephen Grant Novel*; *The River: A Pastor Stephen Grant Novel*; and *Murderer's Row: A Pastor Stephen Grant Novel*.

Keating also is the author of various nonfiction books, and an economist. In addition, he is a former weekly columnist for *Newsday, Long Island Business News,* and the *New York City Tribune.* His work has appeared in a wide range of other periodicals, including *The New York Times, The Wall Street Journal, The Washington Post, New York Post,* Los Angeles *Daily News, The Boston Globe, National Review, The Washington Times, Investor's Business Daily,* New York *Daily News, Detroit Free Press, Chicago Tribune, Providence Journal Bulletin, TheHill.com, Townhall.com, Newsmax,* and *Cincinnati Enquirer.* Keating lives on Long Island with his family.

Made in the USA
San Bernardino, CA
29 October 2016